WHEN THE LIGHTS GO DOWN

It is 1938 and the threat of war looms on the streets of London. But, when the lights go down in the cinema aisles, usherette Daisy Blake is transported to a world of glamour and romance. Daisy falls in love with the handsome organist, Al Dawson. Then war is declared and, just after Al leaves for the frontline, Daisy discovers she's pregnant. Her mother is distraught; she doesn't think Al is right for her daughter and when Daisy's letters to him go unanswered, her mother encourages her to marry John, the cinema's projectionist, to spare her further heartache.

WHEN THE LIGHTS GO DOWN

WHEN THE LIGHTS GO DOWN

by

Pam Evans

Magna Large Print Books
Gargrave, North Yorkshire,
BD23 3SE, England.

British Library Cataloguing in Publication Data.

A catalogue record of this book is
available from the British Library

ISBN   978-0-7505-4768-0

First published in Great Britain in 2016 by
Headline Publishing Group

Published in Large Print 2019 by arrangement with
Headline Publishing Group Ltd.

Magna Large Print is an imprint of Library Magna Books Ltd.

Printed and bound in Great Britain by
T.J. (International) Ltd., Cornwall, PL28 8RW

To my dear friends Dawn and Tony who
show such an interest in my stories
while I am writing them and Tony is a
tremendous help with the research.

Acknowledgements

As always my thanks go to my lovely editor Clare Foss, who is always a joy, and all the team at Headline with a special mention to Clare's assistant Emma Holtz. I think the cover for this book is particularly stunning so thanks to everyone involved. My appreciation, too, to my agent Barbara Levy who still beavers away on my behalf.

Chapter One

'You're very quiet tonight, Daisy,' Bertha Blake observed of her youngest daughter one autumn evening in 1938 when the family were having their evening meal. 'And you look a bit pale, dear. Are you going down with something?'

'I'm feeling fine, Mum,' fibbed Daisy, receiving an admonitory prod under the tablecloth from her sister Mary, who was sitting beside her.

Bertha was a sharp-featured woman with dark greying hair drawn back into a bun and watchful black eyes; very little went unnoticed by her in this house. 'What's all the nudging about? I know when you two are hiding something. So let's hear about it. We don't have secrets in this family. You know the rules.'

Seventeen-year-old Daisy was actually in despair. She'd confided in her sister about the traumatic events of the day but couldn't bring herself to break the news to her parents because she was so ashamed.

'Leave the girls alone, dear,' intervened her father Bill helpfully. 'They're doing no harm.'

'They are up to something, Bill.'

'So what if they are? They're grown women now,' he reminded her. 'They don't have to tell us everything.'

'They're still in their teens and living under our roof so that makes them accountable to us,' she riposted.

'They are old enough to earn a living and pay for their keep every week so I reckon that entitles them to a degree of privacy,' said Bill, who was a skilled worker in an engineering factory. An even-tempered man of solid build, he had light, greying hair, thinning around the edges and bright blue eyes which Daisy had inherited.

'Please don't argue on my account,' said Daisy, desperately trying to summon up the courage to say what she must. 'But yes, Mum's right, there is something I need to tell you.'

Bertha's eyes widened momentarily because that sounded like the forerunner to the sort of news every mother of unmarried daughters dreads. 'Let's have it then,' she urged.

'Er ... well...'

'Come on, spit it out, girl,' said Bertha impatiently.

'I lost my job,' she blurted out, pale with worry and shame.

'Oh.' It wasn't the worst news but bad enough to crease Bertha's brow into a frown. 'That lovely office job of yours ... you've gone and lost it.'

Daisy pushed her corn-coloured hair off her face with her fingers. 'I'm afraid so. I was sacked,' she explained grimly.

Bertha drew in her breath, unable to hide her shock but still hoping for an explanation that would make it respectable. 'Are they cutting down on staff then?'

'No I'm the only one leaving,' Daisy explained, her round sapphire eyes dull and lacklustre. 'Well, I've already left actually. I have to go back on

Friday to get what's owing to me.'

'Sorry to hear that, love,' said her father calmly while her mother clutched her brow dramatically.

'And what happened for you to be instantly dismissed?' demanded Bertha, who had never been even distantly acquainted with tact.

Daisy chewed her lip, knowing her mother would be very upset by what she had to say next. 'I complained to the management and they sacked me for being a troublemaker and said they won't give me a reference.'

Up went her mother's brows. '*You* complained!' she exclaimed. 'That wasn't very sensible, dear. I've brought you up to know your place and it isn't to criticise those who are paying you! People like us do as we're told.'

'She had to do it and I think it was very brave of her,' put in Mary, who was a year older than Daisy and close to her sister. 'If more people had the courage to speak out, maybe things would be fairer for employees, especially women.'

'That's all very well but that was a good job she's thrown away.' Bertha's eyes narrowed. 'So, what exactly did you have to complain about, Daisy?'

This was the part she'd been dreading the most but here goes, thought Daisy. 'There's a man at work, Mr Rumbold,' she began nervously. 'Ron they call him, a married man with a family. Middle-aged and quite high up in the company. One of the big bosses actually...'

'And?' her mother urged.

'Er...' She bit her lip. 'It's *really* embarrassing...'

'Never mind that; just get on and tell us what happened.'

15

'In your own time,' added Bill but he'd stopped eating and was looking concerned.

'Well he...' began Daisy.

'He's been taking liberties with her on a regular basis,' cut in Mary, seeing that her sister was struggling. 'Or trying to.'

'What do you mean by liberties?' Bertha frowned.

'The usual sort; touching her up, trying to kiss her,' explained Mary while Daisy turned scarlet and was rendered speechless.

'Oh dear, that's not very nice at all, is it?' Bertha was clearly shocked.

'It's bloomin' disgusting if you ask me,' stated Mary. 'Daisy's supervisor wouldn't get anything done about it so she went directly to the managing director and reported the man to him. I don't blame her either.'

Bertha's face worked. 'You are usually such a reserved girl too, Daisy,' she said.

'Yes I am, but I couldn't bear what was going on. It reached a point where I was dreading going to work every morning so I took my courage in my hands. Fat lot of good it did me because Rumbold turned it round on me; told them I was making a nuisance of myself with him,' Daisy explained. 'As if I'd fancy a repulsive old bloke like him.'

'I'm really sorry to hear about your ordeal,' sympathised Bertha. 'But couldn't you have just kept out of his way and avoided all of this?'

'Not really because I had to go to his office for various reasons during the course of the working day, to take his post and run errands for him and so on.'

'That's when he tried it on; when he got her on her own in his room,' said Mary, her dark eyes filled with disgust. 'The dirty old devil. Men like him should be locked up.'

'He'll wish he was when I've finished with him,' said Bill, leaving the table and pacing the room. 'I'll be at that office as soon as they open in the morning.'

'No you will not,' stated Bertha.

'I will, you know,' he said.

'What good will it do?'

'It'll let them know that they can't treat our daughter like dirt and get away with it,' he said. 'Rumbold is the one who should be sacked, not Daisy.'

'If you create a fuss you'll make things a damned sight worse because it won't be his reputation that's ruined; it will be Daisy's,' Bertha insisted. 'So the least said about this the better. No one must know outside of this family.'

'I think you should go and sort them out, Dad,' urged Mary, a lively girl and a brunette like her mother. 'They need someone to talk back to them. At least get them to agree to give Daisy a reference or she won't be able to get another office job.'

'I intend to, don't worry.'

'The whole thing is so awful it makes me feel sick,' said Daisy. 'I think Mum is right though. They'll look after their own and paint me black. I just want to try and forget about it.'

'For the moment I think we should all finish our meal before it gets cold,' suggested Bertha in a tone that didn't invite argument.

Silence fell over the room. In this Victorian

house in a terraced row in Hammersmith, London, no one was in any doubt as to who was in charge of the household.

'Mum and Dad are having a right old barney downstairs about him going to your office tomorrow,' Mary said to her sister, the two having escaped upstairs into Mary's bedroom after helping with the washing up. 'I think Dad should do it. We can't just sit back and take what happened lying down.'

'I reckon that's exactly what we will have to do because Mum's right, they have all the power,' said Daisy. 'I've been going over and over it in my mind, trying to work out if I was to blame in some way. I mean, I was polite to him because it's part of the job. But I'm certain I didn't encourage him, Mary. *Not ever!*'

'You don't have to convince me because I know you didn't, I mean why would you?' said Mary who worked behind the counter at the Co-op Grocery Store and thoroughly enjoyed her job.

'But I feel so guilty and kind of dirty...'

'Well you mustn't because you've done nothing wrong,' Mary urged her. 'He's the one who should be feeling bad but you can bet your life he isn't. He won't have given it another thought once the blame was fixed firmly on you.'

'I suppose it's because they blamed me that it's made me feel sort of grubby.'

'Understandable I suppose,' agreed Mary. 'But eventually the memory will fade and with luck so will the feeling. Being realistic, Dad won't go to the office. Mum will see to that.'

'Maybe I should have kept quiet about Rumbold's behaviour and left the job of my own accord; then at least my reputation wouldn't be threatened and I'd get references,' Daisy said. 'I don't know what came over me. I'm not usually that bold.'

'No you're not as a rule. I was amazed when you told me what you'd done. Still, it's time you spoke up for yourself a bit more and you did the right thing morally, no matter how it's turned out.'

'Having plucked up the courage to report him to the head of the department and be told in so many words to put up and shut up, I was so furious I marched into the managing director's office on the spur of the moment and blurted it all out without thinking of the consequences. Now I have no job and no prospects and Mum and Dad are downstairs arguing about it.' She clasped her head. 'Oh Mary, I feel awful.'

'Come on, Daisy, don't let that moron Rumbold do this to you,' Mary said gently. 'I know things seem bad at the moment but you'll come through this. No job is worth that sort of punishment.'

'I know you're right but there's this awful feeling...' She couldn't find the words to describe the way she felt; lonely within herself and set apart somehow.

'Aw, try not to upset yourself too much, kid. I know it was horrible for you but you're not the first girl it's happened to and you won't be the last. You'll get another job, references or not.'

'I shall have to,' Daisy said. 'Mum will be none too happy if I can't hand over my housekeeping money on a Friday. You know what a stickler she is about us paying our way.'

'She'll be all right about it if you have to miss a few weeks. She's only strict about it because she has such a strong sense of fairness and believes in people making a contribution if they're earning which is only right and proper. But if you're not working she'll let you off. She thinks the world of us both even if she is the bossiest mother in London and sometimes drives us mad.'

'Yeah, I expect you're right,' agreed Daisy. 'I'll start looking for another job right away, though. In fact I'll take a peek at the situations vacant in last week's local paper if it's still around somewhere downstairs.' She gave a wry grin. 'When things are quieter down there.'

'Don't risk going down while they are still going at it hammer and tongs.' Mary smiled as she spoke.

'The whole thing is best forgotten,' declared Bertha. 'You know I'm right, Bill, even if you'd rather not admit it.'

'I can't forget a thing like that,' he said, his voice raised. 'Our daughter being insulted in such a vile way. I don't know how you can even suggest that we sweep it under the carpet.'

'Because it will be the best thing for *her*, that's how,' she roared. 'Do you think I'm not sick with fury at that man for doing that to her? Of course I am. I'm her mother so I feel her pain as my own. But I truly believe that she'll be the one to suffer if we make a fuss about it. They have all the power and they've shown very clearly whose side they have taken. Daisy's life will be a misery if she's the talk of the neighbourhood.'

'The firm is on the other side of town,' he pointed out.

'People from round here work there, though, and that sort of gossip has a way of getting around. Daisy won't come out of it smelling of roses, you can bet your life on it. The woman never does under these circumstances. So we need to lie low and let it blow over.'

'But it isn't right.'

'No, but it's the way things are. We owe it to our daughters to protect them,' she lectured. 'A woman's reputation is one of her biggest assets. With that in pieces, not only will Daisy be unable to find a job, she won't get a decent man to marry her when the time comes either.'

He narrowed his eyes on her. 'Are you sure it isn't *your* reputation you want to protect?'

'Mine, yours, all of us,' she replied. 'Of course I want to defend my family's reputation and there's nothing wrong with that. I see it as my duty.'

'But Daisy has done nothing wrong except stand up for herself.'

'And look where it's got her, out of a job and leaving under a cloud. I don't want this nasty business to linger so the least said about it the better. You know I'm right, Bill. You might not like the way things work but that's how it is.'

He saw the determined tilt of her chin, the steely look in her eyes, and he knew he would concede. Bertha was a very controlling woman but she was also a loyal wife and a wonderful mother to the girls even though she did both things on her own terms. She was slavishly devoted to respectability and would go to any lengths to protect her family from any kind of slur. But he was certain she would give her own life for their family if it were ever necessary, which helped him to put up with her domineering ways. One thing they were in agreement about: they both adored their girls, and he supposed there was truth in what she said. Daisy would be the one to suffer from any intervention by him.

'All right,' he finally agreed. 'I'll keep quiet about the disgusting incident. But I'm not happy about it.'

She gave him a watery smile and her face softened. She had never been a pretty woman, even in her youth, but she was striking with her dark eyes and aquiline nose. 'Thanks love,' she said. 'Now we can concentrate on supporting Daisy through this horrid turn of events. We must offer her plenty of encouragement and stop her from losing confidence in herself.'

'Absolutely.'

In nearby Shepherd's Bush, later that same night, employment was very much on eighteen-year-old Al Dawson's mind as he returned home from his second job of the day, playing the piano in a restaurant in the less salubrious outskirts of the West End. He was often out in the evenings, at the keyboard, after working all day in a local factory that manufactured electrical goods.

'How did it go tonight, son?' asked his mother Hester, appearing in a red woollen dressing gown.

'All right thanks, Mum,' he said, smiling at her as he took off his coat and hung it on the hall stand.

'You look worn out, love,' said Hester, a small woman of middle years with a round, pretty face and a thatch of greying blond hair that had more than a passing acquaintance with the peroxide bottle. Her son had dark curly hair and eyes the colour of black coffee.

'Yeah, I am a bit tired but I need to wind down before I go to bed. My music falls on deaf ears because the punters are all talking over their meal but it feels like a performance to me even if I am invisible to my audience. It certainly gets the adrenalin flowing.'

'It *is* a performance,' she pointed out. 'They'd soon notice if you didn't play well.'

'That's true.'

'So what's on your mind, son?' she asked. 'I can tell when something's up.'

'Nothing serious but I finish there at the end of the week,' he said. 'They're cutting the music in the evenings because they reckon it's a waste of money paying me when the place is crowded anyway. But it isn't a problem. Something else will come along. It usually does and it isn't as if I am totally reliant on my musical work for my living.' He omitted to mention that the restaurant manager had decided to have a pianist over the lunch period and had offered Al the job. The fact that he wasn't in a position to take it would upset his mother so he'd thought it wise to keep it to himself.

'It's a pity you can't give up the day job and concentrate on your music,' said Hester.

'Maybe one day I will but I'm fine as things are, and I've got some good mates at the factory,' he

23

said. 'We're lucky to have thriving factories around here in the new industries manufacturing cars and wireless sets. Some people in other parts of the country don't stand a chance of getting a job.'

'I know, but it isn't right that you should be lumbered with your Dad's debts,' she told him. 'It's my responsibility to get them paid off.'

'Mine too and Dickie's.' He was referring to his younger brother, who was seventeen and also worked in a local factory. 'Dad only got into debt because he was trying to provide for his family when he got sick and couldn't work. So we'll pay the money back together.'

Hester sighed, sad at the memory of her beloved husband who had suffered a lingering death from TB three years ago. 'Still, I reckon we'll have paid off within the next few months. Then you can go all out for your music.'

'I'm not sure if I will even then. It's more of a hobby really, something I love to do. The factory pays steady money,' he reminded her. 'I'd be taking a chance if I gave it up.'

'Apart from a few at the top of their game, it isn't easy for a musician to make a decent living but I think you owe it to yourself to give it a try because you're a very talented pianist and you've been properly taught. As you're willing to take almost any booking, anything from pubs, restaurants and local shows and dance classes, I think you stand a fair chance. Now is the time to do it; get yourself established while you're young and single.'

'There's something very comforting about having a regular wage packet each week, though,

Mum,' he told her. 'Which I certainly wouldn't have if I relied on my piano work, not at first anyway.'

'We're two of a kind, you and me, son; music is in our blood. We might never play on a concert platform but we'll always be able to make a few bob at the keyboard. It's what we want to do. I was lucky; I had your dad to support me so I was never totally reliant on the money I earned giving piano lessons. It did help with the family budget though, and of course it's a godsend now that we've lost your dad.'

Al had never known a time when a stream of children hadn't beaten a path to their front door after school for their weekly piano lesson. He himself had been taught by his mother and had managed to work his way through the grades before he'd left school while still finding time to hang out with the other kids in the street. Music was as natural as breathing to him but he'd always enjoyed company and had never had sufficient ambition to shut himself away to practise for long periods, which was why he'd never be a classical concert pianist. The piano was his preferred method of earning a living but, as his mother had said, very few jobbing musicians like him could live by their music alone.

'I'll see what comes along,' he said. 'I'll keep my eye on the noticeboard in the music shop where I go for my sheet music. The manager there is in the know too because a lot of local musicians go in there. He might have heard of something.'

'Meanwhile, do you fancy a spot of supper?'

'I wouldn't mind a cup of tea and a cheese sandwich but I'll get it,' he said. 'You go back to bed.'

'You sit there and relax,' she insisted and hurried from the room before he could object further.

He was very fond of his mother. She had never been like other kids' mums and for a while as an adolescent he'd been embarrassed by her long bright hair and colourful clothes, wishing she looked more mumsy like the mothers of his peers. But he'd grown out of that and now embraced the fact that she was a one-off, full of life and heart. She might not always remember to dust the ornaments but she never forgot how much her family meant to her. He and his brother were her world, especially now that Dad had gone.

'What's going on down here?' asked Dickie, coming into the room in his pyjamas. 'Are you and Mum having a party or something? All this talking and clattering of crockery.'

'I'm just having a sandwich and a cuppa.'

'Mm, I wouldn't mind some of that,' said Dickie. 'Seeing as I can't sleep through all the noise you're making, I might as well have some supper.'

'If there's food about you'd come back from the dead,' joshed Al.

'I'm a growing lad,' said Dickie, who was dark-haired like his brother and similar in looks but thinner and more wiry in build, a feature that created a lot of banter because he had such a large appetite.

'So, have you been out tonight?' Al inquired casually.

'Yeah, round my mate's house listening to records on his gramophone,' he replied.

Al raised his brow. 'Not classical, I assume.'

26

'Jazz. You should play that instead of all those daft love songs.'

'I play what I get paid for and people out for the evening like to listen to something nice and gentle. Not that they listen as such. It's just background music. Anyway, I keep up to date and play all the latest songs.'

'Even so, it must be boring.'

'Not to me.' His brother had never taken to piano lessons so their mother hadn't forced it on him when that had become obvious. 'As soon as we can afford it we'll get a gramophone of our own so you can listen to records at home.'

'That will be good.' Dickie sighed. 'Listening to jazz is the most exciting thing in my life, which shows what a narrow life I lead. At work all day and listening to records in the evening with a mate and a visit to the cinema on a Saturday night. I mean, it's hardly the stuff of dreams is it? One of these days I am going to travel the world.'

'You'll either have to join the navy or go as a stowaway,' Al pointed out patiently. His brother had yearned for excitement since he was quite little.

Their mother re-entered the room carrying a tray. 'Oh, you're up, are you?' she said to Dickie. 'I might have known you'd appear at the first sign of food.'

'I'll get myself something, Mum,' he said amiably, getting up and leaving the room.

'Be careful with the bread knife,' Hester called after him. She'd never quite grasped the fact that her sons were grown up when it came to safety.

She and Al were both smiling as Dickie headed

27

for the kitchen. When he wasn't bemoaning his boring life, he was the dearest boy: warm-hearted and funny. He had kept them all going in the dark days during his father's illness and after his death with his determined spirit and sense of humour.

'He's a case,' said Hester.

'He certainly is,' agreed Al, munching into his cheese sandwich with pleasure.

'Well Miss Blake, you seem to be just the sort of person we are looking for,' said the middle-aged man who was interviewing Daisy for a job in the offices of a food processing factory. 'You have good all-round office experience and a very nice manner. I think you will fit in really well here.'

'That's good news, thank you.'

'So it's just a matter of references now,' he explained airily. 'If you could let me have the name and address of the person to write to at your current firm.'

'Er, I'm not working at the moment,' she said. 'I left a few weeks ago.'

He raised his brows. 'Oh I see.' He leaned back slightly. 'May I ask the reason you resigned?'

She lowered her eyes and didn't reply.

'So you didn't leave of your own accord then.'

'No.'

'What was the reason for your dismissal?'

Her face burned so hard it throbbed. 'It was a personal matter,' she said. 'But it had nothing to do with my work. They were very happy with that.'

'But you'd rather not tell me about it?'

'That's right.' She couldn't bear to go through all that again with a stranger.

'Am I to assume from this that they won't be willing to give you a reference?'

'That is the situation, yes,' she said.

'I see.' He pondered for a moment. 'Obviously this complicates matters. References are standard procedure here. I have rules to abide by and my colleagues to answer to.'

'They didn't sack me for dishonesty or lack of efficiency,' she said in desperation as she had now been out of work for several weeks. 'I really do need a job and I am very honest and hardworking. I promise I won't let you down.'

'Hmm, I'm sure. But as references are the rule here it isn't possible to take this any further, I'm afraid. Thank you for coming anyway,' he said briskly.

'Thanks for seeing me.' She got up and left the room with her head held high even though she wanted to weep.

'It's the same at every interview and I've been to a good few now,' Daisy confided to her sister that evening after dinner in the living room when their parents were elsewhere in the house. 'As soon as the question of references comes up and I say I can't supply them, any chance of a job disappears.'

'Did he tell you for definite that you won't get the job because of it?'

'Yes, references are standard practice,' she said. 'The worst part is, they obviously think I must have done something dishonest to get sacked and not be able to supply references. That's the conclusion they all come to. You can tell what they are thinking.'

'You could always tell them the reason when you go for these interviews,' suggested Mary. 'It isn't as if you've done anything to be ashamed of.'

'No I couldn't do that.' Daisy cringed at the thought. 'Apart from the embarrassment, they'd probably think it was my fault like the people at my last firm; that I led Rumbold on.'

'Mm, there is that, so you've got a problem, kid,' said Mary. 'There are no jobs going at my place either. Even if there were you wouldn't want to waste your office training to work in a shop.'

'Mum wouldn't want me to because she likes the idea of having a daughter who works in an office. But I'm getting to the point where I'll try anything.' Daisy paused. 'It's an odd feeling when you don't have a job; you feel different to other people. Not a part of things. It's very dispiriting.'

Their mother swept into the room and handed Mary some money. 'Take your sister to the pictures,' she said with authority. 'Go out and enjoy yourselves.'

'But I can't go out while I'm not earning,' said Daisy.

'You'll do as you're told,' ordered Bertha. 'You need to get out of this house for a few hours. This job hunting is getting you down and you need cheering up. I won't take no for an answer. So get your coats and go. There's enough money there for ice creams for you both too.'

Daisy was warmed by her mother's generosity

but it would take more than a night out to solve her problem. She did enjoy the cinema though and wouldn't want to hurt her mother's feelings by refusing her offer.

'Thanks Mum,' she said, giving her a hug.

'Yeah, it's good of you,' added Mary.

'Go on then or you'll miss the start of the big picture.'

'We're on our way,' said Daisy, quickly tidying her hair in front of the mirror above the fireplace before heading off to get her coat from the hall stand.

Like most people, the Blake sisters normally enjoyed the entire cinema experience. As well as the film there was the excited buzz of filmgoers in the plush foyer and the glamorous usherettes who showed them to their seats with a torch. Then there was the highlight of the evening in the interval when the ice-cream girl appeared in the auditorium with her tray just as the organist rose up from below and filled the place with music.

This time, though Daisy tried hard to enjoy herself, especially as Mum had treated them, there was a dull ache in the pit of her stomach which had been planted there the day she had lost her job, and it refused to budge. Not even the sight of Fred Astaire and Ginger Rogers tripping lightly across the screen worked its usual magic.

'Good film wasn't it?' said Mary as they made their way out with the crowds. 'You can't beat a bit of Fred and Ginger to cheer you up.'

'They are good,' Daisy agreed.

'It was nice of Mum to treat us, wasn't it?' Mary

31

went on. 'She's a good sort when she's not laying down the law.'

'Yeah, she is. She obviously heard our conversation and was just trying to cheer me up.'

'And I get a free night out as well so it's an ill wind,' said Mary jokily. 'Seriously though, kid. I'd sooner pay for my own pictures and have you back to your old self.'

'I do try not to be miserable,' said Daisy.

'I know you do.' Mary linked arms with her affectionately. 'But I know you too well.'

Crowds were surging towards the exit, most talking excitedly about the film and looking at the posters for forthcoming attractions. This usually gave Daisy a pleasant sensation but tonight she felt distanced from it, faking an interest so as not to spoil things for Mary. Then, while her sister was looking at an advertisement for next week's film, something else caught Daisy's interest and her mood took a slight turn for the better.

'What are you smiling about?' asked Mary as they headed out into the night.

'Just thinking about the film,' fibbed Daisy.

'How are you getting on, Al?' asked the owner of the music shop one Saturday afternoon when Al was looking through the latest sheet music. 'Keeping busy?'

'Not as busy as I'd like, musically speaking, Joe,' he replied. 'I lost the job at the restaurant. They don't want a pianist in the evenings anymore.'

'That's a shame,' said Joe, a slim man with a cheerful attitude and a friendly interest in his customers. A musician himself, he could relate to his clientele.

'Mm. It was a blow but never mind, something else will turn up I expect; it usually does.' He looked towards the music. 'Meanwhile I'm looking for something new to add to my repertoire. I like to keep current. Any suggestions?'

'The new Bing Crosby has just come in as it happens.' Joe picked up some music from behind the counter and handed a copy to Al. 'I haven't even had a chance to put it out yet and you don't get more up to date than that.'

'Hmm. "I've got a pocketful of dreams",' said Al, reading from the front page and looking through the music. 'Yeah, I've heard this and it's quite catchy. I'll take it.'

Joe was thoughtful as he remembered something. He'd heard Al play the piano so knew he could confidently recommend him to anyone. 'There is one job I've heard about that might interest you,' he said. 'I'm not sure if it will appeal to you or if you'll be able to do it as you wouldn't actually be playing a piano but it might fill the gap left by the restaurant job until something else turns up.'

'Oh,' said Al, his eyes brightening with interest. 'You'd better tell me more about it then, hadn't you, mate.'

Chapter Two

Bert Pickles never had the slightest inclination to skive off work because he thoroughly enjoyed his job. Although he was from a humble background, he'd never been short of savvy or ambition. As a schoolboy he'd done any odd job he could find for pocket money, smoothed out his rough edges as he was growing up, learned what he could about business from market traders and picture-house bosses for whom he'd worked in menial employment and clawed his way up to his dream position, the manager of a popular cinema: the Adelphi Picture Palace in Hammersmith.

He'd had a keen interest in movies since the silent films of his youth and that wasn't diminished now that he was middle-aged and earning his living from them; though of course they were all talkies now and cinemas places of luxury and comfort rather than the so-called fleapits of yesteryear.

Although smartly dressed for work in a suit and tie, hair greased like a city gent, Bert had never quite lost the common touch so was very good with people and had a natural aptitude for management as his employers were well aware. No one could get staff to do their job as willingly as Bert did. He had created a good working atmosphere at the Adelphi and couldn't be prouder of the place if it was his own. Indeed his attitude towards the cinema was a proprietary one. Although accountable to his employers who owned the place, the responsibility was all his and he thrived on it.

A full team of good staff was essential to keep the place running at a first-class level. Going to the pictures had never been more popular with the public than it was at present and his aim was to touch every customer's visit with magic. To achieve this end he needed to be fully staffed, which he wasn't at the moment. Still, that could change in the next half-hour or so as he had some applicants to see.

Glancing at his notes with the interviewees' details, he went to his secretary in the adjoining office and asked her to send the first applicant in.

'So, Daisy Blake,' he said, having greeted her in a friendly manner. 'Can you tell me why you want a job as an usherette?'

Being accustomed to the frosty manner of office interviewers, she was surprised by his informal attitude but found it heartening. He looked to be about her father's age and had a gruff voice but a warm smile.

'I need a job and I saw your advertisement in the foyer on my way out of the cinema the other night,' she explained.

'So it isn't a job as an usherette you want in particular then?' he said. 'Just any job?'

She bit her lip. 'Well yes,' she admitted. 'But I do enjoy the cinema.'

'You won't be paid to watch the films.'

'I realise that,' she said. 'I meant I like the atmosphere of a cinema.'

'Hmm,' he said, looking at her. 'The hours are unsocial and I know how you young people like time off of an evening to see your friends. I have a daughter of about your age.' He tapped his fingers on the desk absently. 'I don't want to train you then have you leave after a couple of weeks because you don't like working in the evenings and at the weekend.'

'I'm prepared for the hours,' she said.

'Good.' He lit a cigarette and drew on it. 'So what was your last job?'

She tensed as they approached the stage at which the interviews usually fell apart. 'I've worked in an office since I left school,' she replied.

His bushy, greying eyebrows slid up his brow. 'So why such a drastic change of direction?' he asked, surveying her through a pall of smoke.

Deciding the truth was her best option, she blurted out, 'I was sacked because I complained about one of the bosses who was pestering me inappropriately and I was branded a troublemaker.' She paused and added with an air of defiance, 'I can't provide a reference because they won't give me one so I can't get another office job. Not that I'd particularly want one anyway.'

He pondered this, wondering if she might be trouble because usherettes did tend to attract male attention. 'You will get young fellas flirting with you in this job,' he pointed out. 'Do you think you can handle it?'

'The man at the office wasn't a young fella and he wasn't just flirting,' she said in a firm tone.

'Hmm.' He looked at her thoughtfully. 'You will be expected to be friendly to the customers and put up with a certain amount of banter from male punters. But if anyone makes a real nuisance of themselves you just ask for assistance. We look after our staff here at the Adelphi.'

The difference in his attitude to her last employer was astounding. 'That's nice to know,' she said.

'As an usherette you will play an important role, being in direct contact with the public, in the front line so to speak. As important as the film stars in your own way. Appearance and a good attitude are essential so you will need to be well turned out when on duty and polite. Always greet people with a smile. This cinema is packed nearly every night with people queuing around the block and I want it to stay that way. Going to the pictures is very popular but there are many cinemas in London for people to choose from. We aim to be the best.' He seemed to lapse into thought then became more serious. 'People want to escape from the worries of the real world, I expect, and all this trouble abroad.'

'Mum and Dad think it will blow over,' she said, assuming he was referring to the rise of the Nazis in Europe that was often in the newspapers and on the wireless news.

'Let's hope they are right,' he said.

She nodded, hoping she seemed reasonably intelligent, but she was a young girl too full of her own concerns to worry unduly about something that was happening so far away.

'So how soon can you start?'

'Tomorrow?' She was relieved that nothing more had been said about references. They obviously weren't needed here.

'Excellent. Can you here by twelve so we can get you fixed up with a uniform and show you around backstage and run through your duties before you start work?'

'I'll be here,' she said, rising.

'See you tomorrow then. Oh, and can you ask the next one to come in, please, on your way out?'

'Certainly,' she said and left the room.

There was a good-looking young man sitting on the seat outside the office.

'Mr Pickles said would you go in please,' she told him.

'Thanks,' he said, smiling at her, and she wondered what sort of job he was after.

'So you're Al Dawson,' said Bert. 'Nice to meet you, mate. Joe at the music shop speaks very highly of your musical abilities.'

'He suggested that I contact you.'

'He uses the same pub as me and we often have a chat about things.'

Al nodded.

'Anyway, I understand that you're a pianist and, according to Joe, one of the best there is. The problem is, Al, I'm looking for an organist,' said Bert. 'Have you any experience of the organ?'

'Yes I have. The piano is my chosen instrument but my mother taught me to play the organ when I was a boy so that I could play in church sometimes,' he explained. 'Nobody ever walked out or complained so I couldn't have been too bad.'

'A cinema organ is different to a church organ,

so I'm told,' Bert said. 'Though I'm not a musician myself. Do you reckon you could make a decent job of it?'

'I'm a qualified pianist with some organ experience so I'm sure I'd soon get the hang of it. And Joe at the music shop said he would go through the special effects they have on cinema organs with me if I can't work them out for myself.'

Bert leaned forward and spoke in a confidential manner. 'Cinema organs cost a fortune and I persuaded the owners of the Adelphi to pay out for one because the competition has them and we can't afford to lag behind. The one we have came over from America so is the very latest. But I have nobody to play the bloody thing. Not in the evenings anyway. I have someone in the afternoons but he can't do nights because of other commitments. Organists are very much in demand at the moment and some of them think they can get a bit cheeky.'

Al chuckled at his down-to-earth manner.

'I'm the manager here but I have my own bosses to answer to,' he continued. 'I'll be in dead trouble if I don't get a good organist soon, after getting them to pay up for the organ.'

'I'll be straight with you,' Al began. 'The piano is my preferred instrument but I need to earn some extra cash in the evenings. You want someone to play the organ so why don't you let me see what I can do?'

'Good idea, son,' Bert agreed with enthusiasm. 'Why don't we go down to the auditorium now while it's empty and let you give the beast a try?'

'Lead the way.' Al was enjoying the idea of a

new challenge.

'An usherette,' exclaimed Bertha disapprovingly when Daisy made an announcement over dinner that night. 'You're going to work in a cinema?'

'That's right,' she confirmed brightly. 'I'm thrilled to bits. Oh, the utter relief of having a job to go to again. I can't tell you how good it feels.'

'You didn't say that was where you were going when you went out this morning,' said Bertha.

'I knew you'd disapprove and I really do need a job, Mum.'

'Good for her, I say,' said Mary.

'You should have held out longer for an office job,' admonished her mother.

'I couldn't go on any longer without work, sponging on you and Dad. It wasn't right,' said Daisy. 'Anyway, a change will be good for me.'

'I'd sooner you relied on Dad and me than have you out working at night, coming home at all hours.'

'I think she deserves a pat on the back,' said Bill. 'At least she had the guts to go out and find work and to keep trying when it wasn't easy.'

'Will you be able to get us in for nothing?' asked her sister, laughing.

Daisy looked alarmed. 'I don't think so,' she said.

'Just joking.' Mary grinned. 'You should have seen your face. Anyone would think I'd asked you to steal the takings.'

'It's only a stopgap isn't it, Daisy?' said her mother worriedly, Mary's attempt at humour lost on her. 'Until you find something more suitable.'

'I don't know, Mum,' she replied. 'I haven't thought that far ahead yet. I'll see how I get on. For the moment I'm just happy to be gainfully employed again.'

'You'll get to see all the films for free,' Mary remarked.

'Many times over,' said Daisy. 'I expect I'll get bored stiff with them.'

'I've seen the usherettes sitting at the back when we've gone out early sometimes,' said Mary. 'I suppose they're allowed to in between seeing people in and out.'

'I'll soon find out.' Daisy turned to her mother. 'Be pleased for me, Mum. It's a job and I'm lucky to have it.'

'It's just that you had that posh office job...'

'Which I don't have now so please wish me well in this new occupation.'

'Yeah, three cheers for Daisy the usherette,' said Mary, laughing. 'Hip hip–'

'All right Mary, there's no need to go that far,' Bertha interrupted primly. 'Of course I wish you well, Daisy. Have you ever known me not to wish either of my daughters well?'

'No of course not, Mum,' said Mary.

'We'll all be interested to know how you get on, Daisy,' said her father.

'Thanks, Dad.' Daisy was so relieved to be back in work again, not even her mother's lukewarm response could dampen her spirits, though she was beginning to feel nervous. Her confidence still hadn't recovered since losing the last job in such a degrading way.

41

'Well it's something a bit different anyway,' said Hester on hearing about her son's new job. 'Well done!'

'Might be a bit of fun,' added Dickie. 'Can you play what you like?'

'Up to a point,' Al replied. 'But obviously the repertoire must be popular stuff, guaranteed to please the audience.'

'Is it every night?'

'No, four nights a week and two performances on a Saturday.'

'I shall be very proud of you when I go to the pictures and you rise up from below on the organ,' said Hester.

'Yeah, me too,' added Dickie. 'Well done, mate.'

Al was warmed by their support. He would be playing a cinema organ in the interval when people were talking amongst themselves and buying ice creams but they made him feel as if he would be doing a recital on a grand piano at the Albert Hall.

The Adelphi Picture Palace was large and luxurious. Originally a theatre, it had been overhauled and changed into a cinema a few years before as a result of the huge demand for films. On three floors, there were chandeliers in the foyer, red carpet throughout, soft seats, gilt-edged mirrors and paintings adorning the walls. For an affordable price, people could sink into their seats and forget their troubles as they escaped into the fantasy world of film.

Of course Daisy didn't go in through the sumptuous foyer when she went to start work the next day. She went in the staff entrance at the back and she was so nervous she was trembling.

Something magical happened when she put on her usherette's uniform and looked at herself in the full-length mirror. Usually rather self-effacing, now her confidence was boosted by the image of herself in a red, slimline dress with white trims, gold braiding and buttons and matching pillbox hat worn at a jaunty angle, the smart outfit set off with black court shoes.

'It looks lovely on you,' said Doreen, an experienced usherette Mr Pickles had assigned to fix Daisy up with a uniform and show her the ropes.

'I really like it,' said Daisy.

'Yes, I always enjoy putting my uniform on,' said Doreen, who was similarly clad. 'All the girls say they feel nice in theirs. They are very classy. All part of the smart image the Adelphi likes to portray.'

'I feel really good in it too,' added Daisy.

'You look it too. Make sure you don't have so much as a hair out of place for the manager's inspection though. He's quite strict about the way we look.'

'Inspection?'

'Yes, we have to line up before we go on duty and Mr Pickles gives us the once-over,' Doreen explained. 'If a girl has untidy hair or has overdone it with the make-up she has to go and put it right before she's allowed on duty.'

'Blimey, that seems a bit extreme.'

'Mr Pickles is a perfectionist when it comes to this place. He's a good boss and a lovely man but

43

he likes things exactly right.'

'I'm nervous all over again now,' said Daisy.

'You'll be all right,' said Doreen supportively. 'A few days in the job and you'll feel like you've been here for ever.'

Daisy had no problem with the manager's inspection but the afternoon shift didn't go exactly as she had hoped. She upset some people by putting them in seats that were cheaper than those they had paid for, dropped her torch and had to crawl around in the dark to find it and tripped over a man's walking stick as she was showing him to his seat.

'I'm a flamin' disaster,' she whispered to Doreen when they had a few minutes alone at the back.

'No you're not,' Doreen reassured her. 'You've had a few beginner's hiccups, that's all.'

There was a shushing sound from the auditorium and they both got an attack of the giggles and went outside to recover. During her break before the evening performance when she was in the staffroom, Daisy got to know that Doreen was nineteen, engaged to be married and the wedding was before Christmas.

'So I suppose that means you'll be leaving?' said Daisy, feeling disappointed.

'I'll be doing part-time, just weekday afternoons. My fiancé doesn't earn all that much and it's expensive setting up home. Mr Pickles said it will be all right, though I know married women don't usually go out to work. I've been here for a few years so he knows he can rely on me.'

'I'm glad you're not going to disappear altogether,' said Daisy, who had felt an instant rapport with Doreen and hoped they could be friends.

'That's nice,' said Doreen.

Every experienced usherette had to take her turn selling ice creams in the interval which wasn't popular, Daisy was told, because the trays were heavy and there was always a crowd clamouring to be served, some not very patiently. Those not on ice-cream duty could go to the staffroom.

In the interval that evening Daisy was chatting to Doreen and some of the others in the staffroom when one of the other usherettes rushed in.

'Girls, have you seen him?' she cried excitedly. 'He's absolutely gorgeous. I've just seen him on his way to the stage area.'

'Who?' someone asked.

'The new organist,' she explained. 'Cor, I didn't know they came looking like that. We haven't had one like him before. Come and have a look.'

Out they all trooped and stood at the back of the auditorium as spotlights beamed on to the orchestra pit and the gold-painted organ, with coloured lights on the sides, rose majestically from below to the tune of 'The Music Goes Round and Round', which filled the hall and received huge applause.

'Good evening, ladies and gentlemen, and thank you for giving me such a lovely warm welcome on my first night here at the Adelphi,' the organist said, turning towards the audience, his deep voice resounding through the auditorium. 'I'd like to start off with a medley of songs which I think you

45

will all know and I hope you enjoy.'

More cheers as he turned to the organ, then there was silence as music rose to the rafters. Daisy and her colleagues didn't move; just stood transfixed.

'I don't usually listen to the organist,' said one of the usherettes when they finally went back to the staffroom to finish their break while the auditorium was filled with the sound of 'Begin the Beguine'. 'But I bloomin' well did tonight.'

'I was too busy gawping at him to listen to the music,' said someone. 'Cor what a smasher!'

'I wondered what job he was after,' Daisy mentioned casually.

'Do you know him then?' asked her colleague.

'No, I saw him the day I came for my interview, that's all. He was waiting to go in for his.'

'I intend getting to know him,' said the girl who had brought him to their attention.

Daisy had to admit that she was impressed by his talent. He definitely had an aura about him. And yes, the other girl was right: he was very easy on the eye.

Al wasn't nearly as confident as he seemed. As a cinema organist, you had to be a showman and he'd been fraught with nerves before he'd come on. This wasn't a restaurant or a pub where nobody listened to the pianist. This was a proper audience who wanted to be entertained even though some of them were milling about queuing for ice creams and buying chocolate. Cinemagoers, too, were usually the sort of people who weren't afraid to let the artiste know if they weren't pleased with what they'd paid for so he put his all into his performance and the patter that went with it.

When he'd played the punters out at the end of the film programme and pressed the down button at the side of the keyboard to descend to the lower floor, he felt drained but elated. It was a new experience and one that he'd enjoyed immensely. But he was too buoyed up to want to go straight home. He needed to wind down first and some company to do it with.

Part of an usherette's duties was to check along the seats for left property after the performance and collect rubbish ready for the cleaners in the morning. Daisy was busy doing this with her colleagues when someone appeared and said, 'Hello there, I'm Al, the new organist. Thought I would introduce myself to my new workmates.'

Daisy and Doreen gave him a warm greeting and told him how much they'd enjoyed his music.

'Thanks, that's kind of you,' he said. 'It was a bit nerve-racking at first because the organ isn't my usual instrument. I'm more of a piano man but I enjoyed it.'

Some of the other usherettes drifted over to join in the conversation.

'Look, does anyone fancy going to the café across the road for a cup of tea and chat,' he suggested. 'It would be nice to get to know you a bit better as we're all working at the same place.'

There was a ripple of enthusiasm but some said they needed to go straight home and the conversation was interrupted when a young man Daisy

47

hadn't seen before appeared.

'Wotcha, gang,' he greeted them. 'What's this, a staff meeting or something?'

Doreen introduced the newcomer as John the chief projectionist, a thin, fragile-looking young man with brown, greased hair parted on the side.

'I'm the one nobody knows exists until something goes wrong in the projection room, then there's whistling and booing galore in the auditorium until I get the film fixed. The manager gets into a terrible state. He likes things to be perfect in his cinema.'

People murmured in agreement; they all knew about Mr Pickles' high standards.

'I'm trying to persuade them to come to the café with me for a drink of something and spot of socialising, John, do you fancy it?'

'Yeah, I'm all for that, especially as we have a couple of newcomers here tonight,' said John. 'I would suggest the pub for something stronger but most of us are under twenty-one.'

'Better stick to the café,' said Doreen. 'Do you fancy coming, Daisy? It'll be a good chance to get to know everyone.'

Daisy was enjoying the convivial atmosphere enormously and wanted to go with them but she knew the family would be waiting for her at home to find out how she got on.

'I really need to go home,' she said.

'Just ten minutes,' said Al persuasively.

'All right then,' she said, warmed by the company of these people. She felt part of a team, something she had never experienced with her colleagues in the office.

They all piled into the café and sat round a table chatting.

'You're not the only newcomer,' Daisy said to Al. 'It's my first day today too.'

'Really.' He smiled at her. 'How did it go?'

'Work is work but I enjoyed it,' she replied.

'So you'll be staying then?'

'Oh yes, how about you?'

'The devil drives, I'm afraid, because I need the money,' he said. 'But, yeah, I've had worse engagements.'

He told them that it was his second job of the day and that he lived in Shepherd's Bush and somehow he seemed to be at the heart of this gathering. He wasn't at all pushy but he was interesting and people wanted to hear what he had to say.

Such was Daisy's enjoyment she stayed slightly longer than she intended but finally dragged herself away, feeling happy and, for the first time in ages, looking forward to the next day.

What Daisy wasn't expecting was an argument with her mother as soon as she walked in the door.

'Where have you been until this hour?' Bertha demanded in an argumentative manner.

'Oh, a few of us went to a café after work,' she explained. 'It was lovely.'

'You should have come straight home,' her mother said. 'You knew we would be waiting to hear how you got on.'

'Yeah, I'm sorry about that, Mum,' she apologised, 'but a new organist started today and he

49

suggested we all go to the café to relax and get to know each other. As I was new as well it seemed like a good idea. There were quite a few of us.' Daisy was still glowing from the company. 'Really nice people.'

'Sounds good,' said Mary. 'What was the job like?'

'It went quite well,' she said with enthusiasm. 'I had one or two disasters but I got through it. Nice people and it feels really good to be working again.'

'We're glad all went well for you in your new job,' put in her father. 'So now that you're home safely we'll go up to bed.'

'I didn't mean to keep you up,' said Daisy apologetically.

'You should have come straight home then, shouldn't you?' snapped Bertha. 'You shouldn't be walking the streets at all hours of the night.'

Daisy stared at her, her cheeks burning. 'Evening work is part of the job, Mum,' she pointed out. 'So you'll have to get used to my being out late. I only stayed at the café for about fifteen minutes.'

'I don't want you hanging around cafés at night.'

'I was doing no harm,' Daisy retaliated. 'And I am nearly eighteen.'

'You're a well-brought-up girl from a good home,' declared Bertha. 'What sort of people hang around cafés at this hour?'

'People who work late?' suggested Daisy.

'This organist fella should know better,' continued her mother, disregarding Daisy's comment completely. 'Getting young girls to stay out late. I don't like the sound of him at all. He's probably a dirty old man.'

'He's a similar age to me actually, Mum,' Daisy explained.

'Oh, I thought he'd be older than that,' said Bertha. 'But even so, he's a bad influence.'

Daisy had been feeling buoyant after completing the first day at her new job and getting to know her workmates. Now she felt deflated and suffocated.

'How can you say that when you've never even met him? I do have a mind of my own, you know, Mum.' Daisy was angry now. 'I wanted to go with the others. Nobody influenced me. I am not four years old.'

'Well,' roared Bertha. 'That's all the thanks we get for waiting up for you.'

'Look, I'm sorry, I really am,' said Daisy, feeling trapped. 'I think it will be better if you go on up to bed in future and don't wait up for me.'

'Well,' boomed Bertha again, about to go into a tirade.

'All right, Bertha,' Bill intervened calmly, taking his wife's arm. 'Daisy is home now and all is well. So let's go to bed.'

Bertha allowed herself to be led towards the stairs, muttering about Daisy not having heard the last of this.

'So you had a good time then,' said Mary when she and her sister were alone. 'What about this organist fella? You positively glowed when you mentioned him.'

'He's gorgeous, that's why. All the girls were drooling over him.'

'Good-looking?'

'Very but it isn't just that,' said Daisy. 'He's got a sort of a glow about him. Possibly because he's so talented. The audience loved him.'

'You'll have to go after him then.'

'Don't be silly. He wouldn't be interested in me.'

'Why not?'

'Well I'm just me, aren't I?' she said. 'He can have his pick I expect.'

'Daisy,' began her sister in a tone of admonition. 'You must stop doing yourself down.'

'I'm just being realistic.'

'You're just being you and it's time you broke the negative attitude about yourself.'

'Sorry...'

'There you go again, apologising,' said Mary. 'I hoped we'd seen the end of all that when you spoke up against Rumbold at your last job.'

'It's just a habit, I suppose. But honestly, Al the organist is really special but he doesn't seem at all conceited. He just comes over as an ordinary bloke.'

'Which is what he is. He's a cinema organist, not a world-famous pianist.'

'I suppose so. Anyway, that's my first day in the job over.'

'Tomorrow will be better,' said Mary. 'A new job is never so bad once the first day is over.'

'I agree with you,' said Daisy. 'So roll on tomorrow.'

'That's the spirit, kid.' The sisters made their way upstairs to bed.

When Al got home his mother and brother were still up and eager to know how he got on.

'It was really good,' he told them. 'It felt like show business. Because I was in the spotlight, I suppose, instead of at the piano in a corner somewhere.'

'It is show business,' said his mother. 'Some cinema organists go on to bigger things. They go on the wireless and get famous.'

'That will never happen to me, Mum, because the organ isn't really my instrument so I wouldn't want to take it any further. I can play popular tunes but that's as far as it goes. But I enjoyed it; lovely atmosphere. The audience were very warm.'

'Never mind about the audience,' began Dickie. 'What about the usherettes? Did you get off with any of them?'

'Of course I didn't. It was my first night,' said Al. 'What do you think I am?'

'A man,' his brother replied breezily. 'And some of those Adelphi girls are gorgeous.'

Actually, there was one in particular who had caught Al's eye, a blue-eyed blonde called Daisy, but he didn't know anything about her yet. She might already have a boyfriend. Anyway, to have a girlfriend you needed money to spend on her and he didn't have that at the moment so wasn't in a position to make a move in that direction. Not until Dad's debts were paid off. Neither was he going to mention her to his brother, who would seize on it and pester him about her.

'Maybe they are but you don't start chasing them the minute you start the job,' he said to Dickie.

'Of course you don't,' added their mother predictably. 'You'll get a bad name doing that sort of thing.'

'That wouldn't worry me,' said Dickie.

'Well it would me,' Al came back at him.

'Your brother has got a new bee in his bonnet now,' said Hester, changing the subject. 'Tell him, Dickie.'

'I saw a notice stuck to a lamppost,' he said. 'They want people to join the Auxiliary Fire Service in case war breaks out. I thought I might give it a go. I think I'd quite enjoy being a fireman in my spare time.'

'That's very public-spirited of you,' said Hester. 'But I thought this war business had all been sorted out in Munich by the prime minister. He was talking about peace for our time.'

'I suppose the government don't want to take any chances so they feel they must build our defences just in case,' said Al. 'Things still seem a bit dodgy abroad. According to the papers.'

'I want to do my bit,' said Dickie.

'Don't worry, if war does come both you and I will be called up into the services,' Al pointed out.

'That will suit me,' said Dickie. 'Might get a chance to travel at last.'

'Change the subject, please boys,' Hester implored them. 'I don't even want to think about it.'

'Yeah, let's get back to the lovely usherettes at the Adelphi,' joked Dickie.

'You're out of luck because I'm going to bed,' said Al.

'Do you want a hot drink, dear?' asked Hester.

'I had one at a café after work. I went with some of the others.' He yawned. 'I'll tell you all about it tomorrow.'

So they turned the lights out and headed upstairs.

Bertha and Bill were in bed talking in whispers.

'I really think you should take it easy on the girls or we'll lose them,' said Bill. 'It wasn't right the way you went on at Daisy, especially as she had been out working.'

'She'd been hanging around in a café at an inappropriate time,' Bertha said.

'Which she was perfectly entitled to do after work. I thought the way you carried on at her was most unfair.'

'I was so worried when she was late, it all just came bursting out,' she explained. 'Why do you always take their side against me?'

'Because I want them to stay friendly with us,' he said. 'The way you carry on they'll leave home at the earliest opportunity and not even come back to visit.'

'I'm not that bad, surely.'

'But you are at times, Bertha,' he told her. 'I know you are only trying to keep them safe. But they are grown up now and need to spread their wings a little without having you on their backs the whole time.'

'Oh dear,' she sighed. 'I only ever have their best interests at heart.'

'I know you do, love,' he said kindly. 'But they are sensible girls. Nothing bad is going to happen to them just because you loosen the apron strings a little.'

'I can't seem to let go.'

'You are going to have to because we can't protect them for ever. They'll make mistakes, of course they will, like we all do, but they have to be allowed to take their chances. You mustn't let your past influence the way they live their lives.'

'You're right, Bill,' she finally conceded. 'I do tend to act without thinking but I'll try harder in future.'

'Good girl.' He leaned over and kissed her cheek. 'Goodnight.'

'G'night dear.' She settled down and mulled over what had been said. Bill was a good man. Always saw the best in people. She sometimes thought she didn't deserve him.

Chapter Three

The job at the Adelphi proved to be something of a healing process for Daisy. Having had her confidence crushed by the humiliating circumstances of the unfair sacking and subsequent job rejections, being part of the cinema team made her feel valued and gradually began to nurture her sense of self-worth.

Mr Pickles continued to stress the importance of the usherettes and box-office staff as the Adelphi's front line. But he did it in such a way that everyone wanted to do their best. Proud of the fact that they represented the company, a friendly and professional attitude came naturally to them. Behind the smiles and the glamorous uniforms, though, the usherettes worked hard and were on their feet for long periods. The wages weren't huge either.

But Daisy was far too grateful to be working again, and in a job she enjoyed, to be concerned about such things. There were practical advantages to the job to be taken into account too. Although they worked until late they didn't start early so she didn't have to get up at the crack of dawn. Once a month she had a Saturday off and as cinemas didn't open on a Sunday she had that day to herself too. So, although her mother fervently hoped that the job was just a stopgap until she found something more impressive, Daisy had no intention of seeking employment elsewhere.

The initial rapport she'd felt with Doreen had developed into a friendship and she was also good pals with John the chief projectionist. The three of them were usually early for the shift and had a chat before going on duty.

'We won't see so much of you after this wedding of yours, will we, Doreen?' John said one day when they were talking in the staffroom.

'You certainly won't,' confirmed Doreen. 'I'll be taking it easy of an evening instead of rushing up and down the aisles.'

'I don't know so much about taking it easy,' said John with a mischievous grin. 'By the time you've cooked the old man's dinner and done the washing-up it'll be nearly bedtime. Then you'll have to get supper and clear up after that. You'll probably work less hard if you stay on here for the evening shift.'

'Stop trying to put her off,' said Daisy lightly.

'Just teasing,' said John, who was not a robust man, having suffered with a weak chest all his life. But he was kind, good fun and had a keen sense of humour.

'Nothing would put me off marrying my Alfie,' said Doreen, a plump homely girl with warm brown eyes and curly hair. 'I certainly wouldn't swap time with him for a shift at the Adelphi, as much as I love you all.'

'Now we're hurt, aren't we, John?' teased Daisy.

'We certainly are,' he said, grinning and playing along. 'But to hide my pain I'm going up to my penthouse to prepare to get the show rolling.'

'Penthouse,' laughed Doreen. 'I've seen bigger garden sheds than your projection room.'

'It's like a penthouse to me,' he told her. 'Because it's full of things I understand and care about.'

'It's amazing how the movies work when you think about it,' Daisy remarked more seriously. 'I mean, how a reel of film can create such magic.'

'Indeed,' John agreed. 'It's a subject that's interested me since I was a boy and now that the film industry is developing so fast it's even more engrossing. It isn't that long since films were all silent; now they are all talkies and a few even in glorious Technicolor. Goodness knows what the future holds.'

'You must be quite brainy to understand how it all works,' said Daisy.

'The inventors are the clever ones,' said John, though he was pleased with the compliment because he was very much a background member

58

of the team. 'I was just taught. I didn't think it up all on my own.'

'Even so, you must have a few good brain cells.'

They chatted for a while longer then went on duty but Daisy valued these light-hearted conversations with her colleagues. Doreen had made her feel like a real friend when she said she would have liked Daisy to be at her wedding party and if she had known her when the invitations went out she would have included her. Daisy was very touched.

Doreen and John were the members of the team she was most friendly with but the others seemed to be nice enough. There were sometimes disagreements as in any group of people but usually the atmosphere was harmonious.

Then there was Al Dawson the organist. He was only around in the evenings, except for Saturdays, and came on duty later, ready to do his set in the interval, so she hadn't had a chance to get to know him. But there were these moments when they greeted each other in passing and she felt a reaction flow between them in the way it did when people fancied each other. Though she wasn't worldly, neither was she completely naive. She'd had interest from a boy or two and an invitation usually followed that special look. However this didn't happen with Al.

'It's in their nature for men to look at women in a certain way,' said Mary when Daisy discussed it with her. 'Are you sure you're not making more of it than it is?'

'I always feel a communication with him when I see him,' she said, 'but perhaps I'm deluding myself.'

'He's a very attractive bloke,' observed Mary, who had seen Al at the organ when she had been to the Adelphi with a friend recently. 'You won't be the only girl who fancies him.'

'You bet I'm not,' agreed Daisy. 'The only one of the girls in the team who doesn't is Doreen because she's so taken up with her fiancé.'

'You could always make the first move before someone else does,' suggested her sister.

'That isn't how things are done,' said Daisy.

'There's no law to say you can't break with tradition. What harm can it do?'

'Make me look like an idiot?'

'Not if he's interested in you and at least you'd know one way or the other.'

'I'm not doing that,' said Daisy. *'Absolutely not!'*

A few days before Christmas Mr Pickles swept into the staffroom and made an announcement.

'I'd like you all to have a Christmas tipple with me in my office after the programme tonight if you fancy it,' he said. 'Sorry it's such short notice, kids. I've been so busy it slipped my mind until my wife reminded me and tonight is the only night I can stay late because of family commit-ments. Hope you can make it anyway.'

There was a buzz of approval.

'Can you pass the word around for me, please?' he asked. 'My office after work tonight. See you all there, I hope.'

'That's nice of him,' Daisy said to Doreen after he'd gone. 'He's a real gent even if he is a bit rough around the edges.'

'He always has us in for a drink at this time of

year,' said Doreen. 'It's usually short and sweet because everyone wants to get home. But it's a gesture on the part of the management and there are usually a few sausage rolls and mince pies around. At least he makes an effort.'

'Roll on closing time then,' said Daisy.

That night at the party Daisy was full of Christmas spirit, partly created by the friendly atmosphere but also from a couple of glasses of sherry. She got better acquainted with her lesser-known colleagues as well as chatting to Doreen and John and all the while she was aware that Al Dawson was here and every time she looked at him their eyes met. After a certain amount of this optical shilly-shallying, she decided to take her sister's advice.

'Are you enjoying yourself, Al?' she asked, going over to him.

He nodded. 'Not half. Are you?'

'Very much so,' she enthused. 'I enjoy working here and when we get to have a party I like it even more.'

'That's good,' he said, grinning at her. 'There seems to be a good atmosphere among the staff. I'm a bit of an outsider really as I'm not around as often as the rest of you and I sometimes go to my dressing room in between times. But I always feel part of things because everyone is so nice.'

'I always feel like that too, and have done since my first day here,' she said. 'Your day job in a factory must seem a bit mundane after being here in all your glory.'

'Glory,' he said, laughing. 'How many glasses of

that stuff have you had?'

'Only a couple; not enough to make me say daft things.'

'You've just said the daftest of them all.' His manner was jovial. 'I only play the organ to make some extra cash and I'm not that good. I'm a piano man really. Some cinema organists are brilliant and I really admire them. It takes a very talented person to get to grips with a Wurlitzer with all their extra features.'

'Your musical talent still sets you apart though. Anyone can be an usherette but not everyone can play the organ and people enjoy the music when they go to the pictures.' She looked at his crisp white shirt and elegant dark jacket which he wore with a maroon bow tie. 'Smart outfit too.'

'Yours too,' he said, giving her an approving look. 'They like to project a glamorous image at the big cinemas nowadays, don't they? Going to the pictures is a very popular pastime apparently. Some people go two or three times a week to see what's on at different picture houses.'

They were engrossed in conversation when Mr Pickles tapped a glass with a spoon for silence and said it was time for them to leave because the cinema had to be locked up for the night.

'Thank you all for coming and I hope you've enjoyed our little get-together even though it's been so short. I know you've all got the Christmas spirit but the holiday isn't quite here yet so don't forget to turn up for work tomorrow,' he said to a ripple of laughter. 'If you could drink up and leave your glasses on my desk that would be lovely, thanks. The cleaners will clear up in the morning.

Goodnight all.'

It was then that Daisy heard the magic words.

'Can I see you home, Daisy?' asked Al.

'You certainly can,' she said.

They walked instead of taking the bus as Daisy usually did. It was a cold night with the beginnings of a frost, the streetlights bathing the streets with an amber glow, their voices seeming to echo at this late hour, with the houses mostly dark and silent. As their interest in each other was mutual there was no shortage of conversation.

'I took the job at the cinema as a last resort because I couldn't get any office work and the two things couldn't be more different,' she told him. 'I'm obviously not suited to a desk job but I didn't realise that until I started at the Adelphi. It's quite tiring being an usherette and terrible hours but I'm young so I can take it. It's sociable behind the scenes as well as up front and I enjoy that.'

'Some people just aren't suited to certain jobs. But we all have to work so we just get on with it. I'm not mad about my day job but I'm very glad to have it, especially when you hear about so many people being out of work in other parts.'

'I suppose you'd rather be a full-time musician.'

'You bet,' he said then initiated a quick change of subject because he didn't want to go into his parlous financial situation. 'Are you from a big family?'

By the time they had finished exchanging personal details and other items of interest, they had reached her front gate and she waited expectantly for the goodnight kiss. But he paused awhile then just said, 'See you tomorrow at work then.'

'Oh, right,' she said, surprised. 'Thank you for walking me home.'

'Pleasure,' he said. 'See you tomorrow.'

'Yeah.'

What a lovely man he was, she thought as she headed for the front door; a real gentleman too. At least she hoped that was the reason he hadn't kissed her. Neither had he mentioned meeting again apart from work. Perhaps he would tomorrow. Surely she couldn't have imagined the chemistry between them. She was certain she hadn't and was still glowing from it as she put the key in the lock.

Since the big bust-up with her mother when she was late home on her first night at the Adelphi, her parents usually went to bed before she got back if she was later than usual. So she didn't expect anyone to be around when she came in tonight. But her mother was downstairs waiting for her and she didn't look happy.

'Hello Mum, I thought you'd be in bed,' Daisy said.

'Obviously,' said Bertha.

'What do you mean by that?'

'You thought I would be safely tucked up in bed so that you can come rolling home when you like,' Bertha snarled. 'But I never go to sleep until you're in. I just lie there worrying and you know that very well.'

'I'm later than usual because of a Christmas get-together at work. I couldn't let you know because the manager sprung it on us and it would have been rude of me not to go. Sorry if you've been worried.'

Bertha ignored her apology. 'You've been drinking. I can smell it on your breath.'

'Yeah, I have had a couple of glasses of sherry as it happens,' Daisy admitted with an air of defiance. 'We all had a drink with the manager because it's Christmas.'

'And I saw you at the front gate with a boy,' said Bertha accusingly.

'Yes, that's right, Al walked me home.'

'Not that organist fella.'

'Yes, that organist fella,' said Daisy firmly. 'It was very nice of him, don't you think?'

'No I do not,' her mother stated categorically. 'Boys only take girls home for one reason.'

'Mum,' objected Daisy fiercely. 'That's a horrible thing to say. He was the perfect gentleman.'

'This time maybe.'

Now Daisy was furious. 'So this is going to be my life from now on, is it?' she blurted out. 'Every time I do anything the slightest bit adult like having a drink or being friendly with a boy, I'll have you on my back.'

'Now now, you two,' said her father, coming into the room in his dressing gown. 'You'll wake the neighbours if you carry on like this so keep it down.'

'She's been drinking, Bill,' Bertha informed him in disgust.

He raised his eyes. 'Have you, Daisy?' he asked.

'Yes, I had a glass or two of sherry with the manager and staff after work. Which is all very traditional at Christmas. They even did that at the miserable office where I used to work. I'm sure you and Mum will have a good few to drink over the holiday, won't you?'

'Don't be rude, Daisy,' her father reprimanded her.

'And a boy brought her home,' Bertha put in.

His brow knitted into a frown but he just said, 'I hope he was a decent type.'

'Is that all you have to say, Bill?' ranted Bertha. 'Why don't you tell her that she mustn't do these things?'

He was quiet for a moment then said to his wife, 'Why don't you go back to bed, dear? I'll deal with this.'

Daisy waited for her mother to explode but she seemed to think it over for a while then just said, 'All right but make sure you give her what for. We're a decent family, remind her of that.'

'She knows that and doesn't need reminding,' he said patiently. 'I'll be up in a few minutes.'

'You are the only one in this family Mum listens to,' said Daisy as Bertha shuffled off.

'Your mother and I have been together for a long time so we know each other inside out. I know that she comes on a bit strong sometimes with you girls and I have spoken to her about it. But she means well, you know. She is protective, that's all.'

'Suffocating more like.'

'Now now, you know I won't hear a word against her,' he warned. 'She's always got your and your sister's best interests at heart whatever she does. All right, so she worries rather too much about you but that doesn't make her a bad person and I won't have her referred to as such.'

'I thought it was usually the fathers who were over-protective of their daughters,' Daisy said. 'In this family it's Mum and she overdoes it by miles. I can't do anything without getting into an argument with her.'

'Aren't you exaggerating a little, dear?'

'Not really, Dad. Since I've been working at the cinema, it's been terrible.'

'She's bound to worry when you're out of an evening and if you're late...'

'I couldn't let you know I'd be late because Mr Pickles didn't give us any notice about the get-together,' she explained. 'And as for the alcohol thing, all I did was have a couple of drinks with the people I work with and you'd think I'd come home blind drunk, the way she carried on.'

'What about the boy?'

'What about him, Dad?' she asked. 'He walked me home. Nothing more to it than that. But so what if there was? It's perfectly normal for a girl of my age to have a boyfriend.'

'Yes, I suppose it is. I think your mother is finding it hard to accept the fact that you and Mary are adults,' he said. 'I am aware that she overdoes it and I'll speak to her about it again but please try to be patient.'

'She's the one who needs to be patient,' said Daisy. 'Surely she can trust me to behave myself.'

'She does. It's the outside world she has a problem with, now that you are out on your own. Anyway, I'll have a few quiet words with her and see if I can get her to lay off.'

'Thanks Dad,' she said.

67

'I am trusting you to behave, though.'

'I will, Dad, you know that.'

'Goodnight love.'

''Night Dad.'

'The girls are grown up and you will have to accept it,' Bill said to Bertha when he got back into bed. 'All Daisy did was have a Christmas drink or two at work, like most working people at this time of the year.'

'She's underage.'

'She wasn't in a pub, dear,' he said patiently. 'She'll probably have a glass of something with us on Christmas Day. I'm sure you'll not be offended by that.'

'That's different altogether.'

'If you want to blame someone, blame the manager of the cinema. He gave her the sherry. But I'm sure you won't want to put her job at risk by taking this up with him.'

'Of course not,' she said. 'Did you take her to task about the boy?'

'I didn't interrogate her about him if that's what you mean. She's of an age now to take an interest in boys and to have a boyfriend. It's only natural. She said nothing happened.'

'Like she would admit it,' Bertha said scornfully.

'So you don't trust your daughter.'

'It's the boys I don't trust.'

'Well, you're going to have to change your ways because, as I have told you before, if you carry on like this our daughters will leave home at the first possible opportunity and never come back. They'll marry just anyone to get away.'

'It was all so easy when they were little,' she said wistfully. 'Those were the happiest years of my life.'

'Yes, I know they were, dear,' he said patiently. 'And there was no more caring a mother than you. But time has passed and things are different now and you must adapt to it and try to have a more adult sort of relationship with the girls. Of course you'll always worry about them as all parents do. But I think mothers and grown-up daughters can get on well together in a matier sort of way than when they were little. So try and take it easy on them and you might find yourself enjoying them a whole lot more.'

'It isn't easy, Bill,' she said.

'I know that but you need to try. So let's have no more arguments when Daisy gets home late from work. I don't want to spend all my time being peacemaker when I should be sleeping and I have to be as things are because if I leave you to rant at her you're going to say something that will tear this family apart one of these days.'

'I'll try.'

'That's better,' he said but he had more than a suspicion that this wouldn't be the last time they had this conversation.

'More ructions with Mum again last night then,' said Mary to her sister the next morning when they met on the landing, Daisy en route for the bathroom, Mary on her way back to her bedroom. 'Sorry I didn't come down to give you a bit of support but I was just dozing off when I heard you come in and the argument start and I fell asleep.

69

What was it about this time?'

Daisy told her.

'I suppose Dad smoothed things over as usual,' Mary guessed.

'Yeah, the man is a saint. He's the only person she takes any notice of and he does seem to have a big influence on her,' said Daisy. 'It's usually fathers who come down hard on their daughters but not in this family.'

'Mum does enough for the two of them,' said Mary. 'It's only because she cares about us but it is very annoying, I know.'

'She doesn't seem to do it much to you,' Daisy pointed out. 'You get away with murder.'

'She did when I first started work and going out of an evening but you would have been in bed so you probably didn't hear the rows when I got home. I stood my ground with her, and Dad always used to step in. I suppose she's got used to it now so she's laying off me and concentrating on you. She'll stop doing it to you eventually.'

'I bloomin' well hope so because it's driving me mad.'

Mary was thoughtful. 'It seems to be worse since that business at your last job,' she said. 'Maybe the Rumbold affair reminded her of how vulnerable us girls can be. Then you got a job working in the evenings so perhaps the two combined is over-working her protective instincts.'

'Mm,' pondered Daisy. 'Then of course she saw Al outside. But that's probably for the best. I've no intention of living the life of a nun so the sooner she realises that the better.'

'There was progress with Al then,' said Mary

with interest.

'Yeah, I took your advice and went over to him at the party instead of waiting for him to approach me. We got on really well and he asked if he could see me home. He seemed to like me a lot but didn't ask me for a date. Just said he'd see me tomorrow at work.'

'He'll probably ask you out then.'

'I hope so.'

'Anyway I have to get ready for work now,' said Mary, shivering and pulling her dressing gown closer around her. 'We'll talk about it later on.'

Daisy agreed and headed back to her bedroom.

'You're looking a bit gloomy, Al,' said Hester over breakfast that same morning. 'Are you all right?'

'Yeah, I'm fine.'

'You were later than usual getting home.' This was said as an observation rather than a criticism.

'They had a Christmas drinks do at the cinema after work,' he said, finishing his porridge. 'I didn't know anything about it until I got there. I hope you weren't worried.'

'Of course not, dear. You're a grown man.'

'A party eh,' said Dickie. 'Any decent skirt there?'

'That's no way to speak about women,' admonished his mother. 'So please don't do it in front of me.'

'It's just the way men talk, Mum,' said Dickie.

'Not in this house they don't,' she said. 'Your father never did it because it's disrespectful so don't let me hear it again.'

'All right Mum, sorry.' He turned to his brother.

71

'Any nice girls at the party?'

'All the usherettes were there and most of them are nice,' he replied.

'Anyone special?'

'Wouldn't you like to know.' Al drained his tea-cup and rose.

'Yeah, we would.'

'You're out of luck, little brother,' he said. 'I'm off to work. See you later.'

Hester and Dickie exchanged knowing glances as Al left the room.

The programme had finished that evening, the cinema lights were on and Al was playing the audience out to Cole Porter's 'Just One of Those Things'. He'd been worrying all day about what he should do about Daisy. He thought she was the loveliest girl he had ever seen and wanted to ask her for a date but didn't have the funds for that sort of thing. Girls expected to be taken to nice places and about all he could manage at the moment was a cup of tea and a bun in Lyons. If he left it until he was in a position to splash out he could lose her altogether. There would be no shortage of interest in a girl like her.

He was almost certain that his feelings for her were reciprocated. It had felt good when they were together last night and she'd probably expected him to ask her out. But how could he when he didn't have the cash?

The auditorium had emptied so he pressed the down button on the organ and descended. As he gathered his music together and headed for his dressing room he made a decision.

Daisy was feeling disappointed as she checked among the seats for left property. She had hoped that Al would find her in the staffroom or the auditorium but she hadn't seen him except at the organ. Now the show was over and he'd disappeared. So she must have misread the signals and imagined something that wasn't there.

As she got to the end of a row, deep in thought, she heard someone say her name and when she looked up there he was, smiling at her.

'Can I walk you home, Daisy?' he asked, looking serious.

'Yeah, that would be lovely,' she said.

'I'll wait for you in the foyer then.'

She nodded, all smiles now.

'I have something to say to you,' said Al when they were finally on their way home. 'And you might not like me much when I've told you.'

'Oh dear,' she said. 'That sounds worrying. I hope you haven't murdered anyone.'

'No of course not,' he assured her, looking worried.

'I wasn't being serious.'

'Oh right. Anyway, I'll come straight to the point,' he said quickly. 'It's well ... I like you a lot and I would love it if you would go out with me...' His voice tailed off.

'So, what's for me not to like about that?' she asked.

'Well ... I don't have any spare cash at the moment so I'm not much of a prospect as a boyfriend. I won't be able to take you to nice places.'

'And you think I won't like you because of that? What kind of girl do you think I am?'

'A lovely one but, oh this is so embarrassing...'

'No need to be embarrassed,' she said. 'I'm glad you've told me.'

'You need to hear it all,' he began. 'My father had a long illness and subsequently died but he ran up a good few debts and I'm helping my mother to pay them off. That's why I'm doing two jobs. In the spring the debt will be paid off so I'll be able to splash out a bit then I hope.'

'Oh Al,' she said ardently. 'You don't have to splash out on me. We can go for walks and I can treat you to a cup of tea and a bun in Lyons every now and again.'

He laughed, relieved to have it out in the open. 'That is one of the things I can afford to treat you to. So don't even think of offering.'

'We'll see,' she said.

They walked to Daisy's house hand in hand and at her gate they had their first kiss, a gentle but happy and exciting occasion. Daisy thought her mother was probably spying on her from the window but nothing could spoil this moment for her.

When Al headed off down the street and she made her way indoors, warm inside with joy, she was surprised to find the house in darkness and no sign of her mother. Dad must have finally got through to her, she thought with relief, which was just as well because she was hoping that tonight's embrace was just the first of many.

'Come away from the window, Bertha,' said Bill

74

into the darkness. 'It isn't right to spy on people.'

'But Daisy is out there with that boy again,' she told him.

'So what if she is,' he said. 'Stop snooping and come back to bed, for goodness' sake. Let the girl grow up and live her life. We can trust her not to misbehave.'

Bertha's excessive maternal instincts forced her to intervene in her daughter's affairs. For Daisy's own good, of course. The girl didn't know what was best for her. How could she when she had no experience of life? But, realising that she would seriously upset her husband if she continued her current surveillance, Bertha forced herself away from the window and got back into bed. She had no plans to stand back on a permanent basis though.

Chapter Four

'Do cheer up, Daisy,' admonished her mother. 'Anyone would think it was Doomsday instead of Christmas Day.'

'Sorry Mum,' said Daisy absently.

'Make sure you put a smile on your face when your aunts and uncles come to visit later.'

'Yeah. All right.' She was very vague.

'I don't know what's got into you, going around with a face like a poker on a Christmas Day,' Bertha persisted. 'Is it the time of the month or something?'

'No, I'm feeling fine,' she said. 'I didn't even realise that I seemed miserable.'

'Well you do, so enter into the spirit of the day please. A lot of effort goes into Christmas and I expect people to appreciate it.'

'I do, of course.'

Daisy was in a state of acute longing. For the first time in her life she wanted Christmas to be over so that she could see Al again. The traditions she usually adored – the presents, the abundance of festive food and the visiting relatives – were simply to be endured, so strong were her feelings for him. They had agreed that their romance was too young to involve their families at this stage, and as the festive season was very much a family occasion they simply had to grin and bear it.

'Is it that boy you are moping about? That organist fella. The one who's been seeing you home.'

'Leave the girl alone, Bertha, for goodness' sake,' interrupted Bill, who could see that this was heading towards a full-blown row. 'It's Christmas Day so we don't want any arguments.'

'I'm not looking for an argument,' she came back at him. 'I was just thinking that if Daisy is so keen on the boy we should invite him to Sunday tea some time after Christmas. To give us all a chance to get to know him.'

Daisy recognised the gesture but had strong doubts about it because she suspected that her mother would embarrass her and make Al feel awkward. Sunday tea with the family was more or less standard for courting couples but it was still very early days for her and Al.

But she said, 'Let's see about it after Christmas,

shall we, Mum? Maybe I should get to know him a bit better first.'

'As you wish,' said Bertha while Mary exchanged a look with her sister, understanding flowing between them.

'I've met this girl,' Al told Hester and Dickie as they tucked into their Christmas dinner. 'She's an usherette at the Adelphi.'

Up went his mother's brows. 'Oh,' she said. 'The tone of your voice indicates she might be special.'

'She is,' he confirmed. '*Very* special.'

'Good-looking?' asked Dickie typically.

'Absolutely,' he replied. 'Blonde hair, blue eyes. She has a nice nature too.'

'She sounds lovely,' approved Dickie. 'So when will we get to meet her?'

'You can bring her home to Sunday tea whenever you're ready,' said Hester, who was delighted at the prospect of a steady girlfriend for her eldest. 'Or anytime at all. You know we welcome visitors in this family.'

'I don't want to rush things and risk putting her off,' said Al, though in his heart he was certain that he and Daisy were meant for each other.

'You decide when and we'll look forward to it, won't we, Dickie?'

'I'll say,' he agreed wholeheartedly.

'I didn't half miss you over the holiday,' said Al when he and Daisy were together at last and he was walking her home from the cinema after work.

'Likewise,' she said. 'I thought it would never

end. But I had to put up a front to keep my mother off my back. It isn't acceptable to be anything less than ecstatic in our house on Christmas Day.'

'It's the season to be jolly and all that,' he said. 'But I was thinking about you so much I told them about you. Mum said I should have invited you over but I knew you'd be with your family so I thought I'd better leave it.'

'You were right to,' she said. 'They wouldn't have liked it if I'd gone out. Mum would have really blown her top.'

'Mum and Dickie are keen to meet you.'

'My mother suggested that I invite you to Sunday tea,' she said. 'But I thought it might be too soon.'

'I'm game if you are,' he told her. 'I'll come whenever you are ready and try not to show you up.'

If there was any embarrassing to be done it would be by her mother but loyalty towards her prompted Daisy to just say jokingly, 'You could never do that.'

'So you're an organist at the Adelphi then,' said Bertha as they staggered through that first, nerve-racking Sunday tea.

'Only temporarily,' he said. 'I'm actually a pianist.'

'I thought Daisy said you worked in a factory,' she said, managing to spice the remark with disapproval.

'I do. But I'm a musician as well; it brings in a few extra shillings.'

'It must be nice to be able to play a musical in-

78

strument,' intervened Bill pleasantly, in the hope of ending his wife's interrogation.

'I enjoy it,' said Al. 'I've been playing since I was a little kid. My mother is a piano teacher, a very good one actually, so there is always music in our house.'

'That must be lovely.'

'It's all I've ever known, Mr Blake.' He looked at Daisy's father. 'How about you? What do you do?'

'I'm a skilled worker in an engineering factory.'

'Oh, that's interesting,' Al said and, just to be polite, added, 'It's a good idea to learn a trade. Sets you up for life.'

'Why didn't you learn one then?' demanded Bertha.

'Mum,' hissed Daisy, scarlet with embarrassment, while Bill glared at his wife and Mary struggled with an attack of nervous giggles.

'That's all right,' said Al with perfect manners. 'It wasn't possible for me to learn a trade when I left school, Mrs Blake, because I needed to be earning a full wage, not that of an apprentice.'

All eyes were on Bertha, forbidding her to take this further. 'Oh,' she said. 'I see.'

'I don't think it would have suited me anyway.' He paused. 'The factory work pays the bills. I took the organist job because I like to be involved with music and it's regular extra money. I'm very glad I did too because it's through that I met Daisy.'

'Ah, what a lovely thing to say,' said Mary, beaming.

'Very nice,' added Bill and, turning to his wife

added, 'Isn't it, dear?'

'Yes, yes, of course,' she said flushing guiltily. 'Another sandwich, Al?'

Daisy hoped things might improve now but what an ordeal it was turning out to be.

The young couple went for a walk as soon as they could escape without causing offence, and headed for the river. It was a dry January day with dark clouds rolling across the pale grey skies but there was the usual riverside sense of space and light despite the advanced afternoon. The wind was keen and they were both wrapped up in coats and scarves, their arms entwined.

'Your mother just wants what is best for you,' he said as though reading her thoughts. 'It's only natural she would want to know something about me as we're going out.'

Actually Bertha hadn't been too bad after that first toe-curling grilling. Daisy suspected that her father had managed a few covert words with her in the kitchen. 'I suppose so. I expect your mother will be the same with me when I come to yours for the first time.'

Al gave an odd little smile and said, 'We'll see. Can I tell her you'll come next Sunday?'

The idea of going through the whole wretched rigmarole again next week at his house didn't inspire her with any joy but she was so enamoured with him she said, 'Yeah that will be lovely.'

'Good.'

They stood on Hammersmith Bridge for a while longer, huddled together by the railing, with his arm around her as the incipient dusk began to creep in, the river dark beneath them in the fading light. The air was clear and cold with a familiar hint of urban smokiness.

Al turned and kissed the side of her face. 'I love you, Daisy Blake,' he whispered.

'I love you too, Al Dawson,' she responded.

Standing there with him on this bleak winter afternoon, she didn't think she had ever been so happy.

The Dawson household was completely different to the Blakes', Daisy realised the instant she arrived for tea the following Sunday.

'Lovely to meet you, Daisy. Come on in,' said Hester, beaming, her bushy blonde hair worn with a side parting and clipped with kirby grips. 'Come and sit by the fire.'

'Yeah, come and get warm,' added Dickie. 'I'm Al's brother. Mum and I have been dying to meet you. Seems my brother is smitten with you.'

This earned him an admonitory glare from Al and they all piled into the front room where there was a fire glowing in the hearth and a dining table devoid of food or even a tablecloth.

'How pretty you are, Daisy,' said Hester, ushering the girl into a chair by the fire. 'Such lovely hair.'

'Thank you,' said Daisy. 'Yours is nice too.'

'Oh lor, my colour comes out of bottle I'm afraid, always has done even as a girl,' she said. 'I always wanted to be a blonde but I'm naturally nondescript.' She paused for breath. 'Now make yourself comfortable. I'm really looking forward

81

to getting to know you.'

'Mum,' said Al in a quiet but slightly warning tone. 'What about tea?'

'Oh ... yes, of course,' she said. 'Hark at me, going on. I should have had the tea ready, of course, but I had to go through some exam music with a pupil and the only time I could do it was this afternoon though I don't usually work on Sundays. It won't take more than a few minutes to prepare. Put the tablecloth on please, boys, and lay the table.'

'Can I give you a hand in the kitchen, Mrs Dawson?' offered Daisy.

'Sweet of you to offer,' responded Hester warmly. 'But we don't expect our visitors to work.'

'I'd be very happy to,' said Daisy.

Hester smiled. 'Well, if you really would like to it might speed things up a bit. It's only a case of buttering some bread and setting some cakes out. I've made an apple pie as well. I do hope you like it.'

'I'm sure I will,' said Daisy politely.

'I should wait until you've tasted it before you make a decision,' said Dickie, grinning.

'You might lose some teeth in the process,' added Al.

'Honestly, you boys are awful,' said Hester, not in the least offended. 'You've no idea of the cheek I have to put up with from these two, Daisy.'

'You both look well on your mother's cooking anyway,' she said.

'Thank you dear,' said Hester. 'How lovely to have some support.'

'Oh no, they'll be ganging up against us blokes

now,' joked Dickie.

And so it went on. Chatter and affectionate teasing all the way through tea. Mrs Dawson obviously enjoyed the banter and the apple tart was delicious so the mockery was just a bit of fun.

Later on Mrs Dawson showed Daisy into the back room which had windows on to the tiny garden and was furnished with a piano, a filing cabinet, a desk and chair, bookshelves, framed photographs and potted plants dotted around.

'This is where I earn my living,' she explained. 'This room keeps me sane in troubled times too.'

'Al told me you lost your husband.'

The older woman nodded. 'Saddest thing that's ever happened to me and the boys,' she said, becoming serious. 'But you just have to carry on, don't you?'

'I suppose you do,' said Daisy, but she had no experience of such things.

'This is a very joyful place,' said Mrs Dawson, looking thoughtful. 'Many children sit on the piano stool; some come because they want to learn how to play, others are kids of ambitious parents and the poor babes have no interest. A few pupils drive me mad because they don't practise; others fill me with joy because of their diligence. But always I like to teach and to play and to be involved with music. I am so lucky that I have this thing that is so special to me.'

'Al has taken after you.'

'Yes, he's a fine pianist,' she said. 'It's something we share. Maybe it will never earn us a fortune but we will always have it and I cherish that.'

Daisy stayed until late in the evening and when

it was time to leave she was already anticipating the next visit with relish because the Dawsons were so full of heart and fun to be with.

'Well,' said Al when he was walking her home. 'What's the verdict?'

'They're lovely.'

'You probably think we're a bit of a mad lot, though,' he suggested.

'A little unconventional maybe.'

'We wouldn't know how to be any other way,' he said. 'We never have run with the pack. Our lives have always been interwoven with Mum's musical activity. She's usually involved in some way, either teaching or playing for local shows and so on. Dickie isn't musical but he always wants to go off on some sort of adventure.'

'You and Dickie both look well on it anyway.'

'Mum is the best and has always made sure we were well looked after even though she was busy,' he said. 'She has a very big heart and is a wonderful cook, even though you might not realise it from listening to us.'

'I knew you wouldn't have teased her like that if she really was bad at cooking,' she said. 'Anyway, I tasted her cakes and apple pie.'

'So you won't mind coming again then,' he said brightly. 'These family traditions have to be observed when you're courting, don't they?'

'They certainly do,' she said, enjoying the epithet he had put on their relationship.

Through winter and into spring their sweet but impecunious courtship continued. He saw her home from the cinema every night, they had family Sunday teas, walked miles in the cold just to be alone together and on Saturday mornings they had a treat, a cup of tea and a bun in their local Lyons.

To add to the joy for Daisy was the fact that her mother's attitude towards Al had changed now that she was used to him and she was always pleasant to him. Whether she was pretending to like him because the others did and she didn't want to be unpopular with them, Daisy didn't know. She just enjoyed the fact that there were no more inquisitions; just enjoyable conversation. Both her parents welcomed him into their home and as he was there rather a lot it made things agreeable.

One Saturday morning in May, Al arrived at the teashop with flowers and chocolates for her and asked her if she would like to go dancing that evening as it was her night off.

'I've arranged with Mr Pickles to have the night off too,' he told her. 'He's got someone to cover for me. I'll do the afternoon performance though.'

'Why is this all happening?'

'Because the debt is finally paid off,' he explained joyfully. 'So my wages after rent and housekeeping are my own. I want to make up to you for being such a stingy boyfriend.'

'You've not been stingy,' she said. 'Well, not on purpose anyway, and I don't need to have money spent on me.' She saw the earnestness in his eyes. 'But it would be lovely to go out and have some fun tonight.'

'Good, so the Palais it is,' he said happily. 'What time shall I call for you?'

'I can be ready by seven thirty.'

'I'll be there on the dot.' He looked at her. 'Would you like another bun to celebrate?'

She laughed. 'There's no need to go mad. You've spoiled me enough with the chocolates and flowers.'

He reached across for her hand. 'I could never do enough for you Daisy,' he said tenderly.

She squeezed his hand, imbued with love for him.

It would be difficult for anyone living in Britain to be unaware of the seriousness of the threat of war. If you worked in a cinema it was impossible because the newsreels usually featured Hitler and the troubles abroad. Now, apparently, there were plans for conscription for young men here in Britain in the event of war breaking out. This was being discussed in Parliament.

'It's getting a bit scary now, isn't it, Daisy?' whispered Doreen when they were on duty that afternoon and standing at the back of the auditorium during the newsreel. 'My Alfie will have to go if the worst happens.'

'So will Al I suppose,' said Daisy. 'But I don't think there will be a war. Surely it would have happened by now if it was going to. There's been talk about it for long enough.'

'There is that,' agreed Doreen. 'But Alfie reckons it might come to war because Hitler is such a madman and shows no sign of backing down.'

Daisy shivered at the thought. 'It doesn't bear thinking about,' she said. 'Al's taking me to the Palais tonight so I'm going to forget all about it.'

'That's the best thing. You go and enjoy yourself.'

'I'll do my best.'

'Oh Al, I'm having such a lovely time,' said Daisy as they quickstepped around the floor to music from a well-known dance band, beneath changing coloured lights from the ceiling, the sprung floor crowded with couples enjoying themselves.

'I'm so glad,' he said. 'As that is the whole point of us coming here.'

'I don't have to have all this, though,' she told him. 'I'm quite content with the cheaper way of life. But this is lovely for a change, of course.'

'This sort of thing will be the norm in future, not just for a change. I'm not well off but at least I'll have some money in my pocket from now on.' He exhaled deeply. 'Oh it's such a relief to have the debt finished with. Nice for Mum too. She can relax a bit now.'

'You can be proud of yourself.'

'It was a joint effort,' he explained. 'All three of us put something into the pot every week.'

'So I suppose you'll be able leave your job at the cinema now,' she suggested.

'I could do but I'm not going to,' he replied. 'I rather enjoy it and the extra money will be useful. I want to get something behind me, Daisy, and at least I'll get to see you as you're always there.'

He didn't mention that he wanted to get some money behind him because he wanted to marry her. He couldn't even afford a decent engagement ring at the moment, let alone what it took to set up home. But he couldn't imagine a future without her. He wanted her in his life always.

'I'm glad you'll be staying,' she said.

'I'm pleased too,' he said as the music ended and they left the floor hand in hand.

The next number was a slow waltz and they couldn't have got any closer as they smooched around the floor.

The cinema was packed; every seat taken, even the cheapest at the front of the stalls. It was a Saturday night and the film showing was a sentimental tale called *Goodbye Mr Chips*. Apart from an occasional cough and a rustle of sweet paper from the auditorium there wasn't a sound to be heard as the emotional story and the fine acting held the audience spellbound. The red glow of lit cigarettes could be seen here and there and a pall of smoke hung over everything.

Then the background music stopped, the screen went blank and there was an immediate outcry. People were booing and whistling and slow hand-clapping.

Daisy, who was on duty upstairs in the balcony, heard her name being called by Mr Pickles, who seemed to be in a state of anxiety. He called to her. 'Could you go to the projection room please and tell John that if this fault isn't corrected in five minutes he's sacked. I can't go myself because I have to go on stage and apologise to the punters. Tell him that he'll collect his cards tonight if the film isn't fixed *and quick.*'

'That's a bit harsh, Mr Pickles,' she said. 'I'm sure he's doing his best.'

'His best obviously isn't good enough. The customers are going mad out there.'

'He isn't infallible,' she protested in his defence.

'He's a fully trained projectionist and this cinema is a commercial enterprise,' he ranted. 'I have people to answer to and they won't be best pleased if I have to refund all the ticket money. Anyway you're not paid to argue, so please get on and do as you're told.'

This was a side to Mr Pickles she had never seen before and didn't like but she headed off for the projection room where she found John leaning over the projector, engrossed in what he was doing. There were several other projectors in the room which had only very small windows. Bare light bulbs hung down from the ceiling.

'Mr Pickles sent me,' she told him.

'Is he threatening me with the sack?' he asked.

'He certainly is.'

'How long have I got to fix it?'

'Five minutes.'

'That's not too bad,' he said. 'It's usually two.'

'He's done this before?'

'Every time we have a problem with the film. He gets into a real state and shouts his head off because he has the cinema's reputation to think of and the owners to please. He's a decent bloke normally though.'

'That's what I've always thought.'

'He doesn't mean any of that about sacking me,' he said. 'He'll be back to his old self as soon as I've fixed it.'

'Oh dear.'

'What's up?'

'I gave him some cheek; told him he shouldn't

be so hard on you,' she explained. 'We're all friends here and I wanted to speak up for you.'

He looked at her. 'You mean you put your own job on the line for me?'

'I suppose I did but I didn't realise I was doing that at the time. He just struck me as being unfair and I told him so. It seemed the natural thing to do.'

'I'm touched,' he said. 'If he gives you the sack on my head be it. But he won't.'

'Oh lor, me and my big mouth.'

'You are a diamond even with the big mouth. Don't ever change.'

'Maybe I should.'

'That's it,' he said. 'All fixed. We're back in business. His majesty will calm down now. He always does.'

'I'd better get back to work.' She turned to leave.

'Oh, Daisy.'

'Yeah.'

'Thanks for your support.'

'A pleasure, John,' she said, thinking what a very decent bloke he was.

A few of them went to the café after work that night and John was full of praise for Daisy.

'Your girlfriend is a proper gem,' he said to Al, and told him how she had spoken up for him to Mr Pickles.

'Daisy,' said Al. 'That was very kind of you but also a bit impetuous.'

'Don't worry,' she assured him. 'I won't lose my job over it. I went to see Mr Pickles in his office later to try and smooth things over and he didn't seem in the least bit bothered. Seemed to have forgotten all about it.'

'He does that,' said John. 'He gets all up in the air if something goes wrong but once it's put right he forgets it and moves on. He doesn't hold grudges. He's no pushover though. If someone did something really awful, they'd be out.'

'It's a big responsibility running a cinema,' said someone and it was generally agreed that their boss was one of the best.

Someone else mentioned that they still missed Doreen on the evening shift now that she was married and only worked afternoons.

'I miss her too,' said Daisy.

'You've got me to make up for it,' said Al. 'And we'd better be going soon or we'll have your mum after us.'

'She'll be fine,' said Daisy. 'Now that she knows I'm with you she doesn't worry.'

'I suppose not,' he said.

Even though Bertha was careful to hide it she did still worry excessively about Daisy and was, at that moment, lying in bed fretting about what her youngest daughter might be getting up to out at this hour.

Bertha had welcomed Al into the family rather than alienate the rest of them, although he seemed to think he was God's gift. Personally, Bertha thought Daisy could have done much better for herself. Al had nothing in the way of prospects and was far too good-looking and gregarious to be trusted. Daisy had said something about him paying off his late father's debts which was all very worthy but didn't say much for his family's financial standing.

But as Bill was so fond of telling her, he was young; he had time to make something of himself. Even so, to her mind he wouldn't get rich playing the cinema organ. His mother was a musician too; they sounded an unconventional lot and not her type of people at all. Still, Al did seem to be very fond of Daisy and she of him.

But he was a man and as such a potential danger to her daughter's reputation. Until both her girls were safely married that was always a concern.

She had a sudden thought. Mary wasn't in yet either. She'd said she was going out with some friend from work. Honestly, these girls and the hours they kept. It was no wonder her hair was turning white.

Daisy was just getting into bed when her sister came into her room, positively glowing.

'Who is he?' asked Daisy.

'There isn't a he,' she replied. 'I've been out with a friend from work.'

'This is your sister you're talking to, not your mother,' Daisy reminded her. 'So come on, let's have the truth. A female friend from work wouldn't make you look like that – all pink-cheeked and gooey-eyed.'

'It depends who the friend is,' she said, looking happy. 'But you're right, of course. It is a man. I met him through work though so it wasn't a complete lie. He's one of the regular reps who call to see the manager. He's gorgeous, Daisy, and I absolutely adore him.'

'So when do we get to meet him?'

'I'm not bringing him home.'

'Why not?'

'He's quite a bit older than me; in his thirties. Mum would never approve.'

'I don't see why not,' said Daisy. 'An age difference isn't a crime.'

'Picture the scene, Daisy,' said Mary. 'I invite him for Sunday tea and this mature man turns up instead of the fresh-faced boy Mum and Dad are expecting. I don't think Ray would be impressed with the inquisition either.'

'You can't *never* bring him home.'

'Why not?'

'It's what people do,' she said. 'It's traditional.'

'Mm, maybe it is but I'm not telling Mum and Dad anything about him, not for the moment anyway.' Mary was adamant. 'Maybe further down the line but for now I shall be going out with a friend from work as far as Mum and Dad are concerned. So not a word, Daisy, please.'

'Of course,' she agreed. 'But do I get to know anything about him?'

'His name is Ray. He's six foot tall, has lovely brown eyes and is very smartly dressed. He has a good sense of humour and can't do enough for me. He took me to a restaurant in the West End tonight.'

'Ooh I say.'

'It is lovely, but I'd want to be with him if we just went for a walk or to buy chips.'

'I know the feeling,' said Daisy.

'It's like that for you with Al then.'

'Absolutely.'

'Ray is the one,' Mary said dreamily.

'I must say I did wonder why you were seeing so much of your friend from work but I've been too preoccupied with Al to take much notice.'

'Which was lucky for me because I wasn't ready to talk about it,' she said. 'But I've been seeing Ray for a while now. Long enough to know that I'm in love with him.'

'Really. I'd never have guessed,' said Daisy sardonically, smiling broadly.

'That obvious, is it?'

'Absolutely!'

'I'll have to watch myself in front of Mum and Dad then.'

'You will indeed,' agreed Daisy. 'You'll have to bring him home for a vetting before Mum gets to work it out.'

'Which is enough to put any man off and is why it's a secret, for now anyway.'

Daisy was pleased for her sister. She, herself, was happy and she wanted the same for Mary. It was nice that they both had someone special.

Chapter Five

It had become impossible for most people to be unaffected by the preparations for war that were taking place all around them: the trenches in the parks, the issue of gas masks and Anderson shelters, the predominance of sandbags in the area. But Daisy and Al were too engrossed in each other to pay a great deal of attention, though their time together felt even more precious in this increasingly disturbing environment.

Now that Al had pocket money, they made the most of their day off on Sundays and either took the train to Brighton, or the river at Runnymede for a picnic. Sometimes they went to the West End and spent time in one of the parks.

'I can't imagine a future without you in it, Daisy,' said Al one sunny Sunday afternoon when they were sitting on a bench by the Serpentine idly watching the abundant wildlife and listening to the gentle splash of oars from the rowing boats.

'Nor me without you,' she said. 'But why would we even want to try?'

'Because there is so much uncertainty around at the moment, it makes you wonder,' he explained. 'But I know that, somehow, whatever happens, we'll be together in the end.'

'I certainly hope so,' she said. 'But there isn't a war yet. It might not happen.'

'Maybe there's still a very small chance that it won't.' He sounded doubtful. 'But even if the worst happens, it won't last long, so they say, and we'll be together when it's all over. You and me were meant for each other.'

'I know, Al,' she said seriously.

Had he been in a position to do so, Al would have proposed to her there and then. But he had to get a decent amount of dosh behind him before he could take that step. Anyway, for the moment they were happy being together and in love.

'Shall we have a wander, listen to what the anti-war protestors have to say at Speakers' Corner then go and get some tea?' he suggested.

'That would be lovely,' she said and they made their way towards Marble Arch, hand in hand through the crowds. The atmosphere here was jolly, as though people were determined to enjoy themselves despite the depressing news bulletins.

Bertha suggested that Daisy invite a few friends round to the house for tea to celebrate her eighteenth birthday on the nearest Sunday to it. Nothing formal; just some light refreshments in the late afternoon and a little pleasant conversation.

So it was that Al, John, Doreen and her husband Alfie arrived and they all gathered in the back room with the French doors wide open on to the garden, a small area of lawn well looked after by Daisy's father.

'So this is the Adelphi crowd we've heard so much about, is it?' said Mary after introductions had been made. 'I notice you haven't invited the famous Mr Pickles.'

'He's a lovely bloke but we can do without the boss around when we are off duty,' Al explained. 'He'd be telling us all what to do; he just wouldn't be able to help himself. Cinema management is in his blood. He probably ushers his family into their seats at home of an evening.'

'He'd want to talk to me about the latest projection techniques,' said John.

'Yeah I suppose he might,' said Mary, looking at John with a hint of admiration. 'I think what you do is very clever. I can't begin to imagine how you make it work.'

'Don't tell him that,' said Al jokingly. 'His head will get too big to get in the door of the projection room.'

There was a good-humoured protest from John and laughter from everyone else. Daisy opened her presents – a necklace from her parents, perfume from Al and chocolates and toiletries from the others.

Then there was the birthday cake, a pretty confection with pink and white icing and eighteen candles.

'This is lovely, Mrs Blake,' said John after he had had a taste. 'Did you make it yourself?'

'Oh yes,' she said, flushing with pleasure at the compliment. 'I wouldn't dream of buying a shop cake.'

'You'll have to teach my wife how to make a cake,' said Alfie, teasing Doreen, his hazel eyes full of laughter. 'She could do with a few lessons.'

'Watch it, you,' objected Doreen, slapping him playfully, 'That's a bloomin' insult. In fact, I think it might even be grounds for a divorce.'

They all laughed at this and the party continued. Daisy was touched by the way her friends included her parents in the conversation even though they were of a different generation and had nothing in common. Mum was complimented about her baking and her father about his neat garden. They both positively glowed. When Mum let herself go a little she was good company, observed Daisy. It was a pity she didn't do it more often.

There was even some sherry for the toast. When birthday wishes filled the air as the sun went down over the small suburban garden, Daisy felt a lump rise in her throat. Her happiness was tinged with sadness because this event felt so precious but time would move on and it would disappear into the past. She hoped she never forgot how she'd felt today with family and friends and the man she loved around her.

'It was a good party, Daisy,' remarked Mary later on when everyone had left and the sisters were in Mary's bedroom while she put her curlers in. 'They're really nice people, your cinema lot.'

'Now you know why I enjoy going to work.'

'I certainly do.'

'Mum and Dad were on good form I thought,' Daisy mentioned. 'I wasn't sure about it when Mum suggested the party because she can be so off-putting. But she was as good as gold. It's a pity your Ray couldn't be there.'

'He would have come if I'd asked him I expect but I wouldn't throw him in at the deep end like that. When I do bring him home it will be when there's only the family.'

'I think you're wise. A crowd might be a bit much for a first time,' said Daisy. 'You and John seemed to get on well. You were talking to him a lot.'

'He's an interesting bloke and I was quite impressed,' said Mary. 'Just to talk to obviously. I don't fancy him or anything.'

'Of course not. You've got Ray.'

'Exactly.'

Right up until the final moments of peace, Daisy maintained her optimism that war could somehow be avoided. When the announcement came on that sunny Sunday morning in September telling the nation they were now at war with Germany, the Blake sisters burst into tears while their parents remained composed but seemed quietly bewildered.

'Why did they let it happen?' sobbed Daisy. 'Surely something could have been done to stop it.'

'World affairs are tricky to deal with,' said Bill. 'I'm sure the government did their best to avoid war but it was out of their hands in the end.'

'But how will it affect us?' she asked, looking pale.

'We'll be all right,' her mother assured her, putting up a front. 'We'll just have to get on with it, the same as everyone else.'

'I wonder what happens now,' said Mary.

'None of us knows the answer to that,' said Bertha thickly. 'We'll have to listen to the wireless to find out.'

Bill went to the window to see a crowd in the street. 'But at this moment we need to be with other people, so let's join our neighbours outside.'

'I've got things to do. I have to finish making the blackout curtains and get the dinner ready,' said Bertha, who was naturally unsociable and always kept to herself.

'You can leave everything just for ten minutes or so on a day like today,' he said and headed towards the front door with the women following.

The Dawson brothers were very supportive of their mother, who was in floods of tears on hearing the news. An emotional woman anyway, the outbreak of war was too much.

'You'll be all right, Mum,' said Al, putting his arm around her. 'You've got two strong sons to look after you.'

'It isn't me personally I'm upset about,' she told them. 'It's the whole idea of us being at war and not being a free country. Not only that, you boys will be called up. Both of you now that Dickie has turned eighteen.'

'Mm, you're probably right,' Al was forced to agree. 'But it probably won't be for long. People are saying it will be all over by Christmas.'

'Maybe,' she said, blowing her nose and composing herself. 'But we'll have to get on with it however long it lasts. I'm all right now, boys, so let's go and see how the neighbours have taken it. We need to look out for each other at a time like this.'

'You're right,' said Al, leading the way to the front door.

As well as being told to carry their gas masks with them at all times, the BBC newsreader on the wireless at teatime also announced that all places of entertainment would be closed until further notice.

'Blimey,' said Daisy. 'That means I'm out of a job. Do you think cinemas will be closed for the duration of the war?'

'I shouldn't think so,' said her father. 'But none of us knows what will happen yet.'

'I'll be broke if it goes on for too long,' she said. 'I shall have to look for another job.'

'I can help you out with cash,' offered Al, who was having tea at the Blakes'. 'I've got my day job so I'll be able to manage without the extra.'

Daisy turned and smiled at him. 'That is sweet of you but I'll be all right. I'll look for something else if the cinema stays closed. But I'll go to the Adelphi tomorrow to see if I can find out anything.'

No one mentioned what was uppermost in their minds: the fact that Al would be called up.

'What a peculiar day it's been,' said Daisy when she was saying goodnight to Al at the front gate, the street in darkness as the blackout was now in force. 'I suppose we'll get used to it, whatever lies in store.'

'Of course we will but it might not be too bad.'

'How did your mother take it?'

'She shed a few tears but soon recovered,' he said. 'She's a strong woman even though she tends to be emotional.'

'I suppose she would be upset, having two sons.' Daisy cleared her throat. 'When do you think you'll get called up?'

'I'm young and fit so they'll want blokes like me sharpish I should think.'

'Oh Al,' she said. 'How will I survive without you?'

'The same goes for me having to be without you.' He put his arms around her and held her close. 'But you and I will always be together no matter what and despite having to part for a while.' His voice was hoarse with emotion. 'Yes, I will have to go in the services but the war won't last for ever and when it's over we'll take up where we left off and be stronger than ever.'

'I know,' she said. 'It just seems as though we've been plunged into a dark new world.'

'Dark is the word. Pitch black without any lights.' He put his mouth to her ear and whispered, 'It isn't all bad though. This blackout is a flippin' gift to courting couples. People can't see what we might be getting up to.'

She laughed. 'Al Dawson, you're a wicked man,' she said, teasing him and suddenly feeling normal for the first time that day, thanks to his sense of humour. 'But we won't be getting up to anything different to usual just because it's dark. So forget it.'

'Spoilsport,' he laughed.

Restored to her normal cheerful self she could see that they were all in this together. Families, friends, neighbours and lovers the length and breadth of the country were feeling concerned tonight. Nobody wanted a war but that's what they had and they must get on and do whatever was required of them.

'So give us a kiss before I try to find my way home,' he said.

'Come here then,' she said, drawing him close.

The Adelphi re-opened on the ninth of September and there was a positive stampede. Daisy had never seen such queues. There were a few changes; the weekly and sometimes twice weekly change of films ended so that the same films were shown for longer, many of the advertising posters disappeared and the foyer became a showcase for

102

wartime campaigns. The staff were all trained in the procedure should there be an air raid and taught the basics of first aid.

The biggest change of all came a few weeks after the re-opening when Mr Pickles announced to the staff that the Adelphi would be opening on a Sunday in future to cater for soldiers and war workers who were away from home. No one was forced to work the extra day but it was made clear that it was expected of them in these testing times. Everyone was given a day off in lieu and Monday was Daisy's.

She didn't hear anyone refuse to work on a Sunday. For her personally it meant precious time with Al lost but she knew it couldn't be helped. Everyone was keen to do their bit, including Mr Pickles who seemed to have become something of an ambassador for wartime spirit, encouraging his staff as they coped with the extra numbers and new restrictions. He even went outside for some rousing repartee with the people in the queue.

'It won't be long now, folks,' he'd inform them heartily. 'You'll be glad you waited when you get inside because we have a corking programme for you tonight.' He looked at the buskers who were plying their trade to the cinema queues. 'Though you're not doing too badly for entertainment out here, are you?' He put some money in the tin of a man playing the piano accordion. 'I hope you'll all feel inclined to show your appreciation.'

'He seems to have found a new lease of life since war broke out,' Daisy remarked to Doreen in their break one day.

'The takings will be well up with all these crowds

and Sunday opening,' suggested Doreen. 'That's probably why he's feeling so cheerful.'

'I suppose that's part of it,' said Daisy. 'But I think he genuinely enjoys the chance to be a bit more sociable. He's very good at it too.'

'I think he enjoys it too,' agreed Doreen. 'People in general seem to be friendlier now.'

'You're telling me,' said Daisy. 'Even my mother, who has always gone to great lengths to avoid our neighbours, has been a bit more chatty with them. She even pops next door every now and again.'

'Company is a comfort,' suggested Doreen. 'You can get very morbid on your own.'

'Yeah. We're all in the same boat. Even the rich are as likely to get hit by a bomb as we are.'

'Except that some of them have fled to the country.'

'There is that. But I heard that a lot of them are doing charity work for the war effort.'

'I'm glad to hear it,' said Doreen. 'We can't have people sitting about doing nothing just because they've got plenty of money. Not in wartime.'

'It's all a bit peculiar though, isn't it? I mean, there are all these precautions and warnings and men being called up but life is the same as before for the most part.'

'And long may it stay that way,' said Doreen.

Al couldn't play the organ at the Adelphi every night now because he worked longer hours at the factory, which had gone on to war work, and he couldn't always get there in time. He did his best though and if he couldn't make his shift he came to the cinema later to see Daisy and walk her home. One night in November he was there as usual but seemed quieter than normal. She thought he was probably tired after a very long day.

'You don't have to come every night, Al,' she said as they walked through the dark streets, arms entwined. 'You're up early in the morning for work so I don't mind if you want to have an early night sometimes.'

'I want to come,' he said. 'I feel quite off colour if I don't see you at some point every day.'

'Ah, that is so sweet, but don't be afraid to say if you can't always make it.'

'The thing is, Daisy,' he began uncertainly. 'I won't be able to make it any day after next week, not for a while anyway.'

She turned to him. 'Oh, no! Please say they haven't come yet, your call-up papers.'

'Afraid they have.'

'Oh. Even though we knew it would happen at any time it's still a shock now that it has. I'll miss you so much!'

'I don't mind going to do my bit,' he said. 'It's leaving you that's hard.'

Tears threatened but she tried to be positive. 'You'll get leave I expect and the war won't last for ever,' she said with feigned cheerfulness. 'We'll just have to put up with it, the same as everybody else.'

With the awful threat of parting hanging over them they held each other even closer for the rest of the way.

Hester and Dickie were having breakfast, neither

105

saying much. Al had left on an early train for an army training camp somewhere in Hampshire.

'You'll be going soon,' said Hester. 'And don't tell me you can't wait because I don't want to hear it, not today.'

'I wouldn't dream of it, Ma,' said Dickie, reaching across for her hand. He was hungry for adventure and had never been shy of admitting it in the past but now wasn't the time to remind her. 'I don't want to leave you, you know that. But I'll have to go and do my bit when they send for me.'

'I know that, son.'

'Will you be all right here on your own?'

She put down her porridge spoon and drew on every last bit of energy she could muster. 'Of course I'll be all right,' she said, looking at him directly. 'What do you think I am, some old biddy who relies on her children to get her through life?'

'I was only asking, Ma,' he said. 'There's no need to fly off the handle.'

'Sorry, son. I suppose I'm a bit tense because of Al leaving. But honestly, I'll be fine. I shall keep busy helping with the war effort and my piano pupils, if they aren't all evacuated to the country. Don't you worry about me at all. You and your brother will have quite enough to do without bothering your head about your mother.'

He took her hand and pretended not to notice the tears in her eyes.

'You won't be the only one missing your man, come next week,' Doreen said to Daisy one day in

December when they were having a chat in their break in the staffroom. 'Alfie's call-up papers have come. He'll be gone this time next week.'

'So I'll have to take it in turns in seeing you home,' said John who had walked Daisy home every night from the cinema since Al had left.

'Don't you worry about me,' said Doreen. 'I only live a few minutes' walk away and in the opposite direction to you and Daisy. I'll be absolutely fine.'

'Daisy it is then,' he said cheerfully.

'You don't have to walk home with me, John,' Daisy assured him.

'I want to do something to help as the army doesn't want me.' John had failed the medical for the services because of his weak chest. 'I think Al would be pleased to know that someone is looking out for you.'

'I'm sure he would so I'll make the most of it,' she said. 'Will they make you leave the cinema and go on to war work?'

'I've inquired about that but apparently I'm not fit enough for a war factory. Anyway, the cinema is considered important to public morale and I'm well trained and experienced so I'm allowed to stay on. For the moment anyway. I'd be happy to work in a factory. At least I'd feel as though I was making a contribution.'

'You're making one at the Adelphi,' she said. 'People need the cinema more than ever now, as a means of escape, and you work your magic and create the entertainment. I mean anyone can be an usherette but a projectionist is a highly skilled job.'

'Maybe. But it isn't easy being home when your

107

mates are all going into the services.'

'I'm sure.'

'I've already had a few nasty remarks from people in the street because I'm in civvies,' he said. 'That will get worse when all the boys have gone. I'll stand out like a sore thumb then.'

'Oh John, that's awful. And so unkind. What's wrong with people?'

'You can't blame them. Their sons and husbands have had to go so when they see a young bloke in civvies, all they can see is injustice he told her. 'I don't look as though I have anything wrong with me.'

'You're not the strongest-looking man I've ever met,' she remarked. 'But I know what you mean. You'll just have to grow a few extra skins.'

'I'm already doing so.' He didn't add how much the accusations of cowardice hurt.

'Who was that you were talking to outside last night, Daisy?' inquired Bertha over breakfast. 'I could see you were with someone in the moonlight.'

'John from work,' she replied. 'He walked me home as Al isn't around to do it.'

'That's kind of him,' said Bertha. 'Might as well make the most of it before he gets called up.'

'He won't have to go in the services,' she explained. 'He didn't pass the medical.'

'Ooh, I bet his mates think he's a very lucky bugger,' said her father.

'On the contrary, Dad,' said Daisy. 'All the boys I know seem keen to do their bit. Al and his brother are anyway.'

'There hasn't been such a mad rush to volunteer as in the last war, so they say,' said Bill.

'Anyway, John feels really bad about not going,' she told him. 'He's had a few nasty brushes with people in the street over it apparently.'

'Some people see red when they see a young fella in civvies. They don't bother to wonder why.'

'I think it's really mean,' said Daisy. 'People can't help it if they aren't fit enough to go in the services. Anyone can see that John isn't a strong man.'

There was a general murmur of agreement.

'You won't have to go in the army will you, Dad?' said Mary.

'No. I'm too old, love. I did my time in the last lot. Even if I wasn't too old I wouldn't have to go because mine is a reserved occupation. The factory has gone over to war work.'

They carried on eating their porridge then Bertha said, 'You should bring John in for a cup of cocoa when he sees you home, Daisy. He's always welcome here, civvies or not.'

'I didn't think of it,' Daisy said casually. 'He would have wanted to go straight home anyway after a long day at work.'

'Well if you want to anytime, go ahead. So long as you don't make a noise and wake us all up.'

'Thanks, Mum. I'll bear that in mind.'

'All this talk about the men being called up, I suppose your Ray will have to go, won't he?' Daisy said to her sister when they were in Mary's bedroom after breakfast. She was doing her hair in the dressing-table mirror ready to go to work and

Daisy was still in her pyjamas.

'He's older so he'll probably get called up later,' said Mary. 'I don't know what I'll do without him.'

'I know the feeling only too well,' said Daisy. 'I'm missing Al something awful.'

'I have never been as serious about anyone as I am about Ray,' said Mary.

'Really?'

'Head over heels. The full works and you can take that whichever way you like.'

'You don't mean...'

'I do, as it happens.'

'Oh, Mary.'

'Don't sound so shocked, little sister. I am a fully fledged adult.'

'What you do is your own business, of course, but we're not supposed to do it until after we're married.'

'So what,' Mary said forcibly. 'Don't tell me you and Al haven't ... wanted to.'

'Wanted to, yes...'

'You've been a good girl, have you? Well, I'm not quite as perfect as you.'

'It isn't that I'm perfect, not at all, just that it's been drummed into us not to,' Daisy said. 'I suppose I can't get past that. They make it seem like it's the worst thing a girl can possibly do before she's married.'

'Yeah, they do make a big thing of it but sometimes you just can't fight nature if you love someone. And by God I love Ray.'

'I can't wait to meet him,' said Daisy.

'Yeah, it's time I brought him home. I've been

going out with him long enough now. Mum and Dad won't like the age gap but I can't help that.'

'I can't see anything wrong with it so you'll have my support,' said Daisy.

'Thanks kid.' Mary rose and headed for the door. 'I'd better get off to work and earn my keep. See you later.'

'Ta-ta.'

Christmas passed quietly for the Blakes and in early January food rationing was introduced on certain food items with warnings of more to come. Al had a couple of weekend passes. He didn't make it home for the holiday because of his training but he did write to Daisy often. Still there was no sign of a bomb or invading German soldiers so people took the inconvenience of the blackout and the food shortages in their stride.

Daisy had a lovely surprise one night in early March when she emerged from her shift at the cinema to see Al waiting for her with news that he had ten days' leave. John greeted him then made a diplomatic exit.

'Ten days, Al,' she said excitedly. 'How marvellous! I can't believe it.'

'There is a catch,' he told her sheepishly. 'It's long because it's embarkation leave, so when I go back I'll be going abroad and I won't be home for a while.'

'Oh.' Naturally it was a terrible blow but she tried to be strong. 'Never mind; we'll make the most of the time we have. I'll ask Mr Pickles if I can have some evenings off and I'll make it up when you've gone back.'

'It would be lovely if you could. I want to spend every minute I can with you.'

'Likewise. Where will you be going?'

'No idea,' he said.

'Surely they've told you.'

'No. The army are incredibly secretive,' he explained. 'We probably won't be told until we are on our way though we might get a clue from the kit we are issued with, but that will probably be just before we leave.'

'I suppose it's because they have to be careful that the enemy doesn't get any hint of what's going on,' she said. 'There's a lot of talk about spies at the moment.'

'Secrecy is of the essence in wartime,' he agreed. 'It wouldn't do to let the other side know what we are doing. Lives could be lost that way.'

'Don't even mention that, please Al. Let's just make the most of your leave.'

'Yeah, let's do that and no gloomy talk,' he said, kissing her.

The days passed for Daisy with a mixture of happiness and longing with the dark cloud of parting hovering. No matter how hard she tried, it simply wouldn't go away even though neither of them ever mentioned it.

She managed to get some evenings off and they went dancing at the Palais and spent every other moment they could together. On the penultimate night of his leave they found themselves with the house to themselves at the Dawsons'. Hester was playing the piano for an amateur dramatic society which had put on a show to raise money for the war effort and Dickie had gone out to see some mates.

'Oh, isn't it lovely to be on our own in comfort and warmth?' she said as they snuggled up together on the sofa by the fire. 'We usually have to be out in the cold somewhere to be alone. It's the same for all courting couples. It's a wonder we don't all get pneumonia in winter.'

'I'm not sure your mother would approve,' he said. 'Just us two. Alone in the house together. Tut-tut! Whatever would the neighbours think?'

'None of them knows what a perfect gentleman you are.'

'There is that,' he laughed.

'Seriously though, Daisy, I want to have a chat with you,' he began.

'I'm listening,' she said.

'We've never really talked about marriage.'

'No, we haven't.'

'That's because I've never had anything to offer you but I've always imagined we would get married when the time is right,' he said.

'I've always hoped so.'

'The timing couldn't be worse at this moment with me about to go away but...'

'Yes?'

'Will you marry me when I come back?' he said. 'I really do love you very much.'

'Of course I'll marry you,' she assured him, overjoyed. 'I thought you'd never ask.'

'Trust me to get it all wrong,' he said. 'I don't even have an engagement ring to give you because I wasn't planning on asking you until I get back.'

'A ring isn't necessary, not at this point anyway,'

she said, melting into his arms. 'I'll have that when you come home.' She laughed. 'I'll insist on it then. A whopping great diamond ring.'

'On army pay it's more likely to be a diamond chip,' he said. 'But it will still be given with all my heart.'

'I know.'

They were both totally caught up in the emotion of the moment, close together, isolated from their surroundings by the strength of their feelings for each other. The firelight flickered over the room as passion rose...

Chapter Six

Life seemed bleak for Daisy after Al left, especially knowing that he would be facing danger, but she was determinedly cheerful and found comfort in the camaraderie of her work pals. She particularly valued her close friendship with John and Doreen, the latter having returned to an evening shift at the cinema now that her husband Alfie was away at the war.

The usual atmosphere in the cinema was a kind of gentle excitement. Going to the pictures was an enjoyable everyday pastime, not dinner at the Ritz. But people loved it because they could slip into a world of fantasy and enjoy a break from the harsh reality of increasing shortages, fear of bombs and bad news from abroad as more men were sent overseas. Although the usherettes worked hard, the customers' enjoyment rubbed off on them too, especially as part of their job was to be friendly.

Of great enjoyment to Daisy, too, were the films. Even though they saw only fragments they could usually get the gist of the story and nearly always saw the end because there was a lull in their duties before they saw people out and started clearing up. Staff and punters were equally thrilled when the much vaunted *Gone with the Wind* came to the Adelphi and the queues were longer than ever. Daisy never tired of seeing Vivien Leigh and Clark Gable in this dramatic story set in the Deep South of America during the Civil War. She and Doreen were usually a bit teary at the end even though they knew the last scene almost off by heart.

'Have you heard from Al lately?' inquired John casually as he and Daisy walked home after work one night.

'No, I haven't. Not since he went abroad,' she replied.

'He's probably moving around and hasn't had a chance to write,' he suggested. 'I suppose they still have a lot more travelling to do when they get off the boat. Upheaval all round probably. They could be at the back of beyond somewhere.'

'That's what I thought,' she said. 'Or it could just be delays in the postal service. I'll probably get a few letters all together. It does happen.'

'It must be a hell of a job, getting all the troops' letters delivered.'

'Indeed.'

'I miss Al on the organ,' said John because a

rather tired elderly man had replaced Al. 'The new bloke is quite good but Al had such a way with him.'

'Yeah, he does have a good stage presence,' she said.

'An absolute whizz on the organ too.'

'Anyway John, how are things with you?' she asked as a diversion; talking about Al made her feel sad because the many letters she had sent to him remained unanswered. 'Any special lady in your life?'

'Not at the moment.'

'You're slipping,' she said, teasing him; she'd heard he did have girlfriends from time to time.

'Women prefer men in uniform these days,' he said.

'Not all of them surely.'

'I suppose there must be some who don't. But servicemen are definitely the flavour of the moment.'

'And most of them are away so not much use as a boyfriend,' she pointed out.

'It could just be my guilty conscience making me think that way.'

'Which, as I've told you a dozen times, you shouldn't have,' she told him firmly. 'I can't believe that every girl in London wouldn't want to go out with a civilian.'

'You may be right,' he said. 'I'll have to test the water when I come across someone I fancy.'

They reached Daisy's front gate. 'Are you coming in for a cup of cocoa?' she asked. 'Mum has taken to leaving two cups out with the cocoa tin.'

'In that case I can't really say no,' he said. 'Another ten minutes won't make any difference and I do fancy a hot drink.'

'Good. It will help us to unwind after a busy night at work.' She headed up the path with him following her.

'Hello Mrs Dawson,' said Daisy when Hester opened the front door to her one Saturday in early summer.

'How lovely to see you, Daisy,' said the older woman, smiling warmly. 'Come on in, dear.'

'I don't want to disturb you if you're busy.'

'I did have some pupils earlier but I'm free now,' Hester said, ushering her inside.

'I'm on my way to work so I can't stay long,' said Daisy. 'But I thought I'd just pop in to find out how you are getting along.'

'I'm fine, dear. I've got myself a little job as it happens.'

'As well as the teaching?'

'Yes. This is teaching too but at the school and not piano; just general music and putting together a choir. The male music teacher was called up into the army so I'm standing in for him. It's rather nice to go out to work. It's only a few mornings a week so it doesn't interfere with my home pupils.'

'Good, I'm glad you are all right.'

'We all have to do our bit, don't we?'

'Indeed.'

'Do you have time for a cuppa?' asked Hester.

'Thank you but I'd better not stop,' Daisy said, an unasked question seeming to stand between them. 'I had lunch just before I came out and I don't want to be late for work.'

'As you wish, dear. How are you anyway?'

'I'm fine thanks. But, actually, I was wondering if you'd heard from Al.'

'Oh yes, he writes quite regularly, bless him, and he seems to be taking it all in his stride, doesn't he, though I know they're not allowed to say much.' She saw Daisy's colour rise then watched her turn pale. 'Oh dear, have you not heard from him then?'

'No, not since he went back the last time and I've written to him lots of times.'

Hester was surprised because Al had seemed to be very fond of Daisy; absolutely mad about her in fact. There was even talk, just before he'd gone back off leave, that last time, about them getting married right after the war. Her instinct was to tell the girl that she would write to Al and give him a wigging for not writing to his girlfriend but she knew she mustn't interfere. Al was a grown man and his mother had no right to meddle in his personal affairs. He must have a reason for ceasing contact with Daisy if that was what he had done. Love affairs were complicated things. He was a young, good-looking man. Who was to say that some other girl hadn't taken his fancy? She couldn't quite see how since he was probably in some godforsaken hellhole somewhere but you just never knew with young people.

She was very disappointed by this turn of events because she was fond of Daisy and had hoped to have her as a daughter-in-law eventually.

'It could be the postal service,' she suggested hopefully.

'But your letters arrived.'

'Yes they did but it is just a matter of chance, I think. I probably won't hear from him again for ages then I'll get a few all together. It's the war, dear. Everything has been turned upside down by it.'

'Al means the absolute world to me, Mrs Dawson,' said Daisy, now ashen-faced and stern. 'If he doesn't want me anymore I'll accept it without a fuss even though it will break my heart. But I think he could have told me. To just cut off contact like that is cruel and I am very hurt and disappointed in him. I know there is a war on and there is a lot of disruption but I would have had a letter by now if he'd sent one.'

'I'm sure it's nothing like that, Daisy,' said Hester sympathetically. 'He was mad about you when he left and I can't see why that would have changed so suddenly.'

'Neither can I but people change their minds all the time, don't they? It's the nature of being human, I suppose.'

'Some of them probably do, yes,' Hester said lamely. 'But I'm sure you'll hear from him eventually.'

'I do hope so,' Daisy said with a watery smile. 'I'll let you know if I get a letter.'

'I'd appreciate that, dear.' Hester wanted to put her arms around Daisy and comfort her but didn't feel able to somehow. It was as though they were on opposing sides.

'I'd better go,' said Daisy. 'Duty calls and all that.'

'Still enjoying the job?' said Hester as she showed her to the door.

'Very much so,' said Daisy.

'Good.' Hester opened the front door. 'I'm sure you'll hear from that son of mine soon.'

''Bye, Mrs Dawson.'

''Bye, dear. Come and see me again whenever you like.'

'Thanks, will do.'

Hester knew she wouldn't see Daisy again unless she heard from Al. It would be too painful for her, too awkward for them both. He was their link, their reason for being friends. It was a pity Al had apparently abandoned her because she really did like the girl a lot.

Daisy's mind was taken off her own problem a few weeks later when she went up to bed one night to find Mary sitting on her bed waiting for her. Her face was tear-stained and her eyes red and swollen from crying.

'Mary, what on earth is the matter?' she asked. 'What's happened?'

'He's married,' Mary said thickly. 'Ray is a married man and this thing with me was just a bit of fun.'

'Oh no,' said Daisy, sitting beside her on the bed and putting her arm around her. 'How did you find out?'

'He told me. Came right out with it.'

'What. Out of the blue?'

'No, not exactly. I've been trying to persuade him to come home and meet the family and he's been reluctant,' she explained. 'I suppose my keeping on about it made him realise things were getting too serious on my part and he wanted out.

So that's what led up to it.'

'I see but I'm sure he's very fond of you,' said Daisy in the hope of boosting her sister's shattered confidence.

'He's enjoyed being with me, we've had fun, he said, but he made it clear that he'll never leave his wife. It'll be best if we don't meet again, was his final decision. It hurts, Daisy. It really does. I've never experienced anything like it before. I'd see him on any terms, that's how deeply I am in love with him, but he doesn't want to see me again. His conscience is bothering him suddenly apparently. I'm very ashamed for being a party to him cheating on his wife.'

'You didn't know he was married so you can't blame yourself for that.'

'But I know now and I'd still see him if he'd have me. I'm pathetic, I know.'

Daisy had never seen her sister like this before. She'd always been the strong, confident one. Now it was as though every bit of self-esteem had been stripped away, leaving a trembling wreck of a woman.

'You wouldn't know how to be pathetic so let's have no more of that sort of talk,' said Daisy. 'You've had a terrible shock, that's all. Anyone would be upset by what's happened.'

'I feel as though my insides have been pulled and twisted. I don't know how to carry on.'

'You will though.'

'It's as if my nervous system has been wrecked,' she explained. 'I feel physically ill with it, Daisy. Sick, and my stomach is all tight.'

'Will a cup of cocoa help?'

121

'Not as much as a bottle of gin.'

'We don't have any of that and it wouldn't help in the long run anyway so I'll go and make you some cocoa,' Daisy said. 'And I know you're upset but try not to cry too loudly or we'll have Mum coming in to find out what's up.'

'I don't want Mum and Dad to know, ever,' Mary whispered. 'They'd be very shocked and hurt, especially Mum. Her daughter having an aff-air with a married man; that would be enough to finish her off.'

'They'll notice that something is wrong, though,' Daisy pointed out.

'I shall have to make an effort to put up a front, won't I, in front of them anyway.'

'The pain will pass with time I expect because everything does, so maybe you'll feel better in a day or two,' suggested Daisy though she was no expert on the subject.

'I don't think I'll ever feel better,' Mary said. 'Ray has been my whole life.'

'I know.' Daisy was feeling almost as desperate herself about Al, but now wasn't the moment to mention it. 'I'll get you that cocoa.'

Bertha was in the queue at the butcher's. The other women were chatting but Bertha was quiet because she was engrossed in her own thoughts. She'd heard it said that a mother had a sixth sense when it came to her children. She didn't know anything about that but she did have reasonably good powers of observation and she certainly knew when one of her daughters was pregnant.

After all the trouble she'd taken to raise them

with a strong sense of morality she'd still been let down. You'd think the girl would have the decency to tell her mother rather than pretending that nothing was wrong when it so clearly was. But not her! Oh no! Well, she'd give it a bit longer and if nothing was said, she would confront her about it. Time was of the essence. This mustn't be left so late it couldn't be seen to. Oh dear, this was her worst nightmare come true.

When the cinema newsreels showed shots of British troops at some unnamed location, people searched for their friends and relatives.

'I thought I saw your Al on the newsreel, Daisy,' said Doreen when they were getting ready to go home one night. 'But when the camera went in close I could see that it wasn't him.'

'Oh,' said Daisy, dully.

Doreen looked at her. 'You haven't mentioned him lately. Is everything all right?'

'It's all over between us,' said Daisy and burst into tears.

'Oh love,' said Doreen sympathetically. 'I'm so sorry to hear that. Is it over for definite?'

'Absolutely.'

Doreen exchanged a look with John, who was standing nearby. 'Sorry you're upset,' he said awkwardly.

Daisy wiped her eyes and lifted her head in a determined effort to pull herself together. 'I'll be fine. But best not to talk about it. It will only start me off again.'

'That's fine with us, isn't it, John?' Doreen said.

'Absolutely,' he agreed.

123

But they were both worried and sad for her. She and Al had seemed like the perfect couple.

'I've waited long enough for you to talk to me about it, Mary,' said Bertha one Sunday morning when they were washing up the breakfast things. Bill was working in the garden and Daisy was clearing up in the other room. 'But as you haven't seen fit to do so, I see no other option but to raise the subject.'

'Oh,' said Mary, who was still nursing a broken heart. 'What are you talking about?'

'Don't play dumb with me, my girl,' said Bertha.

'I really don't want to talk about it, Mum,' she said, too miserable to wonder how her mother had found out about Ray. 'It only upsets me.'

Bertha was incandescent with rage. 'Don't want to talk about it,' she exploded. 'Of course we have to talk about it.'

'Why exactly?'

'Because arrangements have to be made of course! Right, so who is the father, and when is the baby due?'

Mary stared at her in astonishment. 'You think I'm pregnant,' she said.

'Of course I do,' her mother said. 'Why else would you be looking so pale and sickly, crying yourself to sleep every night and not eating your food.'

Daisy was on her way into the kitchen and heard this conversation. 'You've got the wrong daughter, Mum,' she said nervously. 'I am the one who is pregnant.'

The silence throbbed like a heartbeat in the

room. Then Bertha said in a shocked whisper, 'You? How can you be? I've seen so sign of that in you.'

'You don't see everything, Mum,' she said. 'You can't see inside of us. I've not been feeling sick or anything.'

'But how can you be pregnant? I mean, there was only Al and he's away.'

'It happened during his last leave.'

'Oh my Gawd, that was ages ago,' Bertha gasped. 'You'll be too far gone to get it seen to.'

'I wouldn't do that anyway.'

Still confused, Bertha turned her attention back to Mary. 'So why have you been mooning around all sickly?'

'She's had a bad experience, Mum, and it's left her feeling poorly,' Daisy answered for her. 'But please don't question her about it because she isn't up to it.'

'Yes yes, all right,' said Bertha hurriedly, far more interested in her younger daughter's dilemma.

'Before you say anything Mum,' began Daisy. 'I know I've let you down and I'm sorry.'

'I should think so too,' she snapped. 'Yes, you have let us down in the worst way possible. I don't know how I'm going to tell your father.'

'Why don't I tell him then?'

'No it'll be better coming from me.' Bertha spoke quickly, as though already thinking ahead. 'There will be arrangements to be made. You'll have to go and stay with my sister in Essex and the baby can be taken from there. No one around here need know anything about it.'

'I'm keeping it, Mum. I'll move away to save

125

you from embarrassment but I'm not giving my baby away.'

'Oh yeah and how do you think you're going to do that?' said Bertha viciously. 'You'll be an outcast wherever you go. No one will employ you even if you could find someone to look after the child while you work.'

'Mum,' said Mary, shaken out of her own doldrums by this turn of events. 'Don't be so horrible to Daisy. She's probably feeling bad enough as it is.'

'I have no idea how I'll manage, Mum,' Daisy continued. 'But I do know that I am going to do my best for my baby.'

'And the way to do that is to get it adopted,' said Bertha. 'The child won't have a chance otherwise.'

'Giving it away isn't an option, Mum.'

'You are being totally selfish, both to the baby and to your family,' her mother ranted. 'We'll all be tainted by the stigma of illegitimacy, the child more than anyone.'

'Surely wanting to love my baby and bring it up with me isn't selfish, is it?' asked Daisy.

'Of course it is,' stated Bertha. 'You have absolutely nothing to offer it except a lifetime of prejudice.'

'Mm. There is that I suppose,' she was forced to agree. 'I was thinking that a mother's love is more important to a child than anything.'

'Under normal circumstances it is but in this case it's just a silly romantic notion on your part. Face up to it, Daisy, it isn't even as if the father of the child is around to step in and save your reputation and offer financial support. He seems to have disappeared from your life altogether. You never even mention him anymore.'

'Yes, he has disappeared and I don't want to talk about it,' she said.

'So the best thing for everyone is to give the baby up as soon as possible after the birth, before you have time to get attached. I shall make all the arrangements. All you have to do is disappear as soon as you start to show and come back afterwards and carry on as normal.'

Daisy felt sick. She knew that some of what her mother said was true, but to give her baby away! How could she possibly do that? 'I can't leave my child to be brought up by a stranger. I just can't do it, Mum.'

'Keeping it just isn't an option so you might as well accept it and be thankful that I am not throwing you out on the street,' declared Bertha. 'It's disgusting what you've done.'

'There might not be anyone willing to adopt,' said Daisy, concentrating on the practicalities. 'I expect there are lots of abandoned children in care; poor little things.'

'We can't worry about that now,' said Bertha. 'Your aunt will look into that in Essex where you will go when the time is right.'

'Don't worry, Mum, I wouldn't dream of staying around here and embarrassing you when my condition becomes even remotely noticeable,' Daisy told her coldly.

'There's no need for any of that empty dramatic talk,' said Bertha. 'We both know you don't have anywhere to go. So you just leave it to me and everything will be all right. I'll make some inquiries and get in touch with your aunt. This time next year you'll have forgotten that any of this ever happened.'

'I doubt that,' she said sadly.

'Blimey, Daisy. You don't half produce some dramas; first the Rumbold affair and now this,' said Mary when the sisters were alone, their mother having gone to see a neighbour about the National Savings collection she had taken on since war broke out. 'It even made me forget my own troubles for a while. Why didn't you tell me?'

'You had quite enough of your own to cope with,' Daisy reminded her. 'Anyway, I don't think I wanted to face up to it. If I kept quiet it didn't seem so real. It bloomin' well does now though.'

'I'll bet,' said Mary. 'Did you mean all that about keeping the baby?'

'I hadn't thought of anything else until Mum put her oar in. Do you think it would be selfish of me?'

'It's no good asking me. I know nothing about such things. But I am certain that if I was pregnant with Ray's baby – and that really would send Mum over the edge and I'm not – I would want to keep it. Surely it's only natural, isn't it?'

'For me it is but I don't want to inflict a lifetime of misery on the kid.'

'A mother's love is worth a lot, Daisy.'

'I've got that in spades and the child isn't even born yet,' she said. 'But I would have to move away. Even if Mum did let me stay, it wouldn't be fair to inflict the scandal on the family.'

'Surely people have other, more important

things, to worry about these days than whether or not someone's kid is born the wrong side of the blanket, with the war getting so serious and the men having to go away to fight.'

'You'd think so wouldn't you, and they probably have but to Mum this is the biggest disgrace of them all and I couldn't do it to her, to all of you.'

'I couldn't care less what people think so it wouldn't worry me in the slightest,' said Mary. 'I'd love having a baby around. I know the circumstances aren't ideal but it would be lovely to have a little one in the family. It would certainly liven things up around here.'

Daisy looked at her sister and smiled tearfully. 'Thank you,' she said.

'What for?'

'For reminding me of the joy in the situation. The ghastly practicalities have rather overshadowed that.'

'Don't ever lose sight of the joy,' said Mary. 'I know it won't be easy and you are in a hell of a situation but if it was me I'd fight tooth and nail to keep my baby. I'll back you whatever you decide to do but I really hope you don't have to go away. I don't want you to have to live in some ghastly hellhole of a place. Anyway, I want to be a part of it. I'll be an auntie for the first time and that's really special.'

Mary had made it seem like a pleasant reality instead of a hellish nightmare. 'You'll be part of it, don't worry. I shall make sure of that wherever I am.'

'Please can I be godmother?' asked Mary.

'Who else would I trust with the job?' Daisy said,

hugging her.

'So I'll be disappearing before long.' Daisy had told John about the pregnancy as they headed home from work. 'But I shall stay for as long as I can still squeeze into my uniform.'

'I shall miss you,' he said. 'And I'm sure Doreen will too. But we'll still see you, won't we?'

She explained the situation to him. 'So I don't know where I'll be if I keep the baby. I certainly won't be able to stay at home.'

'Oh, Daisy that's awful. You'll need your family and friends more than ever at a time like this.'

'I know, but I'm a scarlet woman now and my mother doesn't want one of those around the house. Not unless I do as she says and give the baby away so that I will disappear for a while and come back as though nothing has happened. But supposing there's no one willing to adopt? My baby could be brought up in an orphanage.'

'Have you written and told Al about it?'

'Yes, I have, several times, but he hasn't replied. He stopped writing a while ago actually. He doesn't seem to want me so sure as hell he won't want to know about a baby. Anyway, he isn't around so he wouldn't be able to save my repu-tation. It's very cruel the way unmarried mothers are treated. You don't realise it until you face the prospect of becoming one yourself. According to my mother my child will be an outcast from society if I keep it.'

'Really. Is it that bad?'

'Apparently.'

'You've got a bit of time to think about it, Daisy,'

he said. 'Don't do anything unless you're sure.'

'How can I be sure what's right?' she said. 'My head is telling me I must do what my mother wants and give my baby up. My heart is telling me to keep it no matter how hard it is.' She paused. 'Anyway, let's talk about something else. Discussing my problem makes me feel doomed.'

'We can't have that, can we?' He feigned a cheerful air; but he was worried about her because she was a very dear friend.

John kept a diplomatic silence before re-opening the conversation with discussion of the news of carnage for British troops on the French coast near Dunkirk. Not a wise choice as it was such a depressing subject but it was what everyone was talking about at the moment. John didn't know which was of more concern to him, the news from abroad or Daisy's plight, though he thought it was probably the latter.

A projectionist's job was very intense and all the equipment had to be kept spotlessly clean and well maintained because of the fire risk caused by the heat from the arc lamp and the flammable nature of the film. The latter had to be examined carefully before putting on the projector and cotton gloves were worn to protect the film as well as the operator's hands. The room was well lit and ventilated because of the solvents in the air around the films, though the bright light in here wasn't noticeable in the auditorium.

As the chief projectionist John was scrupulous in his work and expected anyone who assisted him or stood in for him to be the same. A qualified projectionist, who worked as a freelance for various cinemas, covered for him on his day off or if he was away for any other reason.

The day after Daisy had told him about her problems John was still worrying about her when he went on duty. He wanted to help but felt powerless to do so. It wasn't his place to interfere in a family matter but he knew somehow that if Daisy gave her baby up she would never forgive herself.

Maybe he could have a word with Mrs Blake about it, try to persuade her to let Daisy keep the baby. He did get on well with the older woman. But no, his interference might cause even more trouble for Daisy.

The solution came to him with such power as he was watching the film go through the projector, he was overwhelmed. But before the idea had time to take root the film jammed then broke and burst into flames from the heat of the carbon arc light.

With speed he tore the film off, threw it in the floor and emptied a bucket of sand over it, extinguishing the fire while at the same time stopping the motor and turning off the electric arc lamp. Then he went over to the board of switches on the wall and turned the cinema lights on, knowing there would be outrage in the auditorium and Mr Pickles would appear at any moment in a fury.

There was no time to brood; he had to get the show up and running with all possible speed though he had to give the projector time to cool down. Then he would remove the burned film and make a repair and all the wheel surfaces must be cleaned thoroughly. There would be a tiny gap in the sequence of the film but with any luck the audience wouldn't notice and all would be well.

But now Mr Pickles was here with a face like thunder and John had to calm him down and hope he kept his job.

'So what happened in the projection room tonight?' asked Daisy as she and John walked home together. 'Someone said something about a fire.'

'There was a small one but I soon put it out.'

'You could have been hurt.'

'I wasn't though so we don't even have to think about that, do we?'

'They were going crazy in the auditorium because it was a while before the film started again,' she said. 'They take their fury out on us usherettes.'

'Yeah, I'm sorry about that. But getting the show back on track takes a bit of time because there is a certain procedure to go through,' he explained. 'The film is very delicate.'

'What did Mr Pickles have to say about it? Did he threaten you with the sack?'

'No, he didn't. He doesn't do that so much now because it isn't so easy to get staff these days with people going on to war work and into the services. So he needs to hang on to me.'

'We're losing usherettes to war work and the services,' she said. 'Their replacements are mostly older people but there are some school leavers as you've probably noticed.'

'Yeah, I have seen a few kids and grannies about,'

he said.

'They all seem to be good workers.'

'Anyway, moving on to other, more interesting things,' he began, his voice rising with enthusiasm. 'I've thought of a way you can keep your baby and not move away.'

'Oh, I didn't realise you could work miracles.'

'I can't but I'm not bad on ideas.'

'Come on then, what is this idea?'

'You and I get married to save your reputation and keep your baby,' he said. 'I'm pretty sure your mother would approve. She seems to like me.'

Daisy couldn't hide her shock and there was a sharp intake of breath. 'Oh John, you can't be serious.'

'Well yeah, why wouldn't I be?'

'Because it's a huge thing you are offering and we are not in love with each other.'

'No, but we are very good friends and fond of each other,' he said. 'I just thought it might be a possible solution. You get to keep your baby without moving away to somewhere you don't know, away from your family and friends. We would have to live at your place at first though because I don't have the means to set up home at the moment and Mum and Dad's flat is really small.'

'John. Thank you so much for thinking of it. You are so kind to offer yourself up like that and I am very grateful but it really is a crazy idea.'

'I thought you might be annoyed.'

'I'm not annoyed in the least,' she assured him. 'I'm touched and just a bit overwhelmed by your generosity. You obviously haven't thought it through properly though. Apart from landing yourself with someone else's kid, you'd be giving up your chance of marrying for love.'

'There's no one special at the moment,' he said. 'Anyway it is a kind of love, isn't it, friendship?'

'I'm not an expert but I think it's a different thing altogether,' she said.

'Mm, maybe. Oh well, it was just an idea.' He seemed disappointed but brushed it aside. 'I thought we might be able to make it work so that you could keep the baby, that's all. But you're right; it's a silly idea.'

'Oh John, it isn't silly at all and I'm ever so touched by your offer, and yes it would mean I could keep the baby but how can I possibly accept your offer when I don't have those kind of feelings for you? Or you for me?'

'You're right,' he said. 'So let's just forget it.'

'Thanks though. I do appreciate it.'

'It was just an idea that popped into my mind but let's forget I ever mentioned it.'

'I won't do that, John, because it was very kind of you and I'm really grateful,' she said. 'I'm not likely to forget a thing like that *ever*. But I will put it behind me.'

'Good,' he said. 'So let's get back to normal now and talk about ordinary things.'

But there was an odd silence between them for the rest of the journey.

One morning a few days later Bertha received a letter which put her in a cheerful mood.

'I've got good news, Daisy,' she said when Mary and Bill had gone to work. 'I've had a letter from

135

your Auntie May in Essex.'

'Oh yeah,' said Daisy, feeling tense suddenly.

'She's been making inquiries and she's heard of someone who is looking for a baby to adopt and they want a child with connections to someone they know, which is why they are not going through the usual channels. They want a new born so it's perfect for us. This means you can stop worrying about the baby being brought up in an orphanage.'

'Mm.'

'You'll know it's going to a good home.'

'I won't know that. They could get fed up with it when the novelty wears off and be cruel.'

'Now you're just being ridiculous,' Bertha said. 'You're looking for problems.'

'Of course I am. It's my baby we're talking about.' Daisy's voice was rising emotionally. 'You know I don't want to give it up, not to anyone.'

'You don't have a choice I'm afraid,' said Bertha dismissively. 'And this could work out really well.'

There was a silence while Daisy thought things over.

'Actually Mum, I do have a choice,' she said, her voice becoming stronger as she made a sudden decision. 'We don't need to find someone to adopt my baby because I am getting married and keeping it. I will bring my baby up myself.'

Daisy didn't know who was the most shocked by this statement, her mother or herself!

Chapter Seven

For Bertha this surprising news from Daisy was heaven sent. She got to keep her daughter close, the family reputation would remain intact and she would have a grandchild living under the same roof where she could keep a caring eye. Never mind how it had all come about. It was a solution; that was what mattered.

John was the type of man Bertha had always wanted for her daughters: steady, reliable and even-tempered. Much more suitable than glamour boy Al whom she had never approved of despite the act she'd eventually been forced to adopt for the sake of peace in the family as the others all liked him. Al was far too handsome and gregarious to make good husband material.

So she would welcome John into the family and do her utmost to help the young couple have a happy life together, beginning with a hastily arranged wedding.

'Well, you've certainly fallen on your feet, Daisy,' said Mary when she heard the news. 'Who would have thought you'd get an offer like that? John's a really nice man. I'll enjoy having him as a brother-in-law. It means you'll still be around, too, and so will the baby when the time comes. Yippee!'

'It's made you happy so something good will come out of it,' said Daisy.

'Lots of good will come out of it, won't it?' Mary queried, looking concerned.

'It's just a marriage of convenience,' Daisy reminded her. 'Neither of us has the sort of feelings you should have for marriage in the true sense. But it's very good of him to offer and I'm more than grateful.'

'He always seems like a good sort and you won't be the first to marry for those reasons,' said Mary. 'I should think it can work out quite well with the right sort of attitude. It will certainly be a lot better for you than the other option. I'm sure you and John will make a go of it.'

'I shall certainly do my damndest to make it as good as it can be under the circumstances. That's if he hasn't changed his mind by now. I turned him down when he asked me but when Mum said she'd found someone willing to adopt the baby I couldn't face the thought of giving it up.'

'I'm sure you've made the right decision,' Mary said supportively. 'At least things are working out for one of us.'

Daisy looked at her. 'How are you feeling now?' she asked.

'Still very down for most of the time. I cheer up at the thought of being an auntie. I wish it was me providing you with a niece or nephew though.'

'Let's hope that when you do it will be under happier and more traditional circumstances than mine.'

Mary smiled but Daisy knew she was hurting. She hoped her sister would meet someone who was worthy of her before too long. What a pair they were. Neither of them seemed to have any luck with men.

John hadn't changed his mind and was delighted that Daisy had altered hers.

'I'm so grateful to you, John,' she said.

'I don't want our marriage to be based on gratitude, Daisy,' he said in a firm tone. 'I want it to be about affection and mutual respect.'

Of course it would be based on gratitude, she thought. How could it be otherwise? But she said, 'It will be, of course, but I do appreciate what you are doing for me. And that in itself creates respect.'

She realised at that moment the enormity of what she was getting into. She had to make friendship into a normal married relationship in every sense of the word and this would require an enormous amount of effort from them both. She trusted him to do his part. But could she trust herself?

The wedding was at the registry office a few weeks later, a small gathering with only relatives invited. The couple moved into Daisy's bedroom and they lived in with the family, which was the simplest solution as there was so little space. Daisy wanted to shop and cook for John like any other married woman but her mother said that sharing a kitchen would be too awkward and she was quite happy to do it for them all. So Daisy accepted it with good grace and hoped that she and John were able to get their own place at some point in the future, since setting up home was what being married was all about.

Determined to work for as long as possible Daisy was still squeezing into her usherette's uniform in the autumn with the help of a corset. She thought that Mr Pickles was probably turning a blind eye as workers weren't so easy to come by these days. He knew that she and John had got married but the pregnancy hadn't been made common knowledge yet except to the couple's family and close friends.

'You should be taking things a bit easier now and leave me to do the earning,' John was often heard to say, but she wanted to make a contribution for as long as possible. He was a dear man and had given up his freedom for her so the least she could do was make a financial contribution.

Then in September horror struck and the main concern for everyone was staying alive as the Luftwaffe came over every night with their lethal weapons. The bombing started in East London, which was bombed to the ground in raids aimed at the docks, but soon moved west.

'Surely you'll give up work now, Daisy,' said Bertha.

'And give Mr Pickles even more problems? Not likely,' said Daisy. 'The poor man has got enough on his plate with staff not turning up for work and having to give this speech to every house about what to do in an air raid, so while I still can, I'll carry on.'

'You should be in the air-raid shelter with us of an evening,' insisted Bertha. 'Not out at work.'

'It takes my mind off things,' Daisy said.

'And we come home together so she isn't out on her own,' added John helpfully. 'I'll look after her, don't worry.'

'We have to keep going while we can, Mum, or Hitler has won. People find great comfort in the cinema and I like to be there with them.'

'You'll be giving birth in one of the aisles at this rate,' said Bertha.

'Don't worry, I'll resign long before my due time,' Daisy told her with a grin.

'Not many people leave when Mr Pickles gives his air-raid warning speech, do they?' Doreen remarked one evening. 'When the bombing first started most people rushed off. Now hardly anyone goes.'

'They'd rather stay here and watch Clark Gable or Bing Crosby than go home and sit in a cold and damp air-raid shelter and I don't blame them either,' said Daisy. 'It's better than sitting in a hole in the ground with your heart in your mouth.'

'Do the air raids scare you?' Doreen asked.

'Not half; when the siren goes my stomach turns to water but somehow you get through it, don't you?'

'Mm, though not everyone manages so well. One of our neighbours gets hysterical every time the siren goes. They've had to take her to the doctor's for something to calm her down.'

'There'll be a few like that I expect but people don't like to admit that they can't cope as we are all supposed to just get on with it,' said Daisy. 'Not everyone can carry on regardless. I nearly wet myself with fright sometimes. You want to beg God to make it stop, don't you?'

'I'm always doing that,' said Doreen.

'Well, it's nearly the end of the programme and the All Clear still hasn't gone.' Bangs and explosions could be heard. 'So it looks as though we'll be having a late night again.'

'Still, at least we don't have to get up early.' Doreen spoke in a positive manner.

'Exactly,' agreed Daisy. 'So you won't hear me complaining. It's usually quite fun.'

The cinemas were allowed to stay open later during this crisis if people wanted to remain in their seats and one night recently they had showed the whole programme again. Sometimes the organist played to give the projectionists a break.

Tonight the usherettes led the audience in a sing-song with the elderly organist providing the accompaniment. The air was pungent with a combination of cigarette smoke, sweat, greasy hair and cheap perfume. They could hear the thud of explosions but the spirit here brought tears to Daisy's eyes as the assembled company sang their hearts out. 'You are my Sunshine' was especially lively because everyone knew it.

In a sentimental frame of mind she looked towards the organist, a small, white-haired man brought out of retirement because of the war. She didn't see him though; instead she saw Al at the Mighty Wurlitzer in a smart jacket and bow tie, his charisma reaching out and charming the audience. How wonderful he would be now in these dangerous circumstances with his warm and outgoing personality. She felt a rush of emotion and wanted to weep for the loss of her first love. Even though he had let her down, she hoped he hadn't become one of the casualties of war. She so wanted him to be alive and well wherever he was.

Mr Pickles came on stage and announced that the All Clear had been sounded and wished everyone a safe journey home. The organist played the National Anthem to which everyone stood before hurrying out of the building, only a few not waiting until the last note had sounded.

The night was cold and spiced with smoke and cordite as she walked home, arm in arm with John in the dark streets. There was a sharp freshness in the air and a kind of elation within her, to have survived another night of bombing; and with such gusto too.

'Are you tired?' asked John.

'I suppose I must be as it's late,' she said. 'But the atmosphere is so terrific at the Adelphi I feel wide awake. How about you?'

'I was glad we didn't have to show the film programme again tonight, thanks to you and the other usherettes and your sing-song,' he said. 'It does get a bit tedious in the projection room doing another show after the scheduled programmes. We don't mind, because people need entertaining, but it was nice to have a break and to be able to join in the singing.'

'I can understand that,' she said. 'For me it was just like being at a party, everyone singing their hearts out and enjoying themselves.'

'You'll have to start taking more care of yourself with the baby getting close, Daisy,' he suggested.

'All these extra hours can't be doing you much good.'

'People don't have time to take care of themselves much these days. They are all too busy working and trying to stay alive.'

'I know that but you'll need to put your feet up a bit more soon.'

'You sound just like my mother,' she said.

'We're both concerned about you.'

'I know that, John,' she said, feeling suffocated. She didn't want him to behave like her mother. It made her feel trapped, which in turn made her feel guilty. 'It's very good of you both to worry about me and I do appreciate it but you know me, I don't like a lot of fuss. I love my job at the cinema and I really do want to stay on for as long as I can. But don't worry, I'll be forced to give up soon because of the sheer size of my bump.'

'There is that. As long as you're sensible and don't stay too long.' He sounded about forty-five. 'Anyway, another day over and here we still are.' They turned the corner into their street. 'The house is still standing too so our luck is in.'

She knew he was right and she was fond of him but his constant fussing irritated her in a way it hadn't before they got married. She knew it wasn't fair because he was a lovely man and a good husband. She tried to separate her feelings from the reality of her life and constantly remind herself of what he had done for her. She knew she would never love him as she should but she would try harder to do the best she could as his wife.

Hester Blake climbed out of her neighbour's shelter into the dark garden.

'Mind how you go when you come up, Ada; it's pitch black up here. There's no moon.'

'Thanks for staying with me, love,' said Ada, a childless widow of advanced years. 'I do so hate being in the shelter on my own during a raid.'

'That's all right, love,' said Hester. 'I'm on my own now that both my boys are in the army. There's no point in the two of us being lonely in the shelters when we live next door to each other, is there? Company makes a world of difference when the bombs are coming down.'

'Thanks anyway.'

'See you tomorrow,' said Hester and made her way carefully through the gap in the fence that she and Ada had made at the outbreak of war.

Inside the house, which was cold because the fire had gone out, she felt her spirits take a dive. This home that had once been so full of life and laughter was now silent and still. It had been bad enough after her husband had died but now the boys weren't around either, it didn't feel like a home. Of course her sons were of an age to have flown the nest anyway but they would have stayed local and would have called in on a regular basis. Now they were abroad somewhere and she missed and worried about them constantly.

Forcing herself out of the doldrums by remembering that she was lucky to be alive with the terrible bombs pounding down on them every night, she went into her music room. Resisting the urge to play the piano because it would disturb the neighbours at this hour, she looked in her diary to remind herself of the next day's events.

It was a Saturday so she had pupils in the morning and was playing the piano at a church hall for a concert to raise funds for the Red Cross in the afternoon. Later on she would call on Ada, even if there wasn't a raid, because she knew her neighbour would welcome company. Good; there was enough action to keep her going. She tried always to stay busy because activity was vital to her in these worrying times.

She made her way upstairs to bed thinking of her two sons. They were usually in her thoughts, especially when she went to bed in the silent house. She smiled at the memory of Dickie feigning reluctance to go in the army to save her feelings and failing completely. It was only natural he would want to spread his wings; it was a pity he was doing it under such dangerous circumstances.

Her all-consuming loneliness was hard to shift at night. During the day she could keep it at bay with activity but the nights were awful, especially since the bombing had started. Oh well, you're alive despite Hitler's relentless efforts to change that. So cheer up and be grateful, she told herself as she got undressed, shivering.

'I can't pretend it wasn't expected,' said Mr Pickles when Daisy finally went to his office with her resignation. 'I was wondering how long it would be before the brass buttons on your uniform burst under the strain.'

'You knew.'

'Daisy my dear, I realise that I am well past it to

you young people but I haven't yet lost my eyesight and as a father of two I am fully cognisant with the facts of life.'

'Why didn't you say anything?' she asked.

'I didn't want to lose you,' he said. 'You've been one of my best usherettes and I've lost such a lot of staff lately to the services and war work. I knew you would come and tell me when you were ready to go. I didn't want to pre-empt the situation by bringing it out into the open.'

'My mind isn't ready to go yet. I love the job,' she said. 'But my body is protesting.'

'Yes, it's nature's way. You need to take things easy. Make the most of the rest because you won't get much once the nipper arrives, not while it's still little, anyway.'

She did actually think she would scream if one more person told her she must take things easy but as he was her boss she let it pass.

'So I'll work out my week's notice then, shall I?'

'Sadly I suppose you had better, but if you ever need a job in the future at any time you will always be welcome here.'

She stared at him in astonishment. 'What, a married woman with a child?'

'The war is changing things and it will continue to do so the longer it goes on,' he said. 'I know it's still not acceptable in some professions for a married woman to work but this is a cinema, not the civil service. I want good people on my team. If I continue to lose them at this rate, I will be employing only pensioners and school leavers. People of your age are attracted to the services for the adventure and war work because they can make good money working longer hours. And of course there is a lot of patriotism about. People want to help the war effort.'

'Yes, anyway it's nice to know that I'll be welcome but I don't see how I'll be able to come back because I'll have the baby to look after.'

'Of course, I understand,' he said. 'Anyway I'm sure I'll see you before you leave.'

She agreed with him and left feeling rather sad. Still, she had the baby to look forward to and that was very exciting. What had initially been a problem now felt like a joy. She simply couldn't wait to be a mum.

As raid shelters went the Blakes' must surely be one of the cosiest around, thought Daisy, one night in November when the family, minus John who was at work, was ensconced in it during an air raid. Before she had given up work, she had usually been at the cinema during the raids. Now she was a lady of leisure, most of her evenings were spent here. Mum was a natural housekeeper and had extended her talents to their corrugated iron sanctuary.

'Might as well make it as homely as we can as we're spending so much time down here,' she was often heard to say.

A cloth over a box made a table with mugs and a teapot, some family photos were dotted around, there was a candle in a jam jar; cushions, blankets and a pack of cards all helped to make the circumstances more bearable.

'I hope John is all right,' said Daisy, concerned for her husband who was at work.

'There's just one of you to worry about now,' said Mary. 'Before you packed up work we used to sit here worrying about both of you. But I'm sure he'll be all right so don't worry.'

'It's different being here in the shelter because you feel so afraid just sitting here waiting for the bombs,' said Daisy. 'When you're at the cinema with all the people and the atmosphere you feel safe somehow even though you're not.'

'I'll say you're not,' said Bertha. 'One hit and you wouldn't stand a chance in that place. At least down here in the shelter we're underground.'

'I know what Daisy means though,' said Mary. 'It's the company and doing something normal that takes your mind off the bombs. I'm going to the pictures at the weekend with some friends from work, air raid or not. I'm fed up with being stuck down here every flippin' night, just waiting for my end to come.'

'We're all tired of it, dear, but we have to be careful,' lectured Bertha.

'Some people say that if you're meant to go a bomb will get you wherever you are,' said Bill, who had a night off ARP duty.

'I've heard people say that and I think it's absolutely ridiculous,' disagreed Bertha airily. 'If it was true the government wouldn't have gone to all the trouble and expense of providing air-raid precautions.'

'Obviously no one is suggesting that we all go out in the street and let the bombs get us but I can understand people wanting some normality and enjoyment, especially the young people,' he said. 'The dance halls are packed every night so they say, despite the raids.'

'How do you know, Dad?' asked Daisy jokingly. 'I hope you haven't been up the Palais while we thought you were on ARP duty.'

'Of course he hasn't,' said Bertha, who had never quite got the hang of humour.

'Just joking, Mum.'

'Oh, right.'

'I don't know for how much longer I'll be able to climb down here,' said Daisy. 'I'm like a flamin' mountain.'

'More a large hillock, I would say,' said Mary.

'That makes me feel a whole lot better, I don't think,' laughed Daisy.

'It's only temporary,' Mary reminded her. 'You'll soon be your skinny self again.'

'Hooray for that.'

The distant roar of a bomber plane grew nearer and the conversation petered out, despite their efforts to keep it going. It was so close it appeared to be overhead and Daisy felt the breath squeezed out of her. There was an explosion that shook the ground then the drone of the bomber receded.

'I thought we'd had it that time,' said Bertha shakily.

'But here we all are, still here,' said Bill, determinedly cheerful.

No one wanted to talk much after that until the All Clear went and they all climbed out.

'We'll have to get a crane to haul you out soon, Daisy,' said her sister, teasing her as she helped her through the opening.

'If you can find one strong enough.' Daisy felt weak with relief and thankful to have survived yet again but worried about John because the explosion had sounded quite close.

'Thank God you're home, John,' she said, handing him a cup of cocoa soon after he stepped in the door. The others had all gone to bed. 'One of the explosions sounded really near.'

'Yeah, there are fire engines all over the place around the Broadway but we were all right at the Adelphi.'

'Did you have a sing-song?'

'No. We showed the film again and of course the government's wartime information film,' he said. 'Doreen usually organises the entertainment but she didn't feel like it tonight so we got the film rolling again.'

'That isn't like Doreen,' remarked Daisy. 'She usually enjoys getting people going.'

'Mm. She's had a bit of bad news actually,' he said, looking sad as he sipped his cocoa.

Daisy frowned. 'Bad news?'

His mouth tightened. 'Her husband Alfie ... er ... he was killed in action.'

'Oh John,' she said, feeling choked. 'What a terrible shame. They were just starting off on their life together too.'

'I know, it's awful,' he agreed. 'Mr Pickles told her to take a couple of days off but she said she'd rather be working. She needs to keep busy.'

'I can understand that.'

They each lapsed into their own thoughts. Daisy felt sad but knew that this news would go especially deep with John because he felt so guilty about not being in the army and taking his

151

chances with the rest. 'Give her my love and tell her I'll call in at the Adelphi and see her before she goes on duty in the next day or two. She always gets there too early for her shift.'

'I'll tell her,' he said sadly.

'John...'

'Yeah.'

'You're doing a very useful job and helping people here on the home front to cope by showing the films.'

'Home front being the operative words,' he said. 'I should be out there in uniform.'

'We all play our part in different ways,' she said. 'Even if you had passed the medical, as chief projectionist you might have been deferred from military service because cinema is so vital to public morale. Mr Pickles told me once that yours is the only job in the cinema that does qualify for deferment.'

'Thanks for the support, Daisy,' he said.

'But it doesn't really help.'

'Not really, no, but it's good to know you are on my side.'

'Always,' she said, and it was true.

John wasn't the only one who felt lesser as a human being. It transpired the next day that Mary did, too, but for a very different reason. Daisy was talking to her the next evening when they were on their own in the kitchen, drying the dishes after their evening meal.

'Any sign of a new man in your life yet?' asked Daisy.

'Who would want me?'

'Lots of men I should think.'

'No, all I'm worth is a fling with a married man,' she said. 'And too daft to see when I'm being used.'

'Don't put yourself down, Mary,' Daisy urged her. 'Ray was the guilty one. Not you.'

'I know but I should have realised. You know, him only being available to see me at certain times and not wanting to meet the family. I suppose I didn't want to see what was staring me in the face.'

'We all do that from time to time Daisy pointed out. 'Take me for instance. It was ages before I accepted that Al had chucked me. I kept making excuses for him.'

'Mm, there is that,' Mary said. 'Still, you came up smelling of roses in the end.'

'Hardly that.' Daisy was adamant. 'It will never be a marriage of love for either of us but I respect John enormously for coming to my rescue.'

'I should hope so too.'

Their mother entered the room and the conversation came to an abrupt end.

Like most mums-to-be Daisy found the last stages of her pregnancy very wearisome. She was in a great deal of physical discomfort: backache, heartburn and a bladder that seemed to need constant attention. Because of her eagerness to get the baby born and feel comfortable again, time seemed to stand still.

A couple of days after she'd heard the awful news about Doreen's husband, when she was at the local shops with her mother, she decided to go to the Adelphi to offer her condolences to her friend.

'Will you be all right?' asked Bertha.

'I think I can manage a five-minute amble on my own, Mum,' she said, exasperated by all the concern. 'It's nearer from here than it is from home.'

'You are close to your time, dear,' her mother reminded her gravely.

'I've still got a couple of weeks to go,' she said. 'I'll see you later, back at home.'

'All right dear.' Bertha looked worried but joined the queue at the grocer's.

Daisy headed off towards the Broadway in the bitter December day. The cold weather suited her in pregnancy. She'd found the heat at the end of the summer exhausting.

'Oh Daisy, thanks ever so much for coming,' said Doreen when her friend arrived in the staffroom, a basically furnished area with lockers along one wall, chairs and tables dotted about and lino on the floor.

Daisy engulfed a pale-faced Doreen in a heart-felt hug. 'I'm so sorry that I'm here because of such sad circumstances.'

Doreen nodded. 'It's still nice to see you any-way,' she said.

'It must be such a shock.'

'It is, even though I made myself half expect it as he was among the fighting troops. But you can't prepare yourself for something like this. You just have to let the pain come.'

Daisy eased herself down on to a chair. 'I suppose that's all you can do,' she agreed. 'But obviously you'll be feeling terrible.'

'Yeah but being at work is helping.' Doreen's eyes filled with tears. 'You can't even have a funeral to say a proper goodbye under these circumstances. He's buried in a foreign field somewhere.'

Daisy nodded in an understanding manner. 'Anything I can do, anything at all, you only have to ask.'

'I think you've got more than enough of your own to cope with at the moment.'

'At this precise moment I have nothing at all to cope with since everyone is obsessed with my taking things easy and it's driving me nuts.'

'That will stop as soon as the baby is here and you'll be wishing it hadn't,' said Doreen.

'I expect you're right,' she agreed. 'Everyone is being very good, my mother especially, and I do appreciate it but it seems as though the clock has stopped ticking and I'm going to be like an elephant for ever. But I mustn't complain.'

'Because I have had bad news, you mean?'

'Well, yes, something like that does make you count your blessings, doesn't it?'

'The world hasn't stopped turning because I have lost my husband, you know, even though it feels as though it has to me.'

Daisy drew in a sharp breath at the shock of hearing her friend say the words. It was such an awful thing for a young person to have to bear. 'I suppose not,' she said.

Doreen fastened her uniform and put on her red pillbox hat in front of the mirror. 'There. Now

155

I feel better. I feel like a human being instead of a newly bereaved widow.'

'The uniform does have an uplifting effect, I used to find that,' said Daisy, realising that she was feeling uncomfortable with a pain in her lower abdomen.

'You're right. It does.'

'But I must get off and let you go on duty or you'll have Mr Pickles after you.' Daisy heaved herself laboriously to her feet and as she did so she felt something strange that made her look at the floor where there was a puddle. 'Oh my God, Doreen. My waters must have broken.'

Doreen looked shocked; neither of them had any experience of this sort of thing. 'Don't panic,' she said. 'I'll get Mr Pickles.'

'No don't do that,' said Daisy. 'I'll go home.'

But then she felt a pain so strong, she cried out.

'Oh Lor,' said Doreen. 'I'll go and get help.'

'Oh my good Gawd,' said Mr Pickles when he arrived in the staffroom to find Daisy bent over and groaning with pain. 'When I said you were welcome back here any time I didn't mean for you to give birth here, Daisy dear. The cinema is no place for a baby to be born. We need to get you home.'

'I don't think there will be time,' said Daisy as another contraction gathered strength.

Mr Pickles clutched his throat as though about to choke.

'Oh dear, this is no place for a man. We need a nurse or a doctor, someone who knows about these things.' He turned towards the room where

156

people were getting ready to go on duty for the afternoon show. 'Everybody out please. Get your things and go to work. Sorry folks but this is an emergency and Daisy needs some privacy.'

'Shall I get her husband?' suggested Doreen.

'He's got a film programme to put on,' said Daisy. 'But if someone could get the midwife.'

'Tell me where she lives and I'll go and get her right away,' said Mr Pickles, keen to help but not too close to the action.

'Number two Oak Road.'

'I'm on my way and don't worry, Daisy dear,' he said kindly. 'We'll look after you. Between us we'll see your baby safely into the world.'

The last part of that was drowned out by the sound of Daisy's screams.

As cinemagoers flooded into the auditorium, looking forward to the entertainment, they couldn't guess the drama that was going on behind closed doors upstairs at the back of the building in the staffroom.

'How much longer,' begged Daisy. 'I don't think I can stand any more.'

'Yes you can,' said the midwife, a small woman with a sharp voice and a brisk manner. 'A woman's body is built for this and nothing will be sent that you can't cope with but you've not long to go now.'

'Oh God here comes another one,' groaned Daisy, who was lying on the bed in the sick bay with her legs wide open and her knees bent.

'Keep going,' encouraged Doreen, who had been given time off by Mr Pickles to assist.

157

'Don't push, Daisy,' said the midwife.

'I want to. I need to,' said Daisy. 'How am I supposed to stop myself?'

'Just hold on until I tell you.'

'Don't push, do push,' complained a sweaty, distraught Daisy. 'You need to make up your mind.'

'And you need to watch your manners my girl,' said the nurse crossly. 'There are times to push and times to hold back and I say when.'

'Sorry.'

'I should think so too,' said the older woman. 'Right, now you can do it; give me one big push.'

'Come on, Daisy,' urged Doreen excitedly. 'You can do it. That's the stuff.'

After pushing so hard she thought she had probably injured herself, she felt relief and Doreen said, 'You've done it Daisy. You've done it. You clever girl.'

'Yes, you have a beautiful little boy,' added the midwife to the sound of the baby crying. She cut the cord and gave Daisy her slippery little son to hold.

'Thank you,' said Daisy, feeling as though there was no expression of gratitude that could fully describe how she felt at this moment.

Mr Pickles was very excited about it all now that the serious stuff was over. He even had John put a message on the screen announcing the birth of a son to one of the Adelphi's favourite usherettes and her husband the chief projectionist, which created rousing cheers in the auditorium.

Taxis weren't so easy to find as in peacetime but Mr Pickles managed to get hold of one somehow and sent Daisy home in it with the midwife and John, who had been given a few hours off. Bertha had the surprise of her life when her daughter arrived complete with new born son she had decided to call Sam.

'I knew you shouldn't have gone to see Doreen on your own,' Bertha said predictably. 'You should stay home when you're near your time.'

'The job is done now, Mum, and you have a lovely little grandson so let's enjoy it and not worry about the unconventional place of his birth.'

'I'm not so sure,' she said, but she was smiling.

'You can talk later, ladies,' said the bossy midwife. 'But right now I need to get our new mother into bed.'

'I'll put the kettle on,' said Bertha.

Chapter Eight

It was February 1941. Al Dawson was home on leave and desperately worried about his mother because she was living here alone in London during these terrible air raids which had apparently been even more frequent for the latter part of last year. The Luftwaffe didn't come every night now but when they did, boy was it scary!

After Dunkirk he'd been posted to the UK and was currently stationed in Wales. Of course, he'd heard something about the air raids in London while he was away and had been concerned about his mum. But actually being here with her in the thick of it really sent his protective instincts soaring.

'Why don't you go and stay with your sister in Hampshire while this bombing is going on, Mum,' he asked one morning over breakfast.

'Because I don't want to,' she stated. 'I wouldn't want to leave Ada next door for one thing.'

'But she isn't your responsibility.'

'She doesn't have family so who else is going to look out for her except her neighbours?'

'Couldn't she go with you to the country?'

'I'm not going anywhere.' She was adamant. 'I'm a Londoner born and bred and I'm not being chased out of my home because someone wants us all dead.'

'That's not a very sensible attitude, Mum. Not while it's so dangerous here,' he said. 'Now that I've experienced it for myself, I know how bad it is and I want you away from it and somewhere safe.'

'I'll admit it isn't very comfortable here just now but this is my home, where I belong and I have responsibilities,' she told him. 'I have my teaching and I get quite a bit of piano work for shows put on by amateur groups which I wouldn't want to miss because they rely on me. The bombing will come to an end eventually. The raids are less often now so we do get to sleep in our own beds sometimes. It isn't all bad.'

'Even so, Mum, I'd feel easier in my mind if you were safe in the country,' he insisted.

'I appreciate your concern, son, but I'm not going so please don't keep on about it,' she said firmly. 'I'm sick with worry about you and Dickie

160

most of the time but I know you have to get on with what you do, the same as I do. I am not going and there's no point in you trying to persuade me.'

He smiled, despite his worries. She was a gallant soul and he was extremely proud of her. She seemed smaller and more vulnerable than before he went away, probably because he hadn't seen her for a while. 'All right, I won't say any more about it. I'll just worry more when I'm not here.'

'Worrying about each other is par for the course for all of us in these dangerous times,' she said.

'I suppose so.'

'Anyway, have you managed to see any of your mates while you've been home or are they all away?'

'Most of them are, but a couple of the lads from the factory, who are deferred from the services, are around so I'll have a drink with them while I'm home.'

Hester doubted her wisdom in saying her next words but they popped out anyway.

'Have you been in contact with Daisy who you were going out with before you went away?'

'No.'

His manner definitely didn't invite comment so she just said, 'Oh, I see.'

'I've heard that she's married and has a child though,' he went on. 'I ran into someone I know from the Adelphi the other day and they mentioned it to me. She married John, the projectionist.' There was a brief hiatus then, before she had a chance to react, he changed the subject, 'Have you heard from Dickie lately?'

Accepting the fact that talk of Daisy was taboo, she answered his question. 'I get an occasional letter; well more of a note really, just to let me know that he's all right but he never says much and I've no idea where he is.'

'It's a different world in the army, wherever he is, Mum,' he said. 'There isn't always a chance to write letters.'

'I realise that and I'm not criticising him in any way at all,' she said. 'So long as I get a line every now and again from you both to let me know you're still alive and kicking, you won't hear me complaining.'

He smiled, feeling affectionate and wanting to do something nice for her. 'How about I take you out for a drink tonight if there isn't an air raid?' he suggested.

'I don't usually go to pubs,' she said.

'It'll be a nice change for you then, won't it? And a break will do you good.' He gave her a warm smile. 'I'll be proud to have you on my arm.'

'In that case how can I refuse? But only if there isn't a raid.'

'Don't worry, I won't drag you out if there are any bombs about.'

The pub was crowded but they managed to find a seat in the corner. He even managed to get her a glass of sherry.

'We're lucky tonight,' he said as he put his beer next to his mother's sherry on the table. 'I understand that booze is short here at home.'

'Everything is, son.'

'Cheers, Mum,' he said, raising his glass.

'Cheers, son.' She took a sip of her drink. 'Mm. Nice,' she said, taking another large swallow.

'Steady on,' he said, laughing. 'I'll be carrying you home if you go on like that.'

'I'm just getting in the mood. I've decided that I'm going to enjoy myself tonight, Al,' she announced happily. 'It isn't every day I get to go out with my son so I shall make the most of it.'

She did too. After a few more drinks she delighted the pub clientele with her talent at the piano, playing songs that everyone knew and encouraging them to sing along. Seeing everyone smiling and singing, the war seemed far away. Al realised that his mother had transformed this rather gloomy bar, full of bomb-weary customers drinking watered-down beer, into a palace of fun and enjoyment. She was a proper diamond and he was proud of her.

Although Al was ostensibly the same man he had always been, a sociable, happy-go-lucky sort, there was a sadness within him that refused to go away no matter how hard he tried to shift it. He didn't show it; he never would. But it was there and it had nothing to do with the war.

'What a smashing evening, Al,' said Hester when they got home. 'Thanks ever so much, son.'

'There's no need to thank me, Mum, I enjoyed it too,' he said. 'I don't see you often now so it's nice to see you letting your hair down a bit when I do.'

'I certainly did that,' she said. 'I love playing the piano for pleasure and having a good old sing-song.'

'Shall I make you a cup of cocoa?' he asked.

She hiccuped and sat down in the armchair. 'I don't think I could manage it after all that booze.'

'A cup of tea then if we've got enough tea,' he suggested.

'That would be nice but I'll make it.'

'No you won't,' he said. 'You do enough running around for me. Tonight it's my turn.'

'Well, if you insist, thank you love.'

As he left the room, she sank back in the chair blissfully. She'd had a lovely time and even the bombers had managed to stay away. Some mothers she knew said that their sons seemed different when they came home on leave from the war. They were quieter and more withdrawn even though they put up a front. Al had changed too and had hardly said a word about what he'd actually been doing as a soldier.

Her boy wasn't the same man who'd gone away to war. There was a kind of emptiness about him now which she could only guess was a result of the things he'd seen and done in the line of duty. In a few days' time he would be going back off leave, probably to face more horrors at some point. It wasn't surprising the boys seemed different when they came home.

'Here you are, Mum,' he said, putting a cup of tea on the small table near her chair.

'Thank you, darlin',' she said. 'I won't half miss you when you go back.'

'Don't let's think about that yet, Mum,' he said. 'Just enjoy the moment.'

'I'm doing that all right.' She smiled.

Daisy's son Sam was four months old and a handsome child with his mother's blond hair and bright blue eyes. He smiled and chuckled and responded to people now. Although Daisy adored him she couldn't, in all honesty, say that it had been the easiest few months of her life since his birth.

The adjustment to motherhood had been more traumatic than she'd expected. The weather had been cold, everything was in short supply, the baby cried a lot as young babies do and they had all spent a lot of nights in the cold and damp air-raid shelter scared to death as bombs rained down.

To add to that the cinema was staying open even longer to cater for people who wanted to stay in their seats until they were confident it was safe to go home. So John had often been working very long hours and was permanently tired and irritable. He hadn't adjusted well to the baby's presence anyway and being exhausted didn't help.

But now it was spring and the weather had improved, the raids had lessened, the baby was older so settled into a routine and Daisy was optimistic for better things.

'Sam is really coming on now, John,' she said proudly one morning when she took her husband a cup of tea in bed, having been up early herself with the baby. 'Another couple of months and he'll be sitting up.'

'Let's hope he starts sleeping at nights too,' he said bluntly.

'He only wakes up to be fed,' she said defensively. 'And I take him downstairs as soon as he cries so that you are not disturbed any more than is necessary.'

'I know you do. It's just that I get so tired at work with all the extra hours and the broken nights here as well. I feel shattered most of the time.'

'He'll sleep through the night eventually but I can't say when that will be because he's a baby and not a machine that I can turn on and off.'

'There's no need to take that attitude,' he snapped.

'I'm only pointing out the facts, John,' she said. 'I know you are finding it all a bit much.'

'I'm only human.'

'It will probably be easier when he's older,' she suggested.

'Roll on the future then and let's have some peace.'

'You knew what you were signing up for when you married me,' she said.

'I didn't realise that babies caused such havoc.'

'Neither did I but they are not babies for long.'

'Thank God for that.'

Because Daisy's son was everything to her she was hurt by his remarks. She couldn't even say, 'He's your baby as well as mine,' because he wasn't and she hadn't realised it would make so much difference when she agreed to marry John. She had thought they would share in the joy of him like people in normal marriages do. So far, though, that hadn't happened. She'd heard that some men had a problem with babies but things sometimes improved when babyhood ended and a knowing child emerged. Would that happen as

Sam wasn't John's son?

Of course, men were never involved to the same extent as women so maybe John's behaviour wasn't all that unusual. Anyway, he had done well by her and Sam by marrying her and giving them respectability and she would never stop being grateful to him for that. Even if he never warmed towards Sam, her feelings on that subject wouldn't change. Sadly, she and John seemed to have lost their easy-going friendship in the hurly-burly of marriage and parenthood.

'I'll see you downstairs when you're ready then,' she said.

'I'll be down in a minute and thanks for the tea.'

'You're welcome.'

'You shouldn't spoil me.'

'You're worth it,' she said and left the room.

John drank his tea thoughtfully, sad that he had lost his pal Daisy when he had married her. He missed the easy-going relationship they had shared and was at a loss to know how to resurrect it. The marriage hadn't been easy for him from the start and since the baby had arrived, it was barely possible. He couldn't blame the fact that they had so little privacy because he was actually grateful for that. He was fond of the Blake family and when they were all around, talking and laughing, he could forget how isolated he felt when he was with Daisy on her own.

She did everything she could to make things better. He really believed she would do somer-saults if she thought it would make him happy. She was grateful to him and felt in his debt and no matter how many times he told her he didn't want her gratitude she still found ways to try and fill the hole in the marriage – the feelings that weren't there between them. Tea in bed and slippers by the fire certainly wouldn't do it. But bless her, she tried.

Now he was beginning to realise how naive he had been to think they could have a normal marriage. He'd thought friendship would be enough and had been so concerned about Daisy's plight at the time he had jumped straight in with his size nines.

He wanted things to be the way they were before with Daisy; talking about anything and everything, casually caring for each other as friends. But there didn't seem to be a way back, because the marriage had killed the friendship.

Mary came home from work with an announcement a few days later.

'My days at the Co-op are over, until after the war anyway,' she said. 'I'm going on to war work next week. I'm going to be making shell parts and guns at a factory in Acton.'

'Have they started calling people up for war work now?' asked her mother.

'Not yet but I think they will be quite soon,' she said. 'I'm young, strong and childless and I need to do my bit so I went along to the Labour Exchange and that's what they directed me into. Older women can do my job at the Co-op while I get on to essential employment as they call it. At some point soon everyone without dependent children will be expected to work, I reckon. Probably even you, Mum.'

'At my age? Surely not,' she said.

'I don't know what the rules will be as regards age but there are rumours that the government is going to want everyone working at some point to help with the war effort.'

'It'll be hard work for you on munitions, Mary,' her father warned her.

'That's the whole point, Dad,' she responded. 'I want to feel like I'm doing something worthwhile, a job that takes more effort than slicing cheese and weighing up tea every day. Anyway I've got no choice; you go where the Ministry of Labour decides to send you.'

'Surely they won't make grannies go out to work, will they?' said Bertha, worriedly. She hadn't worked outside the home for so long now.

'It depends how long the war goes on for, I suppose,' suggested Daisy, who had put the baby to bed and was enjoying her meal in peace. 'I doubt if they'll ever send really old people out to work.' She looked at her mother and giggled. 'So you'll be all right, Mum.'

'Oi, don't you be so cheeky,' she riposted. 'I might be a granny but I'm not past it by any means.'

'You didn't sound keen on the idea of going out to work so I was just trying to make you feel better.'

Mary saw the joke and giggled too. 'Perhaps you'd better get out there and get yourself a job before they make it illegal not to work. We don't want you getting carted off to prison.'

'Leave your mother alone, you two,' said Bill,

rising from the table with a grin on his face. 'Sorry to rush off but I'm on ARP duty.' He looked towards his daughters. 'And don't tease your mother while I'm out.'

'We'll behave,' said Mary.

'Don't you worry about me, Bill,' said Bertha. 'I'm more than a match for these two. I ought to be. I've been putting up with their cheek for long enough.'

Bill left and the conversation became general. 'No air-raid siren yet,' said Daisy. 'So perhaps we'll have a quiet night and John will be able to get home before the early hours. It's exhausting, the time he has to put in now.'

'Don't tempt fate,' said Mary. 'It's still quite early.'

'If it comes it comes,' said Daisy. 'But I'm keeping my fingers crossed.'

There was a demanding sound from upstairs. 'I'll go,' said Mary, who adored her nephew. 'It'll give me a chance to see my darling boy. I'll soon sort him out. He wants to see his Auntie Mary, that's why he's crying.'

'Thanks, sis,' said Daisy. 'I'll come up if you can't settle him. At least I get to finish my meal in peace.'

'She's very good with him, isn't she?' remarked Bertha after Mary had gone.

'Absolutely!'

'I reckon she'd like one of her own.'

'She has to find the right man first,' said Daisy lightly.

'That didn't stop you, did it?' said Bertha tactlessly.

Daisy didn't dignify that unkind remark with a response but her cheeks burned because it still hurt that Al had rejected her. 'I'll make a start on the clearing up,' she said, finishing her meal and rising.

There were no air raids that night and Mary was still up when John got home from work as he wasn't quite so late. She'd been sewing all evening, renovating an old summer frock to make it look more fashionable, and had only just finished.

'Fancy a cup of cocoa, John?' she asked. 'I'm making one for myself. Daisy's gone to bed. Sam's been a bit restless this evening so she thought she might as well turn in.'

'I'd love a cup, Mary. Ta.'

They sat in the living room in the armchairs by the hearth, with the door closed and speaking in low voices so as not to disturb anyone. She told him about her new job. 'I actually had a fancy to join one of the services,' she confided. 'But I guess I just didn't have the courage to up sticks and leave home.'

'I wanted all that too,' he said. 'I've never quite got over being turned down for the army.'

'Fancied the adventure, did you?'

'It was more to do with patriotism and wanting to be like all the others I think,' he said. 'I still feel like only half a man because I'm not in uniform.'

'You are doing your bit,' she assured him. 'You're doing it in a different way, that's all. You bring comfort to people with the films and that's very important.'

'Nice of you to say so but it won't make any

171

difference to my feelings on the subject.'

'I'd better shut up then, hadn't I?'

'It might be a good idea,' he said with good humour.

They sipped their cocoa in companionable silence. Then she heard herself say, 'Is everything all right, John, between you and Daisy?'

'Yeah, of course. Why wouldn't it be?' he asked defensively.

'Because you're not exactly glowing with happiness when you're together,' she replied. 'I can't help noticing. We live on top of one another here. It's difficult not to.'

'Your parents; have they noticed anything do you think?' he asked.

'Mum is far too grateful to you for coming to Daisy's rescue to worry about whether the two of you are getting on,' she said. 'Dad minds his own business about everything anyway. It isn't as if the two of you are at each other's throats or anything. It's just that I know Daisy so well and I can tell that she isn't happy.'

'Daisy was a good friend and she was desperate to keep the baby so I stepped in,' he said. 'I was fond of her; I still am. I thought it would be all right.'

'But it isn't...?'

'We haven't talked about it but we both know it isn't working,' he said. 'We were such good friends; now that's all gone and been replaced by a kind of mutual irritation.'

'I know you don't get much of a chance to talk on your own here but surely you need to bring it out into the open.'

'There doesn't seem to be any point since nothing can be done about it,' he told her. 'Marriage is for life. I made those vows and I intend to stand by them. We'll just have to try harder to make it work.'

'I don't see what else you can do.'

'Plenty of people do make the best of things in similar circumstances, don't they?' he said. 'Marriage isn't meant to be a picnic.'

'Neither is it meant to be a penance.'

'You just have to get on with things and keep trying, don't you? The same as everything else in life. You can't just give up because you've stopped liking each other. I'm sure a lot of married couples feel the same way as we do. But they accept things and stay together because they've made promises.'

'But you saved her reputation and Sam from illegitimacy,' she reminded him. 'Both those things are irreversible whatever happens between you and Daisy.'

He narrowed his eyes on her. 'Surely you're not suggesting that I leave Daisy. Don't you think she suffered enough when Al let her down?'

'She hasn't spoken to me about it but I don't think she would suffer if you left on good terms,' she said. 'I think she'd actually be relieved. She bends over backwards to please you, John. I've watched her do it and it's too much and not natural. She doesn't do it out of love but gratitude. And it's obvious that you don't feel comfortable around Sam.'

'Oh dear, you've noticed. I was hoping that might improve as he gets older,' he said. 'I've never had anything to do with babies before and didn't realise what hard work they are.'

'I understand,' she said. 'It might be easier for you if he was your own.'

'I don't resent him not being mine and I would never hurt him or be unkind. He's a sweet little thing but the parental interest just isn't there for me. I want to have it but it won't come. I try to make an effort because of Daisy but I just don't feel comfortable around him. Isn't that awful?'

'You're just being honest,' she said. 'You can't force those sort of feelings.'

'Apparently not.'

'People eh. What are we like?' She went on to confide in him about her love affair with Ray. 'I honestly wanted to die when it ended. I felt physically ill. I've never really known what a nervous breakdown actually is but I think I was quite close to having one.'

'I had no idea,' he said. 'Are you over it now?'

'I still have my wobbly moments; he really did break my heart. But I got through it somehow. And here I still am. We live through these things, don't we?'

'Indeed.'

'Now you and Daisy need to get yourselves sorted. Obviously this conversation stays between us.'

'Of course. And thanks for listening. It felt good to bring it out into the open.'

'I enjoyed the conversation too. Maybe you should do the same thing with your wife; talk to her about how you feel,' she said. 'You are both such lovely people. I want you to be happy and if it isn't together then so be it. But if you talk about it maybe you can sort it out another way.'

'I can't promise to do anything right away because it's too serious to be hasty,' he said. 'But I will give it some serious thought.'

They both got up; she took the cocoa cups into the kitchen and rinsed them under the tap, then followed him up the stairs. The creak of the staircase seemed magnified in the silent house.

After months of air raids, Londoners were hardened to the bombing and as the raids had lessened during the spring of 1941 they were beginning to think that perhaps it was coming to an end. But their hopes were dashed on the night of May the tenth when bombs rained down on them in what seemed like a never-ending attack.

'Well, we've had some raids but I've never known anything like this,' said Bertha as she and the girls and Sam were ensconced in the air-raid shelter listening to almost continuous explosions.

'I hope Dad is all right,' said Mary, because Bill was out on ARP duty.

'John too, at the cinema,' said Daisy.

'We'll be fortunate if we don't lose the house at least tonight,' said Bertha.

'Don't say that, Mum,' said Daisy.

'Just being realistic,' said Bertha. 'We're lucky to have managed to have it intact this long. Plenty of Londoners haven't. Staying alive is the main thing.'

'We don't get morbid in this family, Mum, you know the rules,' Daisy reminded her.

'Sorry girls, but it just seems so much worse than usual,' she said. 'I think they've got the whole of the Luftwaffe dropping their bombs on London tonight.'

'Other places might be getting it too,' said Mary.

'Maybe,' she agreed.

Sam, who was wrapped in blankets and asleep on the bench, woke up suddenly and started to cry. Daisy lifted him up and gave him milk from a bottle which he promptly brought up all over himself and his mother. He screamed as she tried to clean him up and he didn't seem able to stop despite her trying to comfort him. He was absolutely beside himself.

'He's very hot,' she said.

'Yes he is,' agreed her mother, feeling his brow.

'He must be running a temperature because his skin is burning. I'll have to take him indoors and try and cool him down with a cold flannel.'

'You can't go out of the shelter while the raid is still on,' said Bertha.

'What else can I do, Mum?' she said as the baby continued to scream. 'He's obviously not well and he must be uncomfortable in those sicky clothes. I brought his milk and a small cloth but I didn't come prepared for him to be ill.'

'It's gone quiet out there,' said Mary. 'Perhaps the All Clear will go in a minute.'

Sam was almost hysterical and still the All Clear didn't come.

'I'll have to chance it and take him in,' said Daisy, her nerves raw. 'I can't just let him suffer.'

The other two women couldn't really argue with that, as worrying as it was. So Daisy left the shelter and hurried to the house carrying her sick child in her arms. Inside she removed his soiled clothing and sponged him with a cool flannel before putting him into clean clothes but still he cried. She held him on her shoulder, rocking him, and could feel his burning skin throbbing through her clothes. Now her natural instinct had taken over and her priority was making him better. The bombing had fallen into second place.

'She's been gone a long time, Mum,' said Mary.

'Yeah. What's keeping her?' said Bertha. 'She must know the All Clear hasn't gone yet.'

'I suppose she's trying to comfort the baby. Anyway, it's quiet now so maybe the raid is over for tonight. There's often a gap before we hear the All Clear. I suppose they have to make sure there are no more bombers on the way before they sound it.'

'I wish that sister of yours would come back down here though,' said Bertha worriedly. 'It could still be dangerous up there.'

'Shall I go and see what's keeping her; make sure she's all right?' suggested Mary.

'Not likely. I'm not having you disappear as well so you stay where you are.'

'All right, Mum.'

Finally Sam had settled and was asleep in Daisy's arms. His fever seemed to have abated too but she had learned from experience that this sort of thing was often intermittent. So now that he had settled she headed for the air-raid shelter.

Almost as soon as she reached the back door she heard the drone of a bomber and knew she had to make a run for it. But her shoe fell off on the back step and hindered her. When she was midway to the shelter the plane seemed to be overhead and she knew she wouldn't make it. Instinctively, she clutched her child to her breast and lay on the ground with Sam beneath her, careful not to crush him but protecting him with her own body.

There was an explosion nearby and the noise of the engine grew distant but by some miracle she and Sam were unharmed. 'Oh thank God,' she said, sitting up and clutching him to her, vaguely aware that she had instinctively put her son's life before her own by lying on top of him. She'd sometimes wondered if she was capable of that and now knew it had come naturally.

'Thank Gawd for that,' said Bertha when she climbed back into the shelter. 'How is he?'

'He's settled for the moment and seems cooler but I'll keep my eye on him because these things usually come and go,' she said. 'Poor little thing.'

'Oh hallelujah,' said Mary as the All Clear sounded. 'That felt like one of the worst raids we've had, ever.'

'They all feel like that while they're in progress,' Bertha remarked drily.

It had actually been the worst night of the war for London, according to the wireless the next day. Some of the city's historic buildings had been hit; Westminster Abbey and St Paul's not for the first time. Every main line railway station was damaged and many Londoners had been killed. Bill and John both returned home unhurt and Sam seemed to get better overnight so the Blake family considered themselves blessed.

Bertha and her daughters wept openly at the destruction when they went for a walk around the town.

'It's enough to make you want to give up,' said Bertha. 'Nine months of bombing we've had now. How much more can people take?'

'They'll take it for as long as it keeps coming,' said Daisy. 'People won't lose their spirit.'

'I don't know so much about those who have lost loved ones and their homes,' said Bertha. 'They can't be expected to grin and bear it.'

'Maybe not but what else can anyone do but keep going?' said Daisy sadly.

'Nothing,' said Mary. 'You just have to hope that it will stop sometime soon. And we must count our blessings that we are all still alive and our home is intact. We also need to find out if there is anything we can do to help the people who haven't been so lucky.'

'Absolutely,' agreed Daisy.

Chapter Nine

Much to the relief of the Blake family and their fellow Londoners, the shocking onslaught from the air on the tenth of May was followed by quiet skies and nights spent snuggled up in bed instead of in the cold and damp shelters. Most people didn't dare to speculate as to whether they had seen the last of the Luftwaffe but just enjoyed the calm while they had it.

Sam grew and thrived that summer and his besotted mum enjoyed him like nothing else in her life. As his awareness and ability developed he became even cuter and his blue-eyed countenance was now complemented by a mop of golden hair. Although he was so much like Daisy he sometimes reminded her of Al in the way he smiled. One of his most adoring relatives was Mary, who delighted in her role as godmother.

Daisy embraced the nice weather, taking Sam out every afternoon to the park or the river or to visit other young mums she had got to know with children of his age. He was very much a family baby though; they all treasured him and relished the chance to spend time with him. All except for John who still struggled to take an interest.

Daisy pretended not to notice because it was easier; in the same way as she carried on regardless with her marriage as though all was well when nothing could be further from the truth. What else could she do? She could hardly demand devotion from John for herself and her son given the circumstances of their marriage. She didn't want it for herself anyway. But she did wish he could show some affection towards Sam.

One night in early autumn John came home from work with a message.

'Mr Pickles asked me if I thought you might be interested in doing a few evening shifts at the Adelphi if your mum is willing to look after the baby,' he said as they were getting ready for bed. 'I said I'd mention it to you.'

'Oh really.' Instinctively Daisy was keen on the

idea and thought her mother would probably welcome the chance to look after her much-loved grandson. As much as Daisy enjoyed being a mum, she thought it would suit her to be working again, albeit just for a few hours after Sam was in bed.

'Yeah. He came to see me in the interval.'

'Hm. I do quite fancy the idea, John,' she told him. 'But would you mind?'

He looked astonished. 'Why on earth would I mind?' he asked. 'It won't affect me.'

Embarrassed by his reaction, she said, 'I thought you might not like the idea of my leaving Sam.'

Again that look of pure bewilderment. 'Whatever gave you that idea?' he asked.

'A lot of men don't like their wives going out to work even though the war has made it less unusual, especially when there is a child involved,' she said, painfully reminded of the abnormality of their circumstances. John found it hard to connect with Sam so he didn't mind who looked after him as long as it wasn't himself. This hurt dreadfully. She realised she'd been clinging to the hope that somehow he might find a way to love him even though he wasn't his. But it hadn't happened and she was very aware of the widening gap between herself and John.

'He'll be perfectly all right with your mother,' he said in an even tone.

'Yes, I'm sure he will,' she said. 'So will you tell Mr Pickles that I'll give it some serious thought and let him know my answer in the next few days?'

'Oh!' He sounded surprised. 'I thought you

would jump at the chance. I know how much you enjoyed that job.'

'I did but my situation has changed and I need to think about it before I make a decision and make sure Mum is happy with the idea.'

'Yes of course,' he said without much interest. 'I'll tell him tomorrow.'

Daisy was indeed thoughtful over the next few days but she was mulling over much more than a few shifts at the Adelphi. Finally having come to a decision, she waited for John's night off, arranged for her mother to listen for Sam who was in bed and told John that they were going for a walk.

'A walk in the blackout,' he said, astonished. 'What on earth for? I'd rather sit and read the paper and listen to the wireless on my night off.'

'You can do that when we get back,' she said, putting her coat on and handing his to him.

'All right, if you insist,' he agreed with reluctance.

'Where's Daisy?' asked Mary when she got home from work, grimy and exhausted.

'She and John have gone for a walk; it's his night off,' explained her mother.

'Why on earth would they want to go out walking in the dark?' queried Mary.

'Probably to talk in private,' suggested Bertha. 'They don't get much of a chance in this house with us lot around.'

'That's true.'

'How was work today?' asked Bertha.

'Gruelling,' she replied. 'I didn't know what real

work was until I started this job and talk about monotonous, assembling parts all day. But they are a nice bunch of women I work with and we have a good laugh so that helps the time to pass.'

'I hope your food isn't too dried up,' said Bertha as she removed the covered plate from the oven. 'I have to warm it up with you working such long hours.'

'Don't worry, Mum, I'm so hungry I'll eat it if I have to lever it off the plate with a chisel.'

'You don't mind working in a war factory then?' said her father, who was sitting in the armchair reading the paper.

'I wouldn't go so far as to say that,' she said. 'But as I don't have a choice I might as well make the best of it.'

'Good girl,' said Bill.

Mary washed her hands at the kitchen sink and tucked into her meal. Hunger was more or less a permanent state in wartime.

'What's all this about, Daisy?' asked John as they headed through the war-torn town towards the river, the air tinged with the smoky scent of autumn. 'I presume we are walking about in the dark because you want to discuss something with me.'

'That's right. I think it's time we had a chat about our marriage,' she said.

'Oh no,' he groaned.

'Don't worry – I am not going to have a go at you or anything but I think we both know we can't go on as we are, even though we soldier on and pretend nothing is wrong.'

'I honestly don't see what else we can do, Daisy,' he said, his tone warm now but worried.

'I think it's time we went our separate ways; now before we grow to really hate each other,' she suggested.

He didn't insult her intelligence by pretending that nothing was wrong but he did sound shocked when he said, 'Daisy that's a huge thing you're suggesting. I can't walk away from the marriage; from us.'

'There isn't an "us". There never has been in that way.'

'But I have a responsibility to you and Sam,' he said. 'I can't renege on that.'

'You can if I ask you to,' she said. 'You know as well as I do that neither of us is happy and that you'd be relieved to be rid of Sam and me.'

'I wouldn't go that far. I'm still very fond of you, Daisy, despite everything,' he said. 'But I can't deny that the marriage is hard going, for both of us.'

'I suggest that we don't do anything legal for the moment; not unless either of us wants to marry again later on in the future because it would be too complicated and expensive,' she said. 'I'm thinking in terms of a mutually agreed parting of the ways. If we do it now, Sam is too young to be affected. If we struggle on until he's old enough to understand he'll be upset by it.'

'I'm really sorry I haven't been able to be a dad to him, Daisy,' he said. 'I've been hoping I might improve when he's older but we've no way of knowing.'

'I'm not blaming you, John, but, because he is

everything to me, it hurts that you don't feel for him even though I know you can't help it,' she said. 'I shiver if a breeze blows on him, that's how strong my maternal love is. But even aside from Sam, the marriage has destroyed our friendship so we don't have anything to base a relationship on now.'

'I know; it's very disappointing.'

'You came to my rescue and I will always be grateful to you for that. But enough is enough. We've both tried and it hasn't worked so let's accept that. Maybe you can go back and live with your parents and I'll stay at home. I am going to ask Mr Pickles if I can take on more shifts than just a couple of evening ones so I should be able to manage financially. If Mum will look after Sam for me that is. I'm not taking anything for granted as regards that but I think she'll be in her element doing that for me. Her kids and now her grandchild mean everything to her. I know she can be very overbearing and speaks her mind a bit too strongly at times but she'd do anything for her family.'

'Well, what can I say, Daisy? You seem to have it all worked out and everything you say is true,' John said sadly.

'I finally faced up to it the other day so you can feel free to leave with my blessing.'

'I don't know what to say.'

'Just say that you'll do it and we can both get on with our lives,' she said.

'On two conditions.'

'Which are?'

'Firstly that I am allowed to send you some

money each month,' he said. 'I took on the responsibility and I don't want to walk away from it.'

'Only a small token payment if you insist,' she said. 'What's the other condition?'

'That you allow me to tell your family of our plans. They have treated me well and I don't want to leave without saying a proper goodbye.'

'It's very brave of you because Mum isn't going to like it one little bit,' she warned him. 'But if it's what you really want, you go ahead.'

'Moving out!' exclaimed Bertha when John imparted the news as soon as they got back. The family was all at home and Sam in bed. 'You can't just walk out on your wife and son.'

'I've asked him to, Mum, and you know very well that Sam isn't his son.'

'Strictly speaking, that's true I suppose,' she was forced to agree. 'But even so...'

'You know why we got married,' Daisy reminded her. 'We thought we could make it work but we haven't been able to so we've made a mutual decision to part, though it was me who forced the issue, not John. I suggested we call it a day. So don't get the idea that John is doing the dirty.'

'Marriage is for life as far as I'm concerned,' said Bertha predictably.

'In a perfect world, yes,' said Daisy. 'But the real world is far from that.'

'Anyway,' began John. 'I didn't want to leave without saying a proper goodbye and thanking you all for your kindness while I've been here. It's very much appreciated. I'm sorry things didn't work out.'

'How is Daisy supposed to manage?' demanded Bertha.

'All that is taken care of,' he said. 'Daisy will tell you about it after I've gone.'

'Well I'm glad you've both faced up to it at last,' Mary approved. 'It's been obvious to me almost from the start that it wasn't working out.'

'If you are both sure, it must be for the best, I suppose,' said Bill, rising and offering John his hand. 'Thanks for helping our girl out when she needed it, mate.'

John shook his hand and turned his attention to Bertha. 'I'm really sorry, Mrs Blake. I know you think I've let you down but I'm very fond of you all.'

'You've got a funny way of showing it,' she snapped. 'I think it's an absolute disgrace. You can't just walk away from your responsibilities. Marriage is never easy but you don't give up just because of a few problems. These things take a lot of effort on both sides.'

'You go and start packing, John,' urged Daisy, taking his arm. 'I'll sort this out after you've gone.'

An awkward silence fell and he seemed reluctant to leave her to face the music on her own. Then Mary said, 'Good luck John. I expect we'll see you around.'

He nodded. 'I won't be too far away. I'll move back in with Mum and Dad on the other side of town, for the time being anyway.'

'Disgraceful,' snorted Bertha.

'I'll go and get my things together,' said John and left the room looking embarrassed, with

Daisy following.

'Well, you've got yourself into some scrapes, Daisy, but this one takes the biscuit,' said Bertha, later on after John had left, Bill had gone out for a pint and Mary was upstairs in the bedroom putting curlers in her hair. 'Husbands don't grow on trees you know. Fancy letting him go. Have you lost your mind?'

'Quite the opposite,' said Daisy. 'I've come to my senses at last. I should never have let you make me feel so vulnerable that I agreed to marry him.'

'Oh, so it's all my fault, is it?'

'Of course not. But you were demanding that I give the baby up because of the family reputation. Marrying John was a way of keeping him. I made myself believe I was doing the right thing because I was desperate at the time. Surely, as a mother yourself, you must know how I felt.'

'It was right for Sam in that he doesn't have the stigma of illegitimacy,' said Bertha. 'And having made that decision you should have seen it through so that the boy has a normal family life with two parents.'

'How many of those will there be by the time this war is done?'

'That's beside the point!'

'Listen to me for a moment, please Mum,' said Daisy determinedly. 'Sam wouldn't benefit from being brought up by two people who hate the sight of each other, which is what would have happened if John and I had stayed together any longer.'

'Oh well.' Bertha sighed heavily. 'It's done now

so we'll have to get on with it, I suppose. Knowing you, you will have worked out how you'll manage.'

'I certainly have. I'm planning on going back to work because I am only prepared to take a small amount of financial help from John and only until I get on my feet. Mr Pickles is desperate for staff because of the demand for war workers so I'd like to go back to the Adelphi.'

'I see.'

'I'm hoping that you'll look after Sam for me while I'm working but I'm not taking it for granted because it's a big commitment and you might not want to do it. It will mostly be evenings when Sam is in bed and a couple of afternoons for me to earn what I need to manage. Don't be afraid to say if you'd rather not. I know it's a lot to ask.'

'And who else would do it?'

'I'm not sure yet but I think I'll be able to get it organised,' Daisy said. 'I doubt if the nurseries are open in the evenings but there are women who look after children in their homes for payment. I suppose they do evenings as well.'

'Nurseries! Paying some stranger to look after my grandson! Don't you dare.'

'But...'

'Of course I'll look after Sam,' Bertha said. 'I don't see why he should suffer just because you can't get your life properly sorted. I might not approve of the way you carry on but I'll always be there for you, for all of you.'

'Yes I know that, Mum.' All Daisy's irritation was swept away by love and gratitude.

Bertha couldn't get to sleep that night. She was thinking about the latest turn of events with Daisy and John and wondering if she herself really had forced her daughter into a marriage that was wrong for her by insisting that she give up the baby. Maybe she had but only with Daisy's best interests at heart and she wasn't to know that it would go wrong. John had seemed like the perfect husband for her. Solid and respectable, not some fly-by-night like Sam's father.

Right or wrong, she always tried to act in the best interests of her family, who were her whole world. She had no real interests outside of the family and that was the way she liked it. Maybe she was a bit controlling at times but that was because she loved them all so much and wanted what was best for them – which wasn't always what they wanted. But she was more experienced than they were about life so obviously she was more able to judge situations with the wisdom of her years.

Still, it wasn't all bad. She was going to have her grandson to herself while Daisy was out working and she would enjoy that very much. When she'd told Bill he'd asked her if she might find it a bit too much. Bloody cheek! What did he think she was, some old girl who was past it? She was in her fifties not her eighties. Well, she'd soon show him. There were women older than her working as clippies on the buses now, up and down those stairs all day, so she was damned sure she could cope with a toddler.

Daisy wasn't the easiest of daughters; always a drama with that one. First they'd had the awful

190

Rumbold business and the unfair sacking, and then she'd got herself in the family way, now there was a failed marriage. God only knew where it would end. But she always came back fighting, that girl. Never one for self-pity. It would be nice if she could get settled with someone who was right for her though.

Neither of the girls had much luck in that direction. Mary kept things close to her chest as far as her private life was concerned. Bertha knew she had been seeing someone a while ago. Mary hadn't realised it of course. She probably thought her mother was too dim to notice. Anyway, it must have ended because she didn't go out all dressed up and come home late now.

'Go to sleep, Bertha,' said Bill beside her and she realised that she must have been fidgeting.

'Sorry love.' She turned over and tried to empty her mind so that she could doze off.

Like most working mums, Daisy was dogged by conscience about leaving Sam but knew he would get the best possible care with her mother. She appreciated how lucky she was to have her as back-up. A feeling of guilt seemed to come with the territory and there was nothing to do but live with it and do what must be done. Anyway, she only worked three afternoons and five evenings so she was around a lot of the time when he was awake.

Despite her maternal worries, she got back into the cinema routine as if she'd never been away and enjoyed it. Most of the staff she had worked with had left, mainly to do war work, but Doreen, who was deferred from war work because of her ailing, dependent mother, was still there and it was good to see something more of her friend.

Shortly after Daisy's return John decided it was time to make a move. He'd been offered a job that his knowledge of film qualified him for in some sort of war research centre. She knew he had wanted to do something more closely connected to the war for a long time so she didn't suspect it had anything to do with their personal affairs. But she felt sad, especially as it was in the north of England somewhere so he would be moving away. He had been such a part of the Adelphi and her life for a long time.

'We'll miss you John,' she said.

'Not half,' agreed Doreen. 'You're part of the furniture around here.'

'I'll be back after the war,' he said. 'You're not getting rid of me for ever and I'll come home every so often to visit until then.'

'Don't forget to call in and see us.'

'Try stopping me.'

Daisy had a private chat with him about maintenance for Sam, which she didn't see as his responsibility now. The boy wasn't his and John had none of the benefits of marriage so why should he pay? She told him that now that she was working she could manage, especially as she was living at home so only had to pay a share of the rent and household expenses. He was reluctant to end the agreement but she promised to let him know if she needed help at any time.

So the split was very amicable but she missed him more than she expected. Not as a husband but the friend she had lost the day she had married him; she had hoped with time they could gradually rebuild their friendship. Now that he wasn't going to be around it seemed like a faint hope.

But life went on and she fell into a steady routine of work and motherhood, even more enjoyable now that Sam was a little boy rather than a baby. Apart from a few isolated air raids the nights remained quiet so the cinema closed at its normal time.

Daisy and Doreen were talking about what was now known as the Blitz one moonlit night in the spring of 1942, as they left the cinema and walked the short distance together before Doreen turned off towards her home.

'John was absolutely worn out from being at the Adelphi for such long hours,' mentioned Daisy.

'We all were,' said Doreen. 'Mr Pickles had to get tough after a while and close up at midnight some nights to give us a break, bombs or not. People were turning up with sandwiches intent on staying all night in the cinema.'

Daisy laughed. 'I suppose it was more comfortable than the air-raid shelter though not so safe.'

'Thank God the raids have stopped, for the time being anyway,' said Doreen.

'Still no sign of an end to the war though.'

'No, but it does make you feel a bit more confident now that the Americans are in it with us.' Doreen was referring to the entry of the United States into the war after the bombing of Pearl Harbor at the end of last year.

'What about the Yanks eh?' said Daisy approvingly. 'Mary and I took Sam to Hyde Park on my Sunday off and the place was teeming with them. Very smart. Lovely uniforms.'

'You're telling me,' said Doreen, 'I went to Hammersmith Palais on my night off for a bit of fun with some friends and there were a lot of them there. You should see them jitterbug.'

'I've heard about that.'

They reached Hammersmith Bridge where they usually went their separate ways; Doreen took a turning near there while Daisy carried on past the bridge.

'Someone doesn't look very happy,' remarked Doreen, looking towards the bridge where a soldier was leaning on the railing staring down into the water.

'Perhaps his girlfriend has given him the push,' suggested Daisy. 'Poor lad. I know what that feels like.'

'What on earth is he doing?' said Doreen as the soldier started to climb on to the railings.

'Oh my God, he's going to jump off,' said Daisy and the two women rushed towards him.

'Come on down, soldier,' said Doreen.

No reply.

'Whatever it is it can't be that bad,' said Daisy.

'It is,' he said, wobbling on the railing then sitting down looking towards the river with his back to them. 'Believe me. So just go home and leave me to it.'

'We're going nowhere,' said Doreen. 'Not until you come down from there.'

'Just tell us what's troubling you,' said Daisy gently. 'And if you still want to go ahead after we've talked it over, we won't stop you. It's your life.'

'I can't tell you,' he said. 'I'm too ashamed.'

Although his voice was distorted with anguish, there was a hint of familiarity about it that Daisy couldn't quite place.

'I've been where you are now,' said Doreen. 'In that black pit of hell. I didn't climb the bridge railings but I did want to end it all for a while after my husband died.'

Daisy was surprised by this because Doreen had seemed very brave and dignified in her grief. You never really knew people, she realised.

'I'm very glad I didn't because things looked brighter after a while,' Doreen continued when there was no response from the soldier.

'That's a different thing altogether,' he said at last. 'You don't have to get out there on the battle-field.'

'That's very true and I am full of admiration for those who do.'

'The army is full of heroes but I'm not one of them,' he said. 'A coward like me has no place among the fighting troops.'

'I bet many a hero feels like a coward some-times,' said Doreen, who had a very gentle speaking voice which this man seemed to respond to.

'I'm due back off leave tomorrow and I can't go back,' he said, his voice breaking. 'I just can't do it so the only thing for me is the river. If I don't go back they'll come after me and that will upset my mother.'

'And you think killing yourself won't?' asked Doreen.

'Probably not as much as deserting,' he said. 'That's the big disgrace.'

'Rubbish,' said Doreen. 'I'm not a mother myself so I can't speak from experience. But I can think of nothing that would break a mother's heart more than the death of a child.'

'Nor me and I am a mother,' added Daisy but Doreen was leading the conversation. She seemed to have a way with her in this dangerous situation.

'Humph,' he grunted.

The soldier shifted and wobbled dangerously.

The two women held their breath but he seemed to steady himself.

'All I'm asking is that you come down and talk to us,' Doreen persisted. 'Then we'll go away and let you do whatever you feel you must.'

His body began to tremble and Daisy knew that he was crying.

'If you can turn carefully a little this way and take my hand I'll help you down,' said Doreen.

He was silent for what felt like for ever, then he moved around slowly and reached for Doreen's hand. Daisy gasped when she saw his face. It was Dickie Dawson!

Hester Dawson was restless and couldn't stop looking at the clock on the mantelpiece in her living room. She got up and wandered into the music room and knew if she could play it would calm her but might also disturb the neighbours as it was late and as this was a terraced house. She reminded herself that her son Dickie was a grown man and entitled to stay out as late as he liked. But it was close to midnight and he had to get up early in the morning to go back off leave.

It was none of her business, she reminded herself repeatedly. He'd probably met some girl and was doing a spot of courting. She should go to bed and forget about him. As that wasn't possible, she wandered from room to room longing to hear the sound of the key in the door. But all remained silent.

Dickie had been his usual garrulous self during this leave, full of chatter and jokes. But sometimes he'd seemed just a little too cheerful and she wondered if some of it was an act. It was awful for these young men, having to go away and fight and lose all control over their lives. Still, it was the same for them all so there was no point in her upsetting herself about it. She did wish Dickie would come home though. God only knew how long it would be before she saw him again after tomorrow. Come on son, show yourself. Let's have a cup of cocoa together before we go to bed.

Daisy and Doreen were now sitting on a garden wall in a residential street with Dickie between them. He'd been shocked when he'd recognised Daisy but she assured him that she thought no less of him and no one would hear about this incident from her. He had been openly sobbing and Doreen had been marvellous with him. She had been told he was Al's brother and also told him no one would hear about this from her.

'Let it all out. We all need a good cry now and then, even you men,' she'd said.

Gradually he became calmer. Then as suddenly as the flick of a switch, he sat up straight, wiped his eyes and said in a strong voice, 'I'm sorry about all this, girls. Now I want to jump in the river because of the embarrassment.'

'There's no need to be embarrassed with us,' said Doreen. 'If I had to go away and fight I would spend my whole life in tears.'

'Me too,' added Daisy.

He gave a small laugh and stood up. 'I'd better go home. My mother will be waiting up for me as it's my last night.'

'Give her my regards,' said Daisy. 'There's no need to tell her the circumstances of our meeting.'

'This never happened as far as we're concerned,' added Doreen.

'I'll do that, Daisy, and thanks, girls. You saved my life,' he said and walked away in that upright way that soldiers have.

'What a lovely bloke,' said Doreen.

'Mm. I think so too.'

'It would be nice to see him again sometime to find out how he got on but he'll steer well clear of us if our paths ever cross again,' said Doreen. 'He won't want to be reminded of his less than finest hour.'

'You're probably right,' said Daisy and the two women went their separate ways.

'Sorry I'm late, Mum. I got chatting to some mates,' fibbed Dickie. 'You shouldn't have waited up.'

'I thought I would as it's your last night.'

'That's nice of you.'

'Shall I put the kettle on?'

'I'd like that, Mum,' he said because he knew it

would please her though he would rather have gone straight to bed. 'I probably won't see you again for a while so we might as well make the most of the time we have.'

She filled the kettle and he sat at the kitchen table.

'I know you and your brother are grown men but I still worry when you're out late.'

It was a blessing she didn't see them in combat, he thought, but said in a casual manner, 'I meant to tell you, I saw Daisy that ex-girlfriend of Al's the other day in Hammersmith Broadway. She sent you her regards.'

'Oh that's nice,' she said. 'I really liked her and was disappointed when they broke up.'

'Yeah, me too,' he said. His mother would never know just how highly he regarded Daisy and her friend Doreen after what they had done for him tonight.

Chapter Ten

It was late autumn 1942 and Bert Pickles was outside the Adelphi in conversation with the waiting crowds.

'When are you gonna get some ice cream in?' asked a woman in a headscarf. 'The flicks ain't the same without a tub or a choc ice in the interval.'

'You can blame the government for that,' Bert replied. 'They've banned the manufacture of it altogether so there's none to be had for anyone.'

'Blimey, that's a bit drastic,' said the woman to a chorus of agreement from people nearby.

'I don't suppose they can help it,' suggested another queuing female. 'Everything has to come second to the war effort.'

'Another one of our pleasures to disappear,' put in someone. 'We'll have nothing left to cheer us up soon.'

'You've still got the cinema,' Bert reminded her. 'And they aren't planning on closing us down as far as I know, though I don't suppose we'll have any ice cream to offer you until this damned war is over. I miss it myself as it happens. I'm rather partial to a choc ice now and then.'

Of course, he didn't mention that the management missed the income from confectionery since rationing. Now ice cream was no longer available at all they were even more depleted. Cigarettes were in short supply too. So the takings were well down on that side of the business. Fortunately they had packed houses most nights, which was a blessing.

'When are you going to get a Betty Grable film in?' asked a man in a dark overcoat.

'As soon as there's one available sir,' he replied politely. 'But you're in for a real treat tonight with Dorothy Lamour in *The Road to Morocco*.'

'Never mind Dorothy Lamour,' said the woman who was clutching the man's arm in a proprietary manner. 'Bob Hope and Bing Crosby are in it and they are always value for money. We can rely on them to make us laugh.'

'You certainly can,' agreed Bert, starting to move on. 'Enjoy the film, madam.'

For all the headaches of this job in wartime, the shortages, the regulations, and the biggest problem of all, finding decent staff with so many people being directed into war work, he still wouldn't want to do anything else. The punters' excited anticipation when they arrived was palpable, and there was always plenty of chatter on their way out. For a few hours they escaped from the harshness of wartime living. Their enjoyment was Bert's too.

At the moment his two biggest assets were Daisy and Doreen, the best usherettes he'd ever had, and they were both deferred from war work because of dependents. With staff like that it wasn't all bad.

'How much longer are you gonna keep us waiting, mate?' asked a young woman further along the queue.

'We'll get you in as soon as we possibly can, I promise,' said Bert in his usual congenial manner.

He was smiling as he headed back inside. Apart from the fact that he enjoyed talking to the people in the queue, he liked to make sure that they didn't give up and go home. It was, after all, the punters who paid his wages. Once you stopped remembering that, you wouldn't last long in the job. People wanted an enjoyable night out and that included good service and friendliness from all the staff. The public paid their money and in his opinion they were entitled to it.

As the war continued and the age range for conscription expanded, most cinema organists were elderly men and women. If a serviceman home on leave offered to do a one-off show they were given a rapturous welcome. There was an air of excitement among the staff one day in the spring of 1943 when news spread that a soldier on leave would be playing the organ for the evening performance.

The interval lights went up and the music of the Mighty Wurlitzer preceded the organ which rose majestically from below to the tune of 'Begin the Beguine' to loud applause. People who had left their seats in search of some form of refreshment stood still to watch and listen. When the piece ended the soldier in uniform turned to speak to the audience and Daisy emitted a gasp of surprise. It was Al Dawson!

'Why didn't you warn me?' she said to Doreen, who was standing beside her.

'I didn't know it was going to be him,' she said. 'Mr Pickles just said a soldier would be playing the organ. We're the only two who know of Al because the rest of the staff weren't here during his time. Mr Pickles wasn't to know that you'd nearly pass out at the sight of him.'

'I didn't nearly pass out,' protested Daisy. 'I was unprepared, that's all.'

'Shush, we're trying to listen,' said someone. 'Have some respect for the soldier.'

Al's performance was up to his usual standard and Daisy realised she still had a strong physical attraction to him. He had lost none of his charisma and the audience thoroughly enjoyed his showbiz banter as well as the music. Daisy thought they would probably rather listen to him all evening than watch the rest of the film programme.

Towards the end of his set he said in that gorgeous deep voice with its Cockney flavour, 'Thank you for giving me such a warm welcome, ladies and gentlemen. It's lovely to be here with you all again. For those who don't know of me, I used to play here at the Adelphi regular before I went into the army so I feel like a friend.'

The applause practically shook the building.

'I'd like to finish with a number you all know and I hope you will feel free to join in. Goodnight and stay safe.'

'We'll Meet Again' filled the auditorium, the audience's singing enhancing the melodious tones of the organ. The music and the current mood of patriotism created a wealth of emotion. Daisy had tears in her eyes but hers were because of a personal sadness as well as the sentimental mood. How could she not have loved him as she had? He was a very loveable man. She thought of her son, *their son,* and was sad that Sam didn't know his father; but she would tell him who he was when the boy was old enough.

Nevertheless for all his charisma and likeability, Al had let her down and broken her heart. Beneath all that merriment and goodwill was a man with a callous streak.

At the end of her shift, Daisy couldn't wait to get out of the building, to be alone with her chaotic emotions. Doreen was chatting to other members of staff about their guest organist so Daisy told her she would walk on and Doreen could catch up when she was ready.

She headed along the corridor towards the staff

exit, so lost in her thoughts she almost collided with someone coming the other way.

'Oh,' she said, finding herself looking at Al's face and lost for words.

He didn't seem very talkative either. 'I'm on my way to the staffroom to say hello to those that I know,' he said at last.

'Most people who were here during your time have left,' she told him. 'Either for war work in the factories or the services. John moved up North for war work. There's only Doreen. But I'm sure she and the others would like to see you. It was a stunning performance.'

'Thanks.'

'I'll be on my way then,' she said coolly. 'It's getting late. 'Bye, Al.'

''Bye Daisy,' he said and watched her head off down the corridor.

He stood still, stifling the urge to go after her and trying to compose himself. Daisy was past history and dragging it up again would only cause pain. He wasn't in the mood to go to the staffroom now, especially as he wouldn't know anyone. But Doreen had been a good friend so he would go and say hello. He knew Daisy was married with a child so was surprised to see her here. As much as he hated to admit it, he'd only been going to the staffroom in the hope of hearing some news of her. Well, he'd seen her now and nothing had changed. Even so, he would show his face and say hello to Doreen.

After more than three years Daisy had thought she had successfully deposited her love affair with

Al into the past. She had come a long way since those heady days; she was a responsible mother now with her life on an even keel. The girl Al had known was long gone. But one brief meeting with him and she felt like a giddy teenager again, wild with desire. Her emotions were not in tune with her intellect because she knew how ridiculous it was with her mind. It was her body that had been out of control.

Thank goodness he had been at the Adelphi for only one night. Her reason told her she didn't want to see him again, *ever*, even as her heart told her she wanted to see him more than anything. She left the cinema and began to walk home. She doubted if Doreen would catch up with her. Along with the rest of the staff she would be busy praising Al for his performance. He was a much admired man. But people didn't know him like she did.

She hurried on her way, determined to put this evening's episode out of her mind.

It was one of those gloriously mellow autumn days in 1943 with misty sunshine and a hint of a chill in the air. Daisy was enjoying a Sunday off. She and Mary had taken Sam to the park that morning and played ball and other games with him and let him have a good run around. He was too young to remember the swings and other playground items that had been taken away for the war effort so he didn't miss them and was just as happy kicking a ball around or playing hide and seek.

Now they were at home, it was lunchtime and Bertha had managed to keep up with tradition by making a Sunday roast despite having only the tiniest piece of meat. They had roast potatoes and swede, plenty of greens and Yorkshire pudding made with dried eggs.

'It's lovely Mum,' said Daisy truthfully.

'Yeah, spot on,' added Mary 'I don't know how you manage to make such tasty meals with so few ingredients.'

'It's a wonder we're not all dead from starvation with this bloomin' rationing,' exaggerated Bertha, who wasn't comfortable with compliments so deflected them.

'You do a good job, love,' said Bill.

'Eat your greens Sam, that's a good boy,' she said.

'Don't like them,' said Sam, now nearly three years old, a bright lad with boundless energy.

There followed a battle of wits between Daisy and her son over the loathed cabbage which ended in a draw with Sam eating half of what he should. Daisy knew when to call it a day and left him to eat the rest of the meal.

'Why do children never like greens, I wonder,' said Mary.

'I suppose some might,' said Bertha. 'But I've never met one. They like sweet stuff.'

'Precious little of that around at the moment,' said Daisy. 'Sam is lucky because his Auntie Mary lets him have most of her sweet coupons.'

'Well, he's just a little kid,' said Mary. 'Children lose out more than any of us to the war. What with the swings being taken away and sweets on ration. They don't have many bananas or oranges like we had when we were children. And all those awful nights spent in the shelter, poor little things.'

'We haven't had a night in the shelter for ages,' Bill reminded her. 'We haven't had many raids at all this year, not like the Blitz anyway.'

'Someone said something about our defences being strengthened,' said Mary. 'So that's good news if the Germans get cheeky again.'

'Don't tempt fate, dear,' said Bertha.

The meal continued in this easy atmosphere and they finished off with baked rice pudding and stewed apple. There was a very strong sense of family that day and Daisy felt blessed to be a part of it. They were so lucky to be intact. Many Londoners had lost their homes and loved ones and here they were all together and in good health. Daisy didn't have a perfect life by any means. She had no love life or father for her son. But she had this band of people she knew she could always rely on. Yes, while Mum could be difficult at times she had many good points too. John had written to Daisy recently and all seemed well with him. She was glad he was all right living in the North.

'Daisy and I will do the washing-up, Mum,' said Mary. 'You can put your feet up.'

'Will you play with me, Gran?' asked Sam.

'Gran is going to have a rest now, Sam,' said Daisy. 'So you amuse yourself for a while.'

'Get your book and I'll read to you,' said Bertha. 'You can sit on my lap.'

'You spoil him rotten, Mum,' said Daisy in a tone of friendly criticism.

'That's what grandmothers are for, isn't it?' she said.

Daisy felt a surge of warmth towards her mother

which was so strong as to bring tears to her eyes. Mum liked things done her way and she could be infuriating at times but she was devoted to her own.

'Go on then, Sam,' said Daisy, starting to clear the table. 'Get that fairy tale book you like. It's upstairs in the bedroom.'

With boundless energy that only a child has, he rushed from the room and Daisy heard him scale the creaky stairs at speed. She found herself wishing that time would stand still or that she could somehow capture the atmosphere here today. It was just an ordinary family Sunday; nothing special. But it felt very precious.

A few days later Daisy was walking through Hammersmith Broadway on her way to work when she found herself face to face with Hester Dawson.

'Doing some shopping, are you?' said Daisy, shaken at seeing Al's mother.

The older woman nodded. 'Hammersmith has a few decent dress shops. I've got some clothing coupons so I'm going to splash out on something new.'

'Are you going somewhere nice then?'

'Nowhere special but I play the piano at various concerts that the amateurs put on and I like to look nice even though no one really looks at me. I've always loved clothes and something new to wear is a real treat these days, isn't it?'

'I'll say it is,' Daisy agreed. 'Anyway, are you keeping well?'

'Mustn't grumble,' Hester said. 'I miss my boys though.'

Feeling a reaction at the mention of her sons, Daisy hoped it didn't show. 'Are they both still abroad?'

'Yeah. They only get home leave occasionally – Al was home a few months ago – so it will probably be years before I see them again.'

'You hear from them though.'

'Oh yes but the postal service is very unreliable so their letters aren't all that frequent.'

Daisy wanted to know how Dickie was after his crisis but didn't know how to couch it without giving anything away.

'I'm sure they keep in touch when they can.'

'Of course they do because they know how I worry about them. Dickie seemed a bit down when he was home last time and I was a bit worried about him. But he was as right as rain when it was time to go back off leave. So that made me feel a lot better.'

'Good,' said Daisy, relieved that all had been well after he had left herself and Doreen that night.

'How about you and the family?' asked Hester. 'Are you all keeping well?'

'We are all fine, thank goodness,' she replied. 'Still alive and kicking.'

'I'm glad, dear,' Hester responded warmly. 'That's all we ask these days, isn't it, to stay alive.'

'It is and some aren't so lucky.'

Hester nodded. 'I heard that you have a baby,' she mentioned lightly.

Daisy smiled at the mention of Sam. 'Not such a baby now,' she said. 'He's nearly three.'

'Aah, how lovely,' said Hester. 'I bet he's a

smasher. If he's like you he will be anyway. I really enjoyed it when my boys were that age. You can look after them and keep them safe.' Her eyes filled with tears. 'When they grow up you can't do that. You have to let them go.'

It wasn't fitting to give her a hug but Daisy wanted to. 'Do you have any relatives living nearby?' she asked.

'No, not nearby. I have a sister but she lives in Hampshire. The boys have wanted me to go and stay with her since the first bomb dropped on London but I'd hate to live away from here. I have my next-door neighbour who I'm very fond of and I see plenty of people in my line of work and I make sure I keep busy. But it isn't quite the same as family.'

'No, I don't suppose it is,' said Daisy, remembering the Sunday recently when she had felt so blessed.

'Anyway, I suppose you stay at home now that you are a mum,' said Hester.

'No, I went back to the Adelphi. My husband and I split up so I'm a working girl again. I'm on my way to work now for the afternoon performance, as it happens.'

'I mustn't keep you then.'

'It's all right, I've plenty of time,' Daisy assured her. 'I've always been an early bird as far as work is concerned though it isn't so easy now that I have Sam. My mother looks after him while I'm at work but I never want to leave him. Even more so now that's he's such a lot of fun. He keeps us entertained, as you can imagine.'

Hester smiled. Although Daisy knew that she

was a strong woman, at that moment she looked so vulnerable Daisy felt a surge of empathy because Hester was obviously feeling the absence of her sons and not having any close family around must make it worse. She longed to tell her that she did have family nearby. She had a beautiful grandson just a few miles away. But how could she do that without breaking Hester's heart by telling her that her son had refused to acknowledge him?

'I'd love to see him,' said Hester.

'Maybe I could bring him to visit you sometime,' suggested Daisy on the spur of the moment. 'Though I'm at work most of the time except for the mornings.'

'I'm usually around in the mornings too,' said Hester. 'Teaching is late afternoon into the evening, though I don't have so many pupils now because some of the kids have been evacuated. So if you fancy a cuppa and a chat any time, do pop in. You'd be more than welcome.'

'Thanks,' said Daisy, 'I'll do that. I'm not sure when but I'll take a chance on you being in.'

'Lovely,' said Hester, looking happy in anticipation. 'But you'd better get off to work now, hadn't you, dear?'

'Yeah, I'll see you soon though. 'Bye for now.'

'Cheerio.'

Mulling the interlude over as she headed for the Adelphi, Daisy felt as though the unexpected meeting had pleased Hester as much as it had pleased herself. It wasn't usually done to stay friends with an ex-boyfriend's mother but these weren't normal times and Al wasn't around. She could feel a mutual affection flowing between herself and Hester and if she and Sam could help to fill a lonely corner for her while her family was away so much the better. Yes, maybe she would feel awkward knowing that Sam was actually Hester's grandson but the older woman wouldn't suffer by it.

She was smiling as she went into work.

The busiest time for the usherettes was usually the beginning of the evening programme. Although people often came in mid-film and stayed to see the entire showing around, the majority preferred to see the whole thing from the beginning. Daisy and her colleagues were up and down the aisles with their torches almost nonstop.

Towards the end of the rush that evening, Daisy was standing by the closed auditorium doors waiting for those still at the pay desk to come and be shown to their seats when she saw a familiar face heading towards her, a middle-aged man with a young woman on his arm.

'Good evening sir,' she said as he handed her two tickets.

'Evening,' he grunted, showing no sign of recognition.

'How are you?' she asked and without waiting for an answer added pleasantly, 'and your wife and children? Are they keeping well in these hard times?'

'Wife and children,' said the young woman, staring at Reggie Rumbold. 'You didn't tell me you were married.'

For once Rumbold was lost for words. 'I'm not, well I am but well er...'

'Ugh, you dirty old bugger,' said his companion, slapping his face and turning on her heel.

'You'll regret this,' Rumbold warned Daisy. 'I shall report you to the manager.'

'For asking after the health of your family?' she said. 'I don't think my manager would find anything offensive in that. Courtesy is part of the job; the management insists on it.'

The older man looked at her with venom in his eyes then turned and hurried after his young companion.

'Who's next please?' said Daisy, smiling, as she took the ticket from a young airman with a girl of about his own age beside him. 'Enjoy the show.'

She would never forget the mental anguish Reggie Rumbold had caused her and that small slice of revenge had felt sweet. Maybe it had saved another young woman from suffering too.

'Good for you,' approved Mary when Daisy got home, found her sister still up and told her about what had happened with Rumbold. 'That dirty dog needs locking up.'

'You should have seen his face when his girl-friend walked off,' said Daisy.

'If looks could kill eh?'

'Exactly.' She paused. 'I won't say anything to Mum and Dad about it. Mum won't see the funny side and it will drag it all up again.'

'I won't say a word.'

Daisy told her about her meeting with Hester Dawson and how she planned to take Sam to see her.

'Ooh Daisy, are you sure that's a good idea?'

213

asked Mary, frowning.

'I don't see that it can do any harm.'

'She's your ex-boyfriend's mother and the grandmother of your son, for heaven's sake,' her sister reminded her.

'She's also very lonely,' said Daisy.

'Now maybe,' said Mary. 'But what about when her sons come home after the war?'

'She won't need me then so I'll stay away.'

'You can't just turn friendship on and off like that, it wouldn't be fair,' Mary opined. 'But it will be awkward when Al comes back if he gets a new woman in his life. She won't want an ex-girlfriend hanging around so you'd have to stay away then.'

'You aren't half making a big thing of it,' said Daisy, peeved. 'All I want to do is pay a visit to a lonely woman. I'll probably only go the once. How would you feel if you were living on your own and all your family had gone away?'

'I might enjoy the peace and quiet.'

'For ten minutes maybe.'

'All right, Daisy, there's no need to get narked,' admonished Mary. 'Anyway, I thought Al's mum was a lively spark, giving piano lessons and out and about playing for various functions.'

'She is and she does,' said Daisy. 'But I think she could still do with a friend. In these hard times, it's up to us all to look out for each other and that's what I intend to do. I can't leave someone lonely because of possible complications years down the line. That's a terrible way of looking at life.'

'I presume you won't tell her who Sam's real father is.'

'Of course not. I can't do that without doing her son down.'

'No you can't,' said Mary firmly. 'Frankly I think you should stay well clear but it isn't my business.'

'You're right about the last part anyway.'

'I think maybe you want to be friends with Al's mother because it makes you feel close to him.'

It hit Daisy like a boxer's glove. Was that the reason? She had always enjoyed the atmosphere at the Dawsons' when she and Al had been together. Maybe she was trying to recapture some of that.

'I'm right, aren't I?' asked Mary.

'I don't know.'

'You've never really got over him, have you?' Mary asked in a kinder tone.

'No. I don't suppose I ever will entirely,' Daisy admitted. 'He was my first love and they say you never forget that. But if I am trying to get to him through his mother I was not aware of that possibility until this very moment.'

'Could be that you're not aware of it but that whole Al era before the war was pretty special to you, wasn't it?'

'Very special but it's in the past and I'm not trying to recapture it as far as I know. Honestly Mary, I really like Hester Dawson and I felt so sorry for her when we met, probably because us lot are all here together, the family intact, and she's on her own. As far as I know that's all there is to it. How can I turn my back on someone who might need a bit of company because I just might be doing it for the wrong reasons? Who knows what will happen to any one of us tomorrow or next year while this war is on? Obviously I won't go anywhere near the Dawsons when Al comes back.'

'I was worried about you getting hurt again, that's all,' said Mary. 'But you must go with your heart on this one. As you say, we should all do what we can for each other.'

'Exactly. I'm glad you can see it that way now,' said Daisy. 'Mum will probably disapprove like mad because past complications make the Dawsons strictly off limits but I don't want to lie to her. She always wants to know where I'm going when I go out so I shall tell her.'

'One of the drawbacks of family life, I'm afraid,' said Mary.

'You're telling me. I don't know how you managed to keep your thing with Ray from Mum and Dad for so long.'

'It took more than a few fibs, I must admit.'

'Anyone else taken your fancy since?' asked Daisy.

'There's a bloke at work who seems to fancy me but I can't summon up any enthusiasm. I think I must be a one-man woman and Ray was that man.'

'Don't say that,' said Daisy. 'Someone will come along eventually.'

'We'll see,' said Mary.

If Daisy had needed evidence that she was doing the right thing in visiting Hester Dawson, she had it in abundance when the older woman answered the door to her, exuding warmth.

'Daisy, how lovely to see you,' she beamed, her

gaze moving downwards. 'And this is your little boy.'

'Yeah, this is Sam.'

'What a sweetie. Hello darlin',' she greeted him with a smile.

''Ello. I've got a scooter at home,' said Sam, who was clutching a well-worn teddy bear. 'It used to be my mummy's when she was little.'

'The same as his teddy,' said Daisy. 'There isn't much in the shops in the way of toys at the moment. So new things aren't as frequent as they used to be.'

'There isn't much of anything around,' said Hester, ushering them inside.

She put the kettle on and gave Sam a glass of milk and a biscuit despite Daisy telling her they didn't need refreshments and she wasn't to use her rations on them.

'Oh my word, isn't Sam like his mum,' said Hester, observing the blue-eyed, blond boy.

'So everyone tells me,' said Daisy, thinking how lucky it was that Sam was like her side of the family. The cat would really have been out of the bag if he'd taken after his dad.

The two women chatted like old friends. Daisy talked about her job and the family, Hester told Daisy about her musical commitments.

'My pupil list has gone down since the war because of evacuation though some of them came back when the bombing stopped,' she said. 'I think the parents try to make things as normal as possible so they send the kids back to lessons when they come home.'

'That's a good thing.'

'For them and for my purse as well as my pleasure. I get a widow's pension and I do all right thanks to my musical work. I would hate not to do it anyway. I do quite a bit of actual playing aside from teaching, for dance classes and choirs and accompanying singers at concerts. So one way and another I manage well enough. I'd go and work on the buses as a clippie if I couldn't manage but I like to stay in my own profession if I can as I'm trained. Music is very therapeutic and I think it's good for morale in these hard times.'

'I agree.'

While the two women were happy to sit and talk, Sam, like most children, wanted to be on the go and wandered off.

'What's that white thing in the other room?' he asked on his return.

'What white thing?'

He pulled at Hester's hand and she allowed herself to be led into the other room with Daisy following.

'Oh, you mean the piano,' said Hester as the boy pointed to the keyboard.

'We don't have one at home so it's something new for him,' said Daisy. 'I know a lot of people have a family piano but Mum and Dad never have. None of us is gifted musically.'

'Shall I show you how it works, Sam?' asked Hester.

The boy nodded enthusiastically.

Hester sat on the stool and played 'Twinkle Twinkle Little Star' and Sam was entranced.

'Again,' he urged.

She played it again and both she and Daisy sang

the words, much to the child's delight. Hester got up and opened the lid of the stool and rummaged through the music in there, taking out a slim music book.

'Here are some tunes that my beginners start off with,' she said and began to play some nursery rhymes while Daisy sang along, encouraging her son to do the same.

'He'll do this sort of thing when he starts school, so this is a taster for him,' said Daisy.

Sam wanted to have a go himself so Hester got another stool she used for pupils and lifted him up to sit beside her. There followed an awful din as he banged the keys and was admonished by his mother.

'I know a song you might like,' said Hester. 'And I know this one off by heart so I don't need the music.'

While Daisy and Sam listened, Hester launched into a popular song that was on everyone's lips at that moment; it was called 'A Paper Doll'. Hester had a good singing voice and gave a lovely rendition with Daisy joining in at the end, less tunefully, and Sam beaming.

'Again,' he cried.

After a few repeats, Sam still wanted more but it was time Daisy made a move because she had to go to work after lunch. Sam didn't want to leave and she practically had to drag him out. But she left with warmth in her heart, having seen the pleasure Hester had derived from the brief interlude. She told her they would come again quite soon and she meant it.

'What's that you're singing, Sam?' asked Bertha when they got home.

'Dole,' he replied. 'La la la dole...'

Bertha looked blank.

'He means "Paper Doll",' explained Daisy. 'Hester played it on the piano and we all sang it about a dozen times. He couldn't get enough of it.'

'I notice he has about the same amount of musical talent as the rest of us,' said Bertha who, to Daisy's amazement, hadn't objected when she'd been told about the proposed visit to Hester's. 'Which is sweet bugger all, bless him. I didn't recognise one note of that rendition which is why I had to ask.'

Daisy laughed. 'He's only three, Mum,' she said. 'He's got plenty of time to improve.'

'Mm. There is that,' she said. 'But don't bank on an improvement as none of us is blessed in that way.'

'I expect he'll have other gifts,' said Daisy. 'He certainly loved the piano.'

'Did he?'

'I'll say. Hester played all the nursery rhymes for him and we had a good old sing-song. She's a cracking pianist.'

'Did she let him have a go?'

'Yeah, she did and you've never heard such a din.'

'I can imagine,' said Bertha, smiling.

'The visit was lovely, Mum,' enthused Daisy. 'And I could tell that Hester enjoyed it. It was good for Sam too to meet someone new and have a musical interlude. He'll be having that sort of thing when he starts school so this is a little taster for him.'

'So will you go to see her again?'

'Definitely. I'll try and go to see her at least once a fortnight.'

'Hmm. I can't say that I totally approve because of the possible complications later on but I can't really see any harm in it for the moment,' said Bertha.

Daisy didn't say a word but she was absolutely astonished.

Chapter Eleven

As the nights drew in and the mornings became chilly, there was a great deal of talk about the Second Front which it was hoped would be the beginning of the end of this long-drawn-out war. High expectations still hadn't converted into action but an air of hopeful anticipation prevailed. People hummed popular tunes and went to see the latest George Formby film but the Allied invasion was on the mind of most.

'I sometimes wonder if this bloomin' Second Front isn't just a rumour put out by the government to cheer us up,' said Bertha one day in December over Sunday lunch. 'Maybe there are no such plans in place at all.'

Daisy and Mary giggled.

'It isn't funny,' objected Bertha.

'We think it is, Mum,' said Daisy. 'Of course there is an Allied Invasion being planned; the government wouldn't make something like that up.'

'We have no way of knowing if we are being told the truth,' she insisted.

'We just have to trust those who are in charge to do the right thing,' said Bill.

'Might they not lie to us to keep morale up,' his wife suggested.

'I shouldn't think so. I expect they are selective about what the public is told. But they wouldn't make up something like the Second Front. There would be riots all over the country when it didn't happen.'

'I suppose so,' Bertha finally agreed. 'But I wish they'd get a move on and do something.'

'They will be doing all sorts of things,' said Bill. 'A thing like an invasion will take a huge amount of organisation so I expect preparations are underway that we know nothing about.'

'Even so, they need to be seen to be doing something,' said Bertha. 'We are all sick and tired of the wretched war now. People want their normal lives back.'

'At least we're not having air raids now,' Daisy reminded them.

'There is that,' added Mary.

A strange and rather awful noise rose above the gloomy conversation. It was Sam singing 'Paper Doll'.

'No singing at the table please, Sam,' admonished Daisy briskly, trying not to laugh.

'Why?'

'Because it isn't good manners.'

He stared at her in that unwavering way children

have and then said, 'Can I sing after dinner?'

'Yes, my darling, you can sing for the rest of the day once you've cleared your plate and left the table.'

'Ooh, Gawd help us,' said Bertha, grinning. 'I've heard cats with more melody.'

They all laughed, including Sam who had no idea what it was all about.

'Don't be mean about my godson, Mum,' said Mary.

'I'm not,' said Bertha. 'I love him to bits, you know that. But the whole lot of us are completely tone deaf. He's just following family tradition. He's truly one of us.'

The meal progressed in similar cheerful vein and Daisy's mind turned to Hester, who would probably be eating her Sunday dinner alone. Her mood dimmed considerably and she hoped with all her heart that Hester's sons were returned to her intact when this awful war was over. She made a mental note to leave for work a bit early and call in to see her briefly on the way.

Predictably, Hester was delighted to see Daisy but she had an unexpected request for Daisy.

'I've had a letter from Dickie and he wants me to find out the address of a girl called Doreen who works at the Adelphi,' she said. 'I've no idea how he knows of her but he wants to write and doesn't know her address. I suppose he must have seen her when he went to the pictures sometime and taken a fancy to her. He knows her name anyway. I wondered if you could help me out.'

'I can as it happens because Doreen is a friend of mine,' said Daisy. 'I'll check with her and if she's happy about it I'll give you the address the next time I call.'

'Thank you dear,' Hester said. 'Sam's not with you today then.'

'I'm on my way to work. So he's at home with the others.'

'It's very good of you take the time to call when you are so busy.'

'I wanted to see you,' said Daisy because the idea of anyone feeling sorry for her would be anathema to Hester. 'Anyway you're busy too. Most people are these days. But we are all entitled to take time to see our friends whenever we can.'

'Indeed.' She nodded. 'Have you time for a cuppa?'

'No, I won't thanks,' said Daisy. 'Duty calls and all that.'

She stayed long enough for a short chat then headed for the Adelphi, glad that she had made the effort to see Hester.

'You've got an admirer,' Daisy said to Doreen when they were in the staffroom about to go on duty.

'Really?' said Doreen with an inquiring grin.

'Dickie Dawson wants your address,' she explained. 'He wants to write to you, according to his mum.'

Daisy expected surprise, puzzlement, even annoyance. So she was astonished by the look of sheer pleasure that suffused her friend's face.

'Oh,' Doreen said, clearly delighted. 'He probably just wants to apologise for what happened that night.'

'He isn't going to be writing to me as far as I know,' Daisy pointed out. 'So I think he might have taken a fancy to you.'

'We'll see what he has to say.' Doreen didn't seem displeased by Daisy's suggestion.

'So I can pass on your address then.'

'By all means.'

Despite the shortage of practically everything, Christmas was a delight for the Blake family because Sam was old enough to enjoy the celebrations. By dint of a huge amount of queuing and ingenuity, the family managed to fill his stocking and have a good few parcels for him to open on Christmas morning. The well-worn decorations were taken out of the attic for the umpteenth year and the house festooned with paper chains.

'Maybe this will be the last wartime Christmas,' said Bertha as they all sat around eating their collective sweet rations on Christmas afternoon while Sam played on the floor with his new toy train that needed winding up every few minutes.

'We say that every year,' said Mary.

'It has to end sometime.' This was Bertha.

'Exactly,' agreed Daisy. 'And they have got this invasion thing planned.'

'Let's hope they get cracking with it in the New Year,' said Bill and looking towards Sam, added, 'Meanwhile let's count our blessings and enjoy the celebrations.'

'Well said, love,' said Bertha to a chorus of agreement from her daughters.

One evening in January the people of London were startled by a noise they hadn't heard for nearly three years: the air-raid siren.

'I don't believe it,' said Bertha, flustered. 'I've forgotten what we have to do.'

'Just get your coat on and go down the shelter with the nipper,' said Bill. 'I'll fetch some blankets.'

'I hope the girls are all right,' said Bertha. 'Mary will be on her way home from work and it's dangerous out there. Daisy should be all right in the cinema. At least she isn't out on the street.'

'Never mind chattering; get yourself down the shelter with the boy pronto,' he said.

She was already getting Sam into his coat over his pyjamas. 'We're going on an adventure,' she told him.

'Can I stay up late?'

'You're not going to have much choice, mate,' she told him.

The Adelphi staff were busy getting into air-raid mode again after the long break. The film had been stopped while Mr Pickles gave his standard speech about people who wanted to leave doing so quietly and the rest being welcome to stay while the film was shown as normal.

'I'd almost forgotten what to say after such a long break without raids,' he confessed to Daisy as he passed her on the way back to his office.

'It'll probably be just a one-off so you won't have to learn it all again,' she said. 'Otherwise you can always revert to putting a message on the screen like we did in the Blitz when the raids were so frequent.'

'Let's hope it doesn't come to that,' he said.

'I'll say.'

Although Daisy was behaving normally, she was actually petrified for her son at home and experiencing frightening mental images of a bomb hitting the air-raid shelter with the family in it. Her instinct was to abandon her duties and run all the way back to the house to keep Sam safe. But she had a job to do so she had to trust the family to do that for her.

She reasoned with herself that if they'd survived the Blitz they could get through this. As she'd said to the boss, it was probably just an isolated incident, she thought, as she headed into the auditorium with her torch to show a couple to their seats to see James Mason in *Fanny by Gaslight*. Her legs felt very shaky, though, and every explosion that echoed through the building she imagined to be a bomb landing on the Anderson shelter at home. She also thought about Hester and hoped she was safely sheltering with the company of her neighbour Ada.

Hester was actually quite a distance from home, playing the piano at an amateur production of *The Pirates of Penzance* to raise money for war orphans.

Her instinct on hearing the siren was to abandon the show and rush to the nearest shelter. She was worried about Ada too. Her friend would be nervous without the company of her neighbour during a raid. Hopefully she would call at one of the other houses; they all knew each other round there.

Expecting the show to be abandoned, she waited to take her lead from the players. But they carried on. A few people in the audience left but the performance continued and Hester stayed where she was at the piano and played her heart out as though nothing much was happening outside. It was frightening but exhilarating too. Almost an act of rebellion. As though to say, 'You can bomb us but you won't break our spirit.' She had never been so frightened but proud in her life.

Although that first air raid didn't prove to be a one-off and they had regular night attacks again, the bombing was nowhere near as severe as the Blitz had been. People complained but they soon got back into the sheltering habit.

Since the resumption of the air raids, Daisy was always on edge in the evenings at work because of Sam. She was either dreading the sound of the siren or imagining the worst at home after it had sounded. However, one evening after the siren went, she found herself with real problems close by when the Adelphi took a hit and part of the ceiling collapsed towards the front of the auditorium.

Absolute pandemonium ensued. People were screaming and calling for help. The house lights went on to reveal clouds of dust. At first Daisy was rooted to the spot with fear but when she heard Doreen say, 'Are you all right?' she snapped out of it.

'Yeah. Are you?'

'I think so.'

'Good, we'd better see what we can do to help,' said Daisy. 'That first-aid course might come in handy now.'

'That's true,' agreed Doreen.

Mr Pickles climbed through the rubble on to the stage and appealed for calm.

'The first-aid people are on their way, folks,' he said to the audience. 'Meanwhile my staff will do everything they can to help you and get you out of the building safely. Thank you everyone and God bless.'

Daisy and Doreen headed through the dust clouds towards the front of the auditorium, dreading what faced them. But as they reached the sixth row back, some debris began to crumble from the damaged ceiling almost directly above them.

'Phew, that was close,' Bertha said to Mary, who was with her in the candlelit air-raid shelter. Bill was out on ARP duty and Sam was asleep on the bunk under a blanket. He stirred when the explosion went off but was sleeping again now.

'I'll say it was,' agreed Mary with the usual mixture of gratitude to still be alive mixed with fear of the next bomb. 'I hope Dad's all right. It sounded very close.'

'They can be deceiving,' said Bertha, more from hope than conviction. 'Sometimes they sound as though they're on your doorstep but they're actually a few miles away.'

'Perhaps the All Clear will go soon.'

'Don't hold your breath.'

'Any tea left, Mum?' asked Mary.

'No love, sorry.'

They sat there in silence, each lost in their own thoughts, until they heard the thud of footsteps coming their way.

'That'll be Bill to see if we're all right,' said Bertha.

''Ello down there,' said a voice that wasn't Bill's.

'Yeah, who is it?'

'I'm a mate of Bill's from the ARP. He's on duty somewhere. I saw him earlier but can't find him now so I thought I'd better come and tell you that the Adelphi had copped it. I thought you ought to know. Bill mentioned that your daughter works there.'

'Oh no, oh my good Gawd,' said Bertha, clutching her head with her hands. 'I must go and see if she's all right.'

'I should wait for the All Clear. Just in case there's more on the way,' advised the man. 'But I have to get off now; plenty to do out here tonight. Hope your daughter is all right. Mind how you go. G'night.'

'Ta-ta.'

'You'll be all right here with Sam, won't you Mary, while I go down to the Adelphi to find out if Daisy is all right,' said Bertha.

'Course I'll be all right but I don't think you should leave the shelter until after the All Clear,' said Mary. 'It's dangerous out there, Mum. Surely you must realise that.'

'Dangerous or not I have to go,' she insisted. 'She's my daughter so I must be there for her. You won't understand until you have kids of your own but you will then. You and Sam will be as safe as you can be here.'

'It isn't us I'm thinking about, Mum, it's you but I suppose you'll do what you want regardless, as you always do.' Mary spoke in an admonitory tone.

'It's all quiet now,' said Bertha, her voice shaking, Mary's criticism lost on her in her concern for Daisy. 'I think the bombers have finished for tonight. Anyway I have to go. I can't just sit here while Daisy might be hurt.'

'You do what you feel you must,' said Mary coolly. 'You will anyway, whatever I say.'

'I won't be gone long,' said Bertha. 'As soon as I know that she's safe I'll be back. If Sam wakes up, give him a cuddle and he'll go back to sleep again.'

'Be careful, Mum.'

'Will do,' said Bertha and climbed through the door at the back of the shelter.

'Are you all right down there?' called Bill.

'Yeah, Sam and I are fine, Dad, but Mum isn't here,' Mary shouted up to him.

'Not there,' he said, sounding shocked. 'Where the hell has she gone with all these bombs around?'

'She's gone to get news of Daisy. We heard that the Adelphi has been hit.'

'That's right. I just came back to tell you that I'm going down there to find out about Daisy but she's beaten me to it.'

'You know Mum, she isn't slow when it comes to her family.'

'Are you sure you're all right?'

'We're fine.'

'I'll go after her then,' he said.

'All right, Dad. Take care. Ta-ta.'

'See you later.'

As his footsteps receded across the garden, Mary shivered. It was frightening being in an air-raid shelter during a raid without another adult. Sam woke up and called for his mother.

'Mummy will be back soon,' she said, stroking his forehead and holding his hand. 'You'll be fine with your Auntie Mary.'

Soothed by her comforting presence he went back to sleep. She felt isolated and alone. Despite her outward confidence she was very frightened but hoped she had it in her to be strong for Sam. Oh, when was that damned All Clear going to come? The distant roar of another bomber gave her the answer. It certainly wasn't going to be for a while yet.

'Oh well, Sam,' she said almost to herself. 'It's just you and me and the Luftwaffe. God help us!'

Bertha was out of breath from running towards the Broadway so she had to slow down, especially as she had the stitch as well. The back streets were empty; people were buried away in their Andersons but the sky was red and fire engine bells rang out over the town. The only thing on Bertha's mind was Daisy and she was praying that she was safe.

Her thoughts turned to Mary and Sam when she heard the distant drone of a bomber draw nearer. Oh dear, perhaps she should have stayed with them but they were in the shelter so unless that took a direct hit they should be safe. Then there was Bill. He was out somewhere. But Daisy would have been inside the cinema on duty when the bomb dropped and more at risk. So she had to focus her mind on getting to the Adelphi.

The plane sounded as if it was overhead now; Bertha had gone beyond fear into a kind of dull acceptance. What happened was out of her control so she had to carry on, drive herself forward. The last thing she heard before the crash was the whistle of the bomb falling. Then she was lifted off her feet and thrown into the air. The thud as she landed jolted through her body and the pain in her head was all-consuming.

Bill lay flat on his stomach when the bomber was overhead and scrambled to his feet after the explosion and carried on towards the Adelphi. There was no sign of wreckage in this street so the bomb must have dropped somewhere else. The buggers were deceiving and often sounded nearer than they actually were.

He carried on, increasing his speed with a sense of urgency and when he was almost at the Broadway, he turned a corner and saw the ghastly signs of an incident in the moonlight, a small crowd and an ambulance. He could hear someone moaning nearby and someone else shouted, 'We'll get to you as soon as we can, luv,' and looking down he saw a person lying on the ground.

Dropping to his knees he could see it was a woman and shining his torch he saw to his horror that it was Bertha, a trickle of blood running from her head.

'It's all right, love,' he said emotionally, holding her hand. 'It's me, Bill. Can you hear me?'

'Bill,' she said. 'Help me, please help me.'

'Of course I'll help you, but I'd better not move you in case I make things worse. The ambulance is here and someone will come to see to you in a minute. I'm sure they won't be long. There must have been a good few casualties I think.'

'Daisy,' she said, sounding distressed.

'Stop worrying. I'm sure she'll be fine but I'm on my way to find out,' he said, stroking her hand. 'You just concentrate on yourself and try to keep calm.'

'Tell Daisy,' she began but her voice died out.

'You can tell her yourself once they've given you something to make you feel better,' he said. 'So stop worrying.'

'Daisy ... the cinema's been hit.'

'I know but I'm sure she'll be fine,' he said with more confidence than he actually felt. He was panic-stricken about his wife and trying to sound calm. He daren't even think about what might have happened to Daisy.

'Eve,' she mumbled, her voice barely audible.

'Eve?' he asked in a questioning manner. 'I don't think we know anyone of that name, love.'

'No, Eve...' she said again, her voice not much more than a whisper and broken with pain. 'Tell Daisy ... tell her ... eve ... tell her I'm sorry. I'm very sorry.'

'No need to be sorry but I'll tell her love, don't you worry,' he assured her.

A booming male voice said, 'All right sir, we'll take over now. If you could stand back please.'

234

Bill did as he was asked and the man got on his knees to Bertha as stretcher bearers moved in.

Daisy was exhausted when she finally got out of the cinema, having looked after a lot of terrified people and tried to calm them. Fortunately she and Doreen had managed to dodge the debris when the ceiling above them had collapsed and it was just as well because they'd been needed to help bring order to the chaos. The two of them had been the last staff members to leave and had waited until every customer had gone either on foot or in the ambulances. By some miracle there were no fatalities but there had been some serious injuries. The All Clear had gone a while ago and the skies were blissfully silent as she left Doreen at her street corner and headed home.

Because it was so late when she got home she was surprised to find that her father and sister were still up.

'Thank God you're here,' said her father shakily and sounding on the verge of tears. 'I came to the cinema but they wouldn't let me in and no one around there knew anything. I couldn't find out if you were all right.'

'We heard it had taken a hit,' added Mary. 'So we've been worried.'

'Is Sam all right?' asked Daisy.

'He's fine,' said Mary. 'He's fast asleep.'

Daisy looked from one to the other. 'So why are you both looking so peculiar? Something's happened.' Her voice rose. 'What's the matter?'

'It's Mum,' said Mary.

'What about her,' asked Daisy. 'Where is she?

In bed?'

Mary stood up. 'I'm sorry Daisy, sorry to have to tell you, but she's dead.'

'What,' she said, puzzled. 'How can she be?'

'She was caught in the blast from an explosion and injured her head,' said her father. 'She died on the stretcher on the way to the ambulance.'

Pale and shaken, Daisy's brain refused to process this so she said, 'What explosion?'

'The Adelphi wasn't the only place to get bombed tonight, you know,' said Mary, flaring up suddenly. 'We've had bombs around here too. Mum went to the Adelphi to find out if you were all right and she was killed because of it.'

Daisy sank into a chair as her legs threatened to give way. 'Oh no,' she said, her voice breaking. 'Oh please tell me this isn't happening.'

'Of course it's happening, you silly cow,' said Mary fiercely. 'And it's all your fault. Mum is dead because of you.'

'Mary,' admonished Bill. 'Now that's enough. Of course it isn't Daisy's fault.'

Heartbroken by this attack from her sister when she was still in shock from the news of her mother, Daisy said, 'Do you really think it's my fault?'

'Yes I do,' she snapped, tears streaming down her face. 'It's always been you as far as Mum was concerned. Daisy this, Daisy that. Now she's dead because a bloody bomb dropped on your workplace and she couldn't keep away. She wouldn't have gone out in an air raid to find out about me if she'd heard the factory where I work had been hit. Oh no. Just you. So I hope you're proud of yourself.'

'Stoppit now, Mary,' said Bill, who was in deep personal despair and could do without his daughters falling out. 'Leave your sister alone.'

'That's right, you take her side too,' said Mary and ran from the room, sobbing.

Realising that her father was in need of consolation, Daisy went to him. 'I'm so sorry, Dad,' she said, putting her arms around him. 'You must be feeling terrible. You and Mum were so close.'

'Yeah,' he said, his voice breaking. 'I haven't taken it in properly yet.'

'I'm sure you haven't.'

'I don't know what I'm going to do without her, Daisy.'

'Nor me,' she said. 'We'll get through it somehow, together. If it's my fault I'm sorry.'

'Of course it isn't your fault,' he said. 'Take no notice of your sister. It's just her grief talking.'

'Yes, I expect so,' agreed Daisy because she didn't want to cause her father any more pain than he had already. But surely those thoughts must have been in Mary's mind for them to have been uttered. Daisy found that notion devastating. It was as though she'd lost her mother and her sister in one blow. But she needed to concentrate on her father for the moment. The poor man would be like a lost soul without Mum. 'How about you sit down and I make you a hot drink, Dad. Even better still, have we got any booze left from Christmas, do you know? I think something stronger is what you need tonight.'

'There might be a bottle in the sideboard,' he said.

'You sit down and I'll see what I can find.' She felt as though she had reversed roles with her parent.

When Daisy went up to bed later, she heard her sister crying in her bedroom. Normally she would have gone straight in but because of Mary's malicious attack earlier she hesitated, wondering if Mary would want her to. Like all siblings they'd had their disagreements over the years but never anything as serious as this. Up until now they had always supported each other in times of trouble. With her sister's cutting words still fresh in Daisy's mind, she decided to leave her alone but her heart was heavy. Never had she needed her sister more than she did at this moment. Sighing heavily, she went into her own bedroom.

Bill was upset about Mary's attack on her sister too. He'd never seen that side of his eldest daughter before. At this time they needed family solidarity, not a divide. But his brain was so dulled by grief, he couldn't really think much beyond how he was going to manage without Bertha. She had been the dominant one of the two, which had suited him. She ran things and he did as she told him. It had worked.

Now he was on his own. He had the girls, of course, but they had their own lives and would fly the nest at some point in the not too distant future. At this moment he couldn't think beyond tomorrow and waking up without Bertha beside him. He had lost his soul mate and had never felt more vulnerable and alone.

Daisy was getting into her pyjamas when Mary came in and closed the door quietly behind her.

'Sorry Daisy,' she said thickly.

'I had no idea you felt like that about things,' said Daisy.

'I don't,' she said. 'Honestly Daisy, I don't know what came over me.'

'The thoughts must have been there or you wouldn't have said them.'

'I don't know what to say except that I could hear myself saying those things but I didn't mean any of them.'

'Sounded to me as though you blame me for Mum's death,' said Daisy.

'Of course I don't. That must have been grief talking. I could just as easily blame myself for not stopping her from going out in the air raid.'

'No one could stop Mum from doing what she wanted,' said Daisy.

'Exactly.'

'Do you really sometimes think she favoured me?'

'I expect there are probably moments when all sisters think that about each other; times when we hate each other fleetingly,' said Mary. 'You've had more dramas than I have so you've been centre stage more: the sacking, the pregnancy and the marriage break-up. I've only had the one trauma and she didn't know anything about that, thank God.'

'I'm so glad you don't really hate me,' said Daisy.

'As if I ever would, not for long anyway.'

'Well, Mum has gone now and somehow we

239

have to carry on without her.'

'God knows how,' said Mary. 'She was at the centre of this family. She might have driven us mad with her bossy ways and slavish respectability but we all thought the world of her and it's hard to imagine life without her.'

'Dad will have to be our priority,' said Daisy. 'It's going to be awful for him. She ruled his life. He'll be like a lost soul without her telling him what to do.'

'Oh Daisy,' said Mary, throwing her arms around her sister. 'I'm sorry I said those awful things.'

'I'll forgive you,' said Daisy. 'We need each other too much to fall out.'

'We certainly do,' agreed Mary.

The following afternoon, there was a knock at the front door, one of many the Blakes had had that day as the news spread and friends and neighbours called to offer their condolences, especially as it was Sunday and a lot of people weren't working. Bill happened to be nearest so he opened the door and found himself looking at a stranger, a woman with bushy blond hair topped with a red knitted hat.

'Hello,' said Hester. 'I'm sorry to bother you but I'm a friend of Daisy's.'

'Are you?' he said dully.

'I heard that the Adelphi was bombed last night and I wondered if she was all right,' she explained. 'I've been there but the cinema is closed because of bomb damage so I couldn't get any information there.'

Bill, who was pale and deeply depressed, said, 'Yeah I suppose it wouldn't be open today.'

'And Daisy?' she said.

'Daisy is all right.'

'Oh thank God,' she said smiling with relief. 'You're her dad, are you?'

He nodded.

'I'm from Shepherd's Bush. I knew Daisy lived in this road but I wasn't sure of the number so I asked a neighbour,' she rattled on, unaware of the tragedy in progress inside the house and finding his offhand attitude rather rude.

'Hester,' said Daisy, hearing her voice and coming to investigate.

'She's come to see if you're all right,' explained her father miserably.

Realising that Hester wouldn't have heard about their bereavement because she was from a different neighbourhood, Daisy took her aside and told her what had happened while her father went back inside.

'Oh my Lord,' said Hester, putting her hands to her head, her cheeks burning. 'Oh you poor things, and there was me chattering on. Oh Daisy, please apologise to your father for the intrusion and offer him my sincere condolences.'

'Come in and tell him yourself,' said Daisy.

'I wouldn't dream of intruding.'

'You wouldn't be. We've had people calling all day. You took the trouble to come and find out if I was all right, the least we can do is offer you a cup of tea.'

'No dear, ta,' Hester insisted. 'I know you are safe and that's what I came for so I'll be on my

241

way. But if there is anything at all I can do please come and see me. Anything at all.'

Already emotional from the bereavement, Daisy welled up at her kindness and put her arms around her. 'Thanks for coming. I'm sorry you were worried about me. It all feels a bit unreal.'

'It's bound to at this early stage.'

'I'll come and see you when things calm down,' said Daisy, drawing back.

'Whenever you're ready, I'll be pleased to see you,' said Hester and hurried away.

It was a small thing; a visit from a friend, but it warmed Daisy's heart. The good wishes of the neighbours had helped too and she hoped they had given her father some comfort. Yet it was later on, when life returned to normal after the funeral, that he would really feel it. They all would.

By the time they finally got their Sunday dinner it was evening and they were all exhausted from the trauma and the visitors. Because Bertha had always made the kitchen her exclusive domain, her daughters weren't brilliant cooks but they managed to produce a reasonable meal.

'You can do better than that, Dad,' said Daisy when her father put his knife and fork down having left half the meal. 'Was it that awful?'

'Sorry girls. It isn't the food. I'm just not hungry.'

'You must eat,' said Mary in a warning tone. 'You need to keep your strength up.'

'I'll finish it later,' he said and meant it because wasting food simply wasn't acceptable these days when it was so scarce.

'We'll make sure you do, don't worry,' said Daisy. 'We're our mother's daughters, remember. Bossiness is in our blood.'

'Too true,' added Mary. 'You'll have two of us on at you from now on.'

He managed a watery smile and changed the subject as he remembered something. 'Your mother was rambling a bit just before she died. She said something about Eve. She muttered something about my telling Daisy about Eve.'

'That's strange because I don't know anyone of that name,' she said. 'Do you, Mary?'

'No.'

'I think that's what she said but her voice was a bit weak and I was in quite a state so I can't be absolutely certain,' he explained. 'It sounded urgent though and she seemed to be very upset about it.' He paused, remembering. 'She said to tell Daisy she was sorry too. That much I am certain of.'

'Sorry about what?'

'She didn't say but it seemed to be connected to this Eve person.'

'Strange,' said Daisy. 'Eve can be short for Evelyn and I don't even know one of those.'

'Maybe it was someone Mum knew,' suggested Mary.

'I've never heard her speak of anyone of that name,' said Bill. 'And I knew all the same people she did. Why would it concern Daisy if it was a friend of hers?'

'Mm, there is that,' agreed Mary.

'Oh well, there's nothing we can do about it

and we have more important things to worry about, like arranging the funeral,' said Daisy.

'I'll see to all that tomorrow,' he said. 'I expect they'll let me have a few days' compassionate leave.'

'I'll help you, Dad,' offered Daisy. 'I won't have a job to go to anyway seeing as the Adelphi is closed.' Through the dark mists of grief, a worrying practicality emerged. 'I don't have a babysitter either.'

'We'll sort out the funeral together then,' sighed Bill, too deeply immersed in his grief to concern himself with his daughter's employment problems.

Daisy felt as if she had lost the structure of her life as well as her mother. Nothing would ever be the same again, that much she was sure of.

Chapter Twelve

As well as the emotional aftermath of her mother's death, Daisy had practical problems to cope with too. She had no one to look after Sam while she went back to work when the Adelphi re-opened after the bomb damage was made safe.

The idea of leaving him with a stranger after losing his beloved gran was unthinkable. But as much as she enjoyed being at home with him, she needed to be earning. Eventually, with the generous co-operation of her father and sister, a partial solution was found. She worked weekends at the cinema when Dad and Mary were around to look after Sam and her father subsidised her wages in return for taking on the job of running the house in place of her mother.

It wasn't ideal but it was manageable. Being on war work, both Mary and Dad were home too late for her to do an evening shift during the week but at least she was earning something. Fortunately Mr Pickles nearly always wanted weekend staff so was happy to have her.

One thing she did realise with something of a shock was how hard her mother had worked running the home and looking after the family. The weekly wash took up most of Monday: boiling, scrubbing, rinsing, mangling and pegging out. Tuesday was hours of ironing; then there was cleaning and cooking. Shopping for food was done every day and always involved queuing separately at the butcher's, grocer's, greengrocer's, baker's and others before dragging the heavy bags home.

'Phew, I'll be glad to get to work at the weekend for a rest,' she said jokingly one night over their evening meal. 'I don't think any of us appreciated how hard Mum worked and how exhausted she must have felt sometimes. I'm worn out and I'm young. Mum was getting on a bit.'

'Apart from helping with the dishes she never asked us to give her a hand with anything, did she?' Mary remarked. 'And she didn't complain about it either.'

'No she never did,' agreed Daisy. 'About other things but never the housekeeping.'

'She probably didn't want us interfering in the way she did things,' suggested Mary. 'I think she was proud of the fact that she ran this house like clockwork.'

'Now I know first-hand what's actually involved, I take my hat off to her.'

'We don't get that sort of service now, do we Dad?' said Mary, teasing her sister.

Bill wasn't very talkative these days and seemed lost in a world of his own a lot of the time.

'Dad.'

'Yeah, what's that?'

'We're just saying what a good housekeeper Mum was,' said Mary.

He nodded. 'Oh yes. Top notch. Always has been. She didn't like interference though.'

'I wouldn't mind some interference,' said Daisy. 'It's bloomin' hard work. I bet you two notice the difference, especially with the cooking.'

'You're doing a good job dear,' said her dad kindly. 'And you do have young Sam to look after.'

'Mum had two little ones at one time and she never seemed to have a problem,' said Daisy. 'Some women around here have five or six kids and they take it all in their stride.'

'I still say you're doing all right,' insisted her father.

'You could do with a few cooking lessons though,' said Mary with a wry grin.

'It can't be that bad,' said Daisy. 'You never leave anything.'

'If you're hungry you'll eat anything,' said Mary 'Even your lumpy gravy.'

'I'll leave you to do the gravy in future then, shall I,' suggested Daisy.

'It would probably be solid if I did it.'

'Don't criticise me then.'

And so it went on; the banter between the sisters in an effort to fill the silence that now prevailed at mealtimes. Daisy realised that her father had to go through the grieving process before he could recover. But he was a changed man at the moment and it made her sad.

By the end of March the air raids had petered out, which cheered everybody up. Because of the cinema newsreels Daisy was able to keep up to date with the war news. There was still talk of an Allied invasion, generally referred to as D-day, but when it was going to happen still remained a mystery to the general public.

The packed houses at the Adelphi in the evenings continued, the cinema bombing if not forgotten at least cast aside. No one bothered much about the ugly look of the temporary repairs to the damage. People had been through too much to worry about trivialities. If a chilly draught found its way in, few people complained, especially if there was an American film showing with all its sunshine and cheerfulness.

'I miss you during the week, Daisy,' said Doreen one Saturday afternoon when they were getting ready to go on duty.

'Do you?' said Daisy warmly. 'That's nice to know. I always enjoy seeing you too.'

'I expect you miss the money more than the company though,' said Doreen.

'I'll say. I hate the idea of Dad having to sub me. But my weekend wages only pay for bare essentials. They don't cover stuff for Sam, clothes and so on. He grows out of everything so fast.'

'Might John help out if he knew you were struggling?' suggested Doreen.

'He would if I asked but I reckon he has done quite enough for me already.'

'Do you keep in contact with him?'

'Very occasionally we write to each other but I am not going to ask him for money,' Daisy said in a definite tone. 'He didn't get anything positive from our marriage, whereas I got respectability for myself and Sam. So I think he deserves to be left alone now.'

'I'm sure your dad is happy to sub you and you have taken over the housekeeping, which is a big job. I know your mum did it without payment, as such, but if she wanted money for anything out-side of the housekeeping your dad would have given it to her. That's how it seems to work in families.'

'Mm, that's true. I'd still like to be self-support-ing though. If I could just work one more day it would make a big difference. Still, I can't so I'll have to make the best of things.'

'How is your dad now?'

'Still very quiet.' Daisy thought about this. 'The only person who seems to cheer him up is Sam. He simply adores him and vice versa. They're like a couple of mates.'

'I think that's lovely,' said Doreen.

'Yeah, it is sweet.' She paused thoughtfully. 'I've been meaning to ask you if you've heard from Dickie Dawson.'

'I've had a few letters from him,' Doreen said. 'He's never once mentioned that night. So I think he just wants someone to write to besides his mother. That sort of thing means a lot to soldiers abroad, I should think.'

'I'm sure it does,' agreed Daisy.

'I'm enjoying it too,' said Doreen. 'I look forward to his letters. He seems like a really nice bloke.'

'Manager's inspection in a few minutes, girls,' said one of the usherettes.

Daisy and Doreen checked their appearance in the mirror then hurried to the foyer.

'Come on, Sam, make up your mind,' said Bill one Saturday afternoon as he and his grandson stood at the counter in a sweetshop near Hammersmith Broadway. 'The lady is waiting and there are a lot of people behind us in the queue.'

The little boy pointed to the jar of pear drops on the shelf. 'Those please,' he said.

'Are you sure now?' asked Bill, as his grandson was inclined to change his mind about his precious sweet ration after having already taken ages to choose.

'Yes, Granddad.'

Miraculously the sale went ahead without alteration and the two left the shop, Sam clutching his favourites, almost colliding with a woman walking by outside.

'Hello Sam,' she said with obvious delight at seeing him. 'How are you, darlin'?'

'Fine thank you,' he said.

'Lovely manners,' Hester said, smiling at Bill. 'His mum does a good job.'

Bill looked blank.

'I'm Hester, a friend of Daisy,' she informed

him. 'I called at your house once when you'd just lost your wife. Bad timing but I didn't know.'

'I vaguely remember,' he said, the bright hair seeming to strike a chord.

'How are you now?' she asked.

'So-so.'

'It takes a while,' she said sympathetically. 'I went through the same thing myself a few years ago. I know how hard it is.'

'This little fella helps a lot,' he said.

'I'm sure he does; he's a proper smasher.'

'His mum is at work so I'm in charge,' Bill explained. 'My other daughter and I look after him together.'

'Yes, Daisy did mention it.'

'I love having him,' Bill told her.

'I bet.'

'We're going to the park now. He likes to see the ducks on the pond and have a good run around.'

'I'll leave you to it then,' she said brightly. 'Don't eat all your sweet ration at once, Sam.'

He held the bag out for her to take one.

'Oh that is so kind of you, Sam. But I wouldn't dream of nicking any of your precious sweets. You're a very good boy for offering though.' She turned to Bill, smiling. 'A little gem. You must be so proud of him.'

'Very,' he said. 'Daisy does a good job.'

'I expect you have a part in it too.'

'Only a small part,' he said. 'His mum makes the rules. It's my job to spoil him.'

She laughed, turning slightly as if to go. 'Enjoy yourselves at the park, boys. Bye-bye Sam.' She bent down and kissed his brow. 'Be a good boy for your granddad and I'll see you soon.' She turned to Bill. 'Cheerio.'

'Ta-ta.'

As he walked away, holding Sam's hand, Bill realised that he was smiling. For the first time since Bertha's death he had a glimpse of normality; a break in the dark clouds of grief that had consumed him since that terrible night. It was only a hint but it was a start.

'So how come you have a middle-aged woman as a friend?' Bill asked Daisy the next morning at breakfast, having told his daughter about the meeting with Hester.

'As far as I know there are no rules about age with regard to friendship, Dad,' said Daisy.

'Of course not but people usually pal up with persons of around their own age, don't they? It's only natural. Did you meet her at work?'

'No. She's my ex-boyfriend's mother. You remember Al, don't you, Dad?'

He stared at her in astonishment then glanced at Sam, who had finished his breakfast and was playing with his toys on the other side of the room. 'Are you sure that's a good idea?' he said.

'I know it isn't usual to stay friends with someone under those circumstances and I didn't after Al and I broke up. But I just happened to run into Hester in town sometime after and realised how much I liked her. I felt sorry for her too because both her sons are away at the war and she's on her own so I started to go round there.'

'I take it she doesn't know about the boy?'

'Of course not.'

251

'I told Daisy it was a mistake to keep in touch with her ex's mother, Dad,' said Mary.

'I was just thinking that it might be awkward when Al comes home, that's all,' said Bill.

'That's what I think too,' added Mary.

'Hester is an innocent party in all this,' Daisy pointed out. 'She doesn't know anything about why Al and I broke up. She told me that Al has never spoken to her about it. I doubt if many men talk to their mother about their love life. It could have been a mutual agreement between Al and me for all she knows. That's probably why she doesn't think she is being disloyal to Al because, as far as she knows, there's no bad feeling between us.'

'Maybe,' said Mary.

'When Al comes home, God willing that he does, I'll stop going round there.'

'Just like that.'

'Of course not,' said Daisy. 'Hester is an intelligent woman. She'll understand how awkward it would be and she won't want me to go round if Al is there. If she still wants to see me we'll meet in Lyons for a cup of tea or something.'

'She seems very fond of Sam.'

'She loves him to bits.'

Bill lapsed into thought. 'She is his grandmother and she doesn't know it.'

'That's right,' Daisy confirmed.

'Doesn't she deserve the truth as she clearly loves the bones of the boy?' suggested her father.

'I can't tell her without breaking her heart,' she said. 'She would be devastated to know that her son turned his back on me when I was pregnant.'

'Mm, I can see that that might be a problem,' he agreed.

'The whole thing is a bit of a mess,' said Daisy. 'But what are we supposed to do? Leave people to be lonely because of complications in the past that are not of their doing? This is wartime, Dad. Can you imagine how awful it must be not to have anyone close when the bombs are raining down? She knows lots of people because of her work and she's a sociable lady, but her loved ones aren't around. She only has her elderly neighbour.'

'Yes, I can see how you got into this,' he said. 'She seems nice enough. Looks a bit brassy though.'

'Compared to Mum, a vicar's wife looks brassy,' said Daisy.

'That's not a very nice thing to say about your mother,' Bill admonished.

'It wasn't meant in a bad way, Dad,' said Daisy. 'Mum made a point of looking thoroughly respectable and dressing the same way as her peers. Hester flies in the face of tradition and goes for a different look with make-up and bleached hair. Don't be fooled by it though. She has a heart of gold.'

'I could see that from the way she is with Sam.'

'I'm fond of Hester and don't go to see her only because I feel sorry for her. I enjoy her company and will be sad when I can't see her any more if that's the way it works out. At least I can give her company until her sons come home. I'll worry about the rest when the time comes.'

'It does seem awfully sad that the little 'un can't know his grandmother, especially as she is the only granny he has now,' said her father.

'Please don't make me feel worse than I already do, Dad.'

'You've nothing to feel bad about. It's that son of hers who is to blame for all this. If he'd done the right thing by you there wouldn't be a problem.'

'There's no point in harking back to that,' Mary put in. 'Things are as they are. The important thing is that Sam is with people who love him. Who knows what tomorrow may bring? We might have bombs raining down on us again and all we'll want then is to live for another day.'

'Cheer us up, why don't you?' said Daisy with irony.

'Just pointing out the facts,' said Mary. 'Let things be for the moment. As you pointed out, Daisy, this is wartime, the rest is all just speculation.'

Neither Daisy nor her dad could argue with that.

Bill wasn't comfortable with glamorous women. In fact he'd never known any to speak to. Bertha, bless her, had always had a plain appearance with hair taken back severely. Even as a girl she'd worn dark colours and never so much as a smidgen of make-up. So to find himself unexpectedly in conversation with the flamboyant Hester Dawson that day had been something of shock.

She was a good-looking woman, there was no doubt about that. But her appearance was hardly suitable for a grandmother. They were usually severe to look at in black clothes and hair in a bun. Odd that she had seemed quite down-to-earth and friendly. He would have expected someone like that to be full of airs and graces. But what possessed a woman of that age to dye her hair and wear such bright colours, he wondered. All the other women in his age group that he saw around were of a matronly appearance.

Oh well, it took all sorts to make a world, and he probably wouldn't come up against her again, not if he saw her first anyway. Odd to think that she was Sam's real grandmother though. That made the two of them grandparents to the same child. How far-reaching the consequences were of unbridled passion, he thought, realising that for the second time in his life. Still, things were as they were and there was nothing to be done about any of it, except perhaps avoid the dazzling Hester Dawson.

As it happened Mary was proved to be right about the possibility of further bombing. Not very long after that conversation and a week after D-day finally happened, the Blakes and their fellow Londoners found themselves, once more, in fear for their lives. Grotesque flying robots, soon known as doodlebugs, came chugging noisily across the Channel at all hours of the day and night and fell out of the sky when their fuel supply ran out, obliterating everything where they landed.

'This is worse than the flamin' Blitz,' Mary said one Sunday morning when they had just seen one fly overhead, terrified that it might stop and fall on them. 'At least the air raids had a beginning and an end. These vile doodles just keep coming.'

'Where has the booble gone?' said Sam, who couldn't quite manage the 'd'.

'Far away from here, darlin',' fibbed Daisy so that he wouldn't be frightened.

'When will another come?' asked Sam, who had no idea of the danger and thought it was all some sort of an exciting game.

'Not for a long time we hope,' said Daisy.

Even as she spoke the distant rumble of another became audible and they all prepared to take cover in the shelter. But it flew over without cutting out. Daisy felt a pang of guilt for being relieved that someone else would cop it.

After a couple of weeks people adjusted to this new horror and treated it as an irritation rather than a terror, though naturally they were afraid because these things were lethal and caused much death, damage and injury. Life and work went on more or less as normal, though everyone became very adept at diving for cover when they heard a spluttering engine.

In September a new kind of weapon arrived and these gave no warning; they just dropped out of the skies. One fell in nearby Chiswick and the shock of the blast was heard for miles. At first the government stayed silent about the cause of these mystery explosions that were heard across London several times a day and were rumoured to be gas explosions. It wasn't until November the public were finally told by Mr Churchill that a new weapon, a rocket known as the V2, was in operation and they were even more powerful than the doodlebugs.

'And there was us thinking the war was almost

over,' said Bill drily.

'I think it is, Dad,' said Mary. 'Our boys are back over there and making progress, according to the news anyway.'

'Yeah, I know,' he sighed. 'It's just that the end seems to be such a long time in coming.'

'But there are signs of a return to normality,' said Mary. 'We now have half lighting instead of full blackout.'

'These rockets are just Hitler's last push,' said Daisy. 'He knows he's on the losing side.'

'Sorry girls,' said Bill. 'I know I'm a misery lately. I'll try to be a bit more cheerful.'

'It's all right, Dad,' said Mary. 'We don't mind you being a bit down under the circumstances.'

'We'll forgive you,' added Daisy.

Bill was touched by their support. Many people had lost loved ones; in some cases whole families had been wiped out by the bombing. He had lost his wife but he still had two lovely daughters and a grandson he adored, which made him a very lucky man. He must remind himself of that more often.

Mr Pickles had his worried face on, Daisy noticed, when she went on duty one Saturday and happened to pass him on her way to the staffroom.

'Everything all right, Mr Pickles?' she asked, feeling she knew him well enough to ask.

'No it certainly isn't, Daisy,' he burst out.

'What's happened now?' she asked because a large cinema like the Adelphi had its fair share of problems; everything from trouble with the plumbing and the electrics to the projector breaking down or a delay in the films reaching them from the supplier.

'You know me, Daisy. I like the public to have their money's worth when they come to the Adelphi. The full works.'

'Indeed you do, Mr Pickles,' she said truthfully. He was one of the most conscientious people she knew. 'And you usually achieve it too.'

'But how am I expected to put on a decent show for the public when I'm permanently dogged by staff problems?'

'Is someone leaving then?'

'They've already gone and left me in the lurch good and proper,' he said, red-faced and looking as if he was about to explode.

'Oh dear,' she said.

'No warning. Just came to tell me that he won't be coming in tonight or any more at all. That's what you get with casual staff; cash in hand people who aren't on the payroll so they don't have to give notice. But you'd think he would have had the decency to give me time to find someone else, wouldn't you?'

'Yes,' said Daisy cautiously.

'I mean, a Saturday night at the flicks is important to people,' he went on. 'They look forward to it and deserve the full works. They pay to come in so are entitled to the whole cinema experience.'

'Who is it who has left then?' she asked.

'Gordon, the Saturday organist,' he told her. 'He only does one night a week and he can't even manage that now, apparently.'

'He is getting on a bit in years, Mr Pickles,' she reminded him. 'I suppose it's got to be too much for him.'

'Mm, I realise that he's no spring chicken. But people don't want to work on a Saturday night, that's the truth of it,' he said. 'They want to go out enjoying themselves.'

'With respect, Mr Pickles, I think Gordon is a bit past the Hammersmith Palais.'

'He isn't past the pub though, is he?'

'I suppose not,' she said. 'But if people didn't want to go out enjoying themselves you and I would be out of a job.'

He looked at her directly. 'Yes. You're quite right of course, Daisy,' he agreed with a wry grin. 'I can always rely on you to keep my feet planted firmly on the ground. I was just letting off a bit of steam, that's all. Truth is, I like to give the customers their money's worth and that includes music in the interval. I know some people don't even listen to it but others do and it's part of the programme and the general atmosphere. How on earth can I find another organist by tonight?'

She mulled this over. 'No promises, Mr Pickles, but I might just be able to help you with that. But you will have to give me half an hour or so off.' She was rewarded by a hint of hope on his worried face.

There was always an extra buzz in the cinema on a Saturday night. Even though Sunday working had become commonplace throughout the war, some people could sleep in and those who couldn't still enjoyed a night out on a Saturday. Often filmgoers saved their sweet coupons for the weekend and made a real treat of it.

Tonight's big film starred Carmen Miranda and the audience sat patiently through the B film and the newsreel and war information short until the interval when the decorative Mighty Wurlitzer rose from the depths with a small woman at the keyboard playing 'Happy Days are Here Again'.

There were rousing cheers and the organist then launched into 'The White Cliffs of Dover'.

'She looks familiar,' Doreen said to Daisy as they stood at the back listening.

'She's Al's mother,' Daisy explained. 'You probably met her when he worked here. She did come in sometimes to see the films and he liked to introduce her to anyone who was around. They are very close.'

Doreen looked at Daisy quizzically. 'I know you're friendly with her,' she said. 'So did you have a hand in her being here at the organ tonight?'

'I did as it happens.' She smiled. 'Poor Mr Pickles was at the end of his tether earlier when Gordon left without warning so I went round to see if Hester might be interested and was available. I knew she'd played an organ before and was used to an audience so I thought it was worth a try.'

'She's good.'

'Very,' agreed Daisy. 'She is an experienced musician. Plays the piano beautifully too.'

'Looks as though she's enjoying herself,' said Doreen, her eyes fixed on the organist who looked rather attractive in a bright red dress which suited the colour of her hair.

'She's a natural like her son.'

'He might have to fight with her for his job back

when he comes home.'

'I don't suppose he'll want it,' said Daisy. 'He always had his eye on bigger things. I'm not sure she would want it as a permanent job either.'

'No?'

'No. She has plenty of other musical commitments and probably wants Saturday nights to herself. She's just helping out until Mr Pickles can find someone else,' Daisy explained. 'It's only one night a week anyway. Saturday night is the most difficult night of the week to find someone because musicians are in demand at weekends apparently.'

'In that case she might be here until the war is over and things get back to normal and musicians come out of the services,' said Doreen.

'You could well be right.'

It seemed strange to Daisy to think that the end of the war really was in sight at last. They had waited so long it was hard to take it in as a certainty. She wondered if Al would come back to work here after he was demobbed. Seeing his mother up there at the organ reminded Daisy of the days when he had been there and they had been so much in love. Such happy times; sadly now long gone along with all the romantic notions.

'She's certainly got a talent and the guts to put it over,' remarked Doreen as Hester turned and spoke to the audience, thanking them for giving her such a warm welcome then played out with 'We'll Meet Again'.

'Must be where Al gets it from.'

'Sure to be,' said Doreen.

The applause was so loud and heartfelt it brought tears to Daisy's eyes. Like most people, her emotions had been sensitised by the war and sentimental music usually caused a lump in her throat. Well done, Hester, she said silently. You've made a lot of people happy tonight, especially Mr Pickles.

Chapter Thirteen

Bill Blake woke up with a start to find himself trembling. Sitting up in bed he realised that he was sweating but the bedroom was freezing, this being the middle of winter. It was that damned recurring dream again, the one in which Bertha was angry with him and telling him so as forcefully as she had done when she was alive. It seemed very real, though in life he had never been afraid of her as he was in the dream.

He lay back down and pulled the covers up, shivering and feeling depressed. Bertha's last moments haunted him often, which he thought was probably the cause of the returning dream. She had been trying to tell him something and he knew it had been vital because he had been familiar with every single feature of her personality.

Whatever it was she had wanted him to deal with it. But how could he when she'd been taken before being able to tell him what it was? He'd been over it in his mind repeatedly and trawled through his memory for anyone called Eve. But he had never known anyone with a name even vaguely resembling it.

There was nothing to be done so he had to put it behind him and move on with his life, but it wasn't easy. In fact, it was hard going at every level without Bertha. They had been together for such a long time and understood each other completely. Maybe they hadn't always liked each other but there had been deep affection between them. She was the governor in the marriage and that suited them both.

Now that the dream was fading he could be more rational about things. Yes, Bertha had wanted him to do something for her; until his dying day he would be convinced of that. But as he had no way of finding out what it was there was no point in beating himself up about it.

Wide awake now, he forced his mind on to other things and the one part of his life guaranteed to cheer him up: his grandson Sam. Four years old and a little smasher. Chatty, endlessly curious and bounding with energy, you always knew when he was around. But Daisy was firm with him and not afraid to discipline him at the expense of popularity.

He played outside the house in the street with the other kids now and would be starting school in the autumn but he still loved going to the sweetshop and the park with his granddad at the weekend. It was the highlight of Bill's week too. It was Saturday tomorrow so he would take him in the afternoon after work in the morning. That was something to look forward to, he thought as he finally drifted off to sleep.

There was a very good music shop in Hammer-smith with an excellent supply of sheet music including that for the accredited exams. Hester had a pupil who wanted to do Grade One so she took the bus to Hammersmith on Saturday afternoon to get the music. She wouldn't stay to look around the shops because she was playing the organ at the Adelphi later on, which was one of her favourite events of the week. Getting off the bus and heading along King Street she heard a child's voice call her name and, turning, she saw Sam with his grandfather.

'Hello darlin',' she said to the boy with a beaming smile, moving closer to him.

He offered an open paper bag to her.

'Have you been getting your rations again,' she said. 'No thank you, love. You keep them for yourself.' She moved her gaze to Bill. 'Hello there.'

'Wotcha,' he said.

'How are you?'

'Not so bad.'

'I'm on my way to the music shop,' she explained, as though that was necessary. 'They have the best stock of sheet music in West London here in Hammersmith.'

He just nodded because the odd popular tune was about the limit of his musical knowledge.

'Looks like the war is finally drawing to a close,' she said by way of conversation. 'The blackout is being abolished completely from Monday. I heard it on the news before I came out.'

'It's all over bar the shouting. Now that British troops have crossed the Rhine and the Americans and Russians have advanced from other directions Hitler doesn't stand a chance,' he said. 'The V bombs seem to have stopped coming too.'

'Thank Gawd for that, I say,' she said. 'They've even got Union Jacks on sale.'

'Really?' he said. 'I only come to the shops on a Saturday for the little un's sweets so I haven't seen any yet.'

'Oh yes, people can't buy them fast enough so they'll probably run out before long,' she said, adding with a smile, 'But shortages are nothing new for us so we'll take that in our stride.'

'Indeed. I think we might have some flags and bunting stashed away in the attic somewhere,' he said vaguely.

'There is going to be one hell of a party when we finally get the news we've waited so long for.'

'Not half.'

She looked at Sam, who was happily sucking a sweet. 'It'll be lovely for the little ones. About time they had a treat. All Sam has ever known is wartime.'

Bill nodded, then, seeing her lean down and look at Sam with such obvious affection, he was reminded of the connection she had with the child that she knew nothing about. Keenly aware of how much he valued his own close relationship with his grandson, he wasn't comfortable with the fact that she was deprived of hers.

'Something wrong, Mr Blake?' she asked, noticing his sudden frown.

'No no, nothing wrong.'

'I must be getting along,' she said, realising that whatever was troubling him was private. 'I'm working tonight.' She leaned down to Sam and smacked a kiss on his forehead. 'Ta-ta, darlin'. See you soon I hope.'

'Ta ta,' he responded sweetly.

'Cheerio, Mr Blake,' she said and headed off, disappearing in the crowds.

Daisy certainly hadn't inherited her sunny nature from her father, thought Hester, as she hurried towards the music shop. She couldn't quite make out if he was distant because he had things on his mind, whether he was naturally remote or he just didn't like the look of her.

He wouldn't be the first person to disapprove. She'd had plenty of snide remarks, mostly from women, reminding her of the difference between mutton and lamb. Her husband used to love her bright appearance and he was the only one whose opinion really mattered to her; and the boys of course. But they didn't seem worried by their mother's unconventional look. Occasionally they teased her about it but always in good fun.

Still, Daisy's dad had recently lost his wife so it could be grief that made him so distant. Whatever the reason it was none of her business. She certainly wasn't going to worry about it especially as Saturday night was her favourite time of the week. The job at the Adelphi wouldn't be for ever and nor would she want it to be but she was enjoying it while it lasted. The war would soon be over too. Oh happy days!

Bill was deep in thought as he and Sam headed for the park. Some things were best left in the past. But Hester Dawson's blood tie to her grandson was not one of them. It was wrong that she should be deprived in this way because of someone else's past wrongdoing. She had every right to know about her real connection with Sam. He would feel the same whoever she was.

It was almost time for Daisy to go to work when he and Sam got home. But Bill managed a few words with his youngest daughter while his grandson went to play outside.

'I've already told you, Dad, I can't tell Hester the truth about Sam without breaking her heart.'

'But it isn't right,' he persisted. 'She obviously thinks the world of the boy.'

'I know she does and it hurts me not to be able to tell her but I'd sooner it was me hurting rather than her.'

'Surely there must be some way around it,' he said.

'If there is I don't know of it,' she told him. 'Not without causing someone pain.'

'Oh, you're not worrying about that again, are you, Dad,' said Mary, entering the room and getting the gist of the conversation. 'Why not let things be? No good can come from raking it up as nothing can be done to change the situation. Anyway, you don't even know the woman.'

'I was thinking of Sam as well as her,' he said. 'John took no interest in him and your mother is no longer with us, sadly. I can see how fond Hester Blake is of Sam and it seems such a pity for both of them that she can't have her rightful place in his life.'

'I entirely agree with you, Dad,' said Daisy sadly. 'But in all honesty I can't see any way around it. Please don't enter into it against my wishes.'

'As if I would,' he said, outraged. 'I think you know me well enough to know that I don't interfere.'

'Yes I do know that, Dad, but you do seem particularly upset about this.'

'I like things to be right and fair, that's why,' he told her.

'In a perfect world they would be,' she said. 'And Sam's background is far from that. But we all love him to bits and give him the best life we possibly can. Surely that's the most important thing, isn't it?'

'Yeah, I suppose so.' He seemed to calm down. 'I can see that it's awkward so I'll try and forget about it.'

'I think that would be best,' said Daisy.

'Well, I'm going to the shops to see if I can find something to wear for the victory celebrations,' Mary announced. 'I've been saving my clothing coupons.'

'How exciting,' said Daisy. 'I'd come with you if I didn't have to go to work.'

'We don't have victory yet,' Bill reminded them.

'Any time now, though, Dad,' said Mary. 'It's about time you had something new to wear too. You never get anything now that Mum isn't here to nag you into it.'

'I'm always clean and tidy.'

'Don't worry, Dad, we won't drag you to the shops kicking and screaming,' said Daisy.

'I'll see you later then,' said Mary.

'If you see anyone on the street selling flags or bunting, will you get some?' asked Daisy. 'There weren't any around when I was at the shops. They'll be sold out I expect. Everybody wants them.'

'Will do,' said Mary. 'See you later.'

'Ta-ta,' said Daisy. Although she hadn't shown it, she often found herself concerned about Hester not having a proper relationship with her much-loved grandson. But as far as she could see there was no possible solution.

There was excitement in the atmosphere, thought Mary, as she arrived at the Broadway and headed down King Street. Everything was shabby but people were smiling and an air of expectancy was palpable as they waited for the announcement to tell them that the war was over. A few men were selling Union Jacks on the street and she decided to get some before they sold out, then she would hit the dress shops. Fortunately there were a few inexpensive, fashionable ones around here. If she couldn't find anything she would go to Oxford Street next weekend.

'Hello stranger,' said someone and looking up she found herself face to face with Daisy's husband.

'John,' she said, smiling, instinctively pleased to see him. 'Haven't seen you for years.'

'I'm back now,' he explained. 'The job in the North has finished now the war is over, all bar the shouting.'

'Lovely to see you,' she said. 'Are you pleased to be back?'

'Not half,' he said. 'I'm a Londoner through to the bone.'

'I'm the same.'

'How are the family?' he asked.

She paused for a moment then said, 'Have you got time for a cup of tea?'

'What a good idea,' he said and they headed for a nearby Lyons teashop.

'I'm very sorry to hear that,' he said when she told him they had lost her mother.

'I guessed you would be, which was why I didn't want to blurt it out on the street.'

'I always got on very well with your mum.'

'Yeah, I know you did,' she said. 'And she with you. You were her idea of the perfect husband for Daisy. Steady, reliable and in regular employment.'

'Am I really that boring?' he said with a wry grin.

'That wasn't what I meant. You're a good bloke. Daisy was lucky to have you.'

'I don't mind if people think I'm boring, Mary. I am what I am. As it happened I didn't turn out to be the ideal husband for Daisy though, did I?'

'Sadly no.'

'How are Daisy and Sam?' he asked.

'Both fine,' she said. 'Sam is an absolute smasher. He's four now and keeps us entertained most of the time. We all adore him. He's Dad's little pal too. I think he's been a real comfort to Dad since we lost Mum. Someone else to take an interest in and to love.'

John sipped his tea looking sad. 'It was a shame it didn't work out for Daisy and me. I was never

270

able to feel affection for Sam. It just wasn't in me.'

'Babies aren't the easiest of things,' she said. 'But that's all long gone. He starts school in September. He's a lovely boy. The image of his mother.'

'Daisy and I write to each other occasionally,' he said. 'She always says she's fine.'

'She is. She only works weekends at the cinema since we lost Mum because there's no one to look after Sam. She won't let him go to a stranger.'

He looked worried. 'She should have let me know if she was short of money.'

'She thinks you did more than enough for her by giving her and Sam respectability and she'll always be grateful to you for that and wants nothing more. Anyway, she manages, especially as Dad helps out in return for her running the house. When Sam goes to school she'll probably get a little morning job as well as the cinema so she's doing all right. You've no need to worry.'

'I still feel guilty about leaving but don't know what else I could have done, especially as it was Daisy's idea.'

'It was the right thing. I saw the two of you getting more miserable with every passing day. Daisy is much happier now. So are you by the look of it.'

'Yes, I am. It was a bad time for us both back then. Anyway, how about you?' he asked. 'Are you still single?'

She nodded. 'You?'

'Still on my own. I've been out with a few women over the years but it's never worked out.'

Suddenly she found herself wishing that he

271

wasn't her brother-in-law and they could stop talking about the family and the past. She'd always liked him and found him attractive even though she'd never allowed herself to admit it. Her sister's husband? Not likely! But he was free now in every way except legally and Daisy certainly didn't want him.

'Will you and Daisy get divorced eventually?' she inquired casually.

'I should think so though we haven't ever discussed it. If one of us meets someone else and wants to remarry we shall have to,' he replied. 'But I understand it's a long-drawn-out and complicated business. We've no plans at the moment.'

She nodded then changed the subject because this wasn't the moment to be anything other than his sister-in-law; maybe there never would be a time. 'It's looking good as far as the war is concerned, isn't it?' she said.

'Any day now we'll get the news we've waited nearly six years for.' He glanced at the flags poking out of her bag and added, 'I see you're prepared.'

'Too true. It's been a long time coming and I'm ready to cheer my heart out.'

'You and the rest of the nation I should think.'

'I can't wait to see what Sam makes of it all,' she said, smiling at the thought. 'There will be street parties the length and breadth of the country.'

'There certainly will.'

'Anyway, I'd better get off,' she said. 'I want to find something to wear for the celebrations. I've been saving up my clothing coupons in expectation.'

'You could always just wrap yourself in a Union

272

Jack,' he suggested jokingly.

She laughed. 'There will be a few exhibitionists who'll do that I expect. People will certainly let their hair down and I don't blame them. Anyway, I must dash. Nice to have seen you again, John.'

'And you, Mary. Give my regards to Daisy and your dad. I would come round to the house but it's a bit awkward and I'm sure Daisy would rather I didn't.'

'I don't know about that, John,' she said. 'You must do what you think is best.'

'I'll give it some thought.'

'Ta-ta.'

'Cheerio.'

As she went on her way, she wondered if he had ever thought of her in any other way than as a sister-in-law. They had always got on well when he was living with them. Oh well, she might never know the answer to that. He really was a nice man though.

'I think there are some flags up in the attic,' Bill told them the next morning over breakfast, which was lingered over, this being Sunday. 'Might be some bunting too. They'll be a bit dusty and will need a wash but the more we have the better. We want to make the house and the street look festive like never before. There will be red, white and blue everywhere once we get the news we're waiting for. I'll go up and have a look later on.'

'I'll go up there, Dad,' offered Daisy. 'I'm smaller and more agile than you.'

'If you're offering, I won't say no.'

'You won't catch me volunteering to go up

there,' said Mary with a wry grin. 'It's far too dusty for me. The place will be full of cobwebs.'

'Coward,' laughed Daisy.

'The stepladder is in the cupboard under the stairs,' said Bill. 'I'll get it out after breakfast.'

'That's another dusty hellhole,' said Mary, laughing.

'Oi, do you mind,' objected Daisy. 'I cleared it out only the other day.'

'It's still a magnet for dust and spiders,' said Mary.

'I think we'll have to put you on housekeeping duty,' said Daisy. 'That'll cure you of being so finicky.'

'I will be looking for a job now the war's over,' Mary said. 'But I'll steer clear of housekeeping.'

'Will you go back to the Co-op?' asked Daisy.

'I hope so but I'm not sure if they'll have a job for me as there will be thousands of women pouring on to the jobs market now that war work is finished. The Co-op might want to keep the older women they took on to replace people who went on to war work.'

'Surely they will have to stand back for people like you who were forced to leave to go into a factory.'

'They probably will. I'm still needed where I am for the moment anyway, helping them to clear up ready for the change back to normal manufacturing.'

'I wonder if many of the married women who went out to work will revert to normal and stay at home now they're not needed,' said Daisy.

'I hope so otherwise it might be difficult to find

employment for us single girls who don't have anyone to support us,' said Mary.

'I should call in at the Co-op and find out where you stand,' suggested Daisy.

'I've kept in touch while I've not been working there and I think I'll be all right. And talking about jobs finishing with the war, I ran into John in town yesterday and his war job has ended. He's back in London for good.'

'Oh. Is he all right?' asked Daisy with genuine interest because she still regarded him as a friend.

'He seemed fine. He sent his regards. We had a cup of tea and chat in Lyons actually. It was nice to see him again. I always got on well with him.'

'So did I until I married him.'

'No regrets?'

'That he left? No, it was a mutual decision.'

'I suppose you'll have to think about getting a divorce at some point.'

'I wouldn't have the faintest idea of how to set about it. But, yes, I suppose we will have to look into it sometime in the future. We can't stay legally married for ever.'

The subject came to its natural conclusion and Sam said, 'Can we go and find the flags now, Mummy?'

'You're not coming up there with me, darlin',' she told him firmly. 'I think we can all do without you falling off the ladder and breaking both your legs.'

The idea of this amused him and he giggled helplessly. 'Can you get them soon?' he asked when he'd calmed down.

'When I've finished my breakfast,' she said.

275

'He's getting into the party mood already,' said Mary.

'Children have no sense of time,' said Daisy. 'They want things instantly. He'll pester the life out of me until I do go up and get the perishin' flags.'

'When is the party, Mum?' asked Sam.

'Soon we hope,' said Daisy.

'When is soon?'

'Not long.'

'No more questions, you little pest,' said Mary, smiling at him affectionately. 'Finish your porridge and pipe down.'

'Can you keep him occupied while I'm up in the attic and please don't let him climb up the ladder?' asked Daisy.

'I'll take the ladder away while you're up there,' suggested her father. 'Just to make sure there are no accidents.'

'Good idea, Dad.'

'Mummee ... have you found the flags yet?' Sam shouted up to the attic.

'Yes, I have found some.'

'Are you coming down then?'

'In a minute,' she replied. 'I'm just trying to find some more decorations and sort things out a bit up here. Why don't you go and keep Auntie Mary company.'

'She's washing the dishes.'

'Oh, well go and stay with Granddad then,' she said. 'I won't be long.'

'All right, Mum.' He trotted off to find his grandfather.

'Are you all right up there, Daisy?' Bill shouted up to the attic more than half an hour later. 'You've been up there for ages.'

There was no reply.

'Daisy,' he called more urgently. 'What are you doing up there, for goodness' sake?'

There was a long silence then she replied thickly, 'I'll be down in a minute, Dad.'

'Have you fallen and hurt yourself or something?' he said. 'You sound funny.'

'I'm perfectly all right, Dad,' she assured him.

'Why don't you come down then?'

There was a short silence then she said, 'I'm coming now so could you put the ladder up and keep Sam well away from it please?'

'Will do,' he said, getting the ladder and putting it into place for her to use.

She threw the flags and bunting down ahead of her so that her hands were free, then came down.

'They'll need a good wash,' she said on reaching the floor. 'But they should add a bit of colour to the proceedings.'

'Well done,' he said. 'You've managed to find quite a lot. I didn't realise we had so many.'

'They built up over the years after past celebrations, I suppose.'

'Is something the matter?' asked Bill, looking at her more closely. 'You look a bit pale.'

'It's probably the dust,' she fibbed. 'I'm fine. I'll put these in the sink later and give them a good scrubbing. They'll be as good as new when I've finished.'

'Are you sure you're all right?' he asked again.

'You seem a bit strange and look rather peaky.'

She wanted nothing more than to tell him about her shocking discovery in the attic. But now, with the victory celebrations expected any day, wasn't the time. It wouldn't be fair to spoil such an important and happy event for the family. They deserved to enjoy something they had all waited so long for. Besides, she needed more time to make sense of what she now knew.

Chapter Fourteen

Even when the BBC informed the public that Hitler had killed himself, there was still no official announcement regarding the end of the war. People were ready and waiting with flags, bunting and street parties organised.

After an agony of delay and rumours, the news finally came that Tuesday 8th May would be celebrated as VE Day and it would be a national holiday as would the following day.

The atmosphere was indescribable. It was a kind of glorious chaos and a deeply moving experience for Daisy. After six years of fear, threat and grief, they were free. People were out on the streets, dancing, singing and hugging each other. Even normally reserved souls, who usually avoided their neighbours, were out well-wishing. Complete strangers chatted like old friends. The end of a world war was a huge event and Daisy was aware that history was being made. She was proud to know that in years to come she would be able to say, 'I was there. I was a part of it.'

The actual celebrations were a riot of fun and excitement. Red, white and blue bunting fluttered in the breeze over the trestle tables weighed down with sandwiches and cakes and around which sat the beaming children of the street, most in fancy dress which had been pre-arranged along with the party when the war had seemed likely to end. Between them Daisy and her sister had found enough material among their old clothes to make Sam a Robin Hood outfit, aided by their mother's old treadle sewing machine and bags of imagination. He really looked the business in it.

The merrymaking went on long after the children had gone to bed. People were singing, dancing and knocking back the booze until the small hours though the Blakes were in bed before that. Daisy was glad she had decided to leave the dark discovery in the attic unspoken. Dad and Mary deserved today and its memories unspoiled.

'I think the celebrations might have been a bit too much for Sam,' said Daisy to her sister the following Sunday when she and Mary were in the kitchen preparing lunch. 'He hasn't been himself at all this past few days.'

'Ah bless him,' said Mary. 'I suppose the excitement got to him even though he doesn't understand what it's all about.'

At that moment the boy appeared and clung to his mother's skirts, crying.

'Aah, don't you feel well, darlin',' said Daisy and to her sister, 'He isn't usually clingy.'

279

'No, he certainly isn't,' agreed Mary. 'You go and sit down and give him a cuddle and I'll take over here.'

'Thanks, sis.'

Daisy picked him up and took him into the living room where her father was reading the newspaper. She sat down and lifted her son on to her lap. He cried softly. She did all the usual checks: felt his brow and glands, looked at his tongue and checked for a rash with measles in mind but all seemed well.

'I expect he's just tired,' she said to her father.

'Perhaps it's all been a bit too much for him,' added Bill. 'Maybe if he has a sleep he'll feel better.'

He did not sleep but seemed miserable for the rest of the day and during the night he became feverish and was vomiting. By early in the morning he had developed a rash and his throat was red and sore. The really alarming thing was his tongue, which was white-coated with red around the edges. Daisy knew enough about children's diseases to know that in a few days the whitish coat would peel off leaving the boy with a strawberry-red tongue.

'Could you go for the doctor please, Mary?' she asked. 'I'm almost certain that Sam has scarlet fever.'

'What makes you think that?' asked her sister.

'Look at his tongue,' she said.

Mary did so. 'Bloody hell, I think you're right,' she said. 'That's definitely strawberry tongue in the making. I'll go for the doctor now.'

'Try not to worry, Daisy,' said her father but

they both knew they were just empty words. Scarlet fever killed many children every year because there was no cure.

In the evening of that same day, Daisy and her sister were crying with their father not far off as they stood outside the closed isolation ward looking through the window at Sam, who was in bed being cared for by nurses and unaware of anyone at the window. To add to their pain he was crying and there was absolutely nothing they could do about it. They weren't allowed in because this was one of the most contagious of diseases.

To see your child, the love of your life, sick and needing you and being powerless to be with him was excruciating. The worry that had seemed so all-consuming to Daisy just before VE Day now seemed unimportant in comparison. She had been told that everything was being done for Sam but they couldn't commit themselves on his chances of survival because of the possibility of complications such as pneumonia and meningitis which so often happened with this disease.

'You should think about going home, my dear,' said a senior nurse, appearing at Daisy's side. 'There's nothing you can do for him; the nurses are doing everything they can.'

'He needs his mother,' she said desperately, tears streaming down her face. 'He's crying for me.'

'He's crying because he's ill and he feels bad and he doesn't understand,' said the nurse. 'He'll get used to the nurses. They'll look after him, I promise you.'

'Not like I do.'

'You must let go of him for a little while and trust us to do our best for him.'

'Is he going to die?'

The nurse's expression was unreadable. 'I can't answer that at the moment,' she said. 'All I do know is, we will do our very best to make sure that doesn't happen.'

'He's in the best place, love,' said her father thickly.

'Yeah,' added Mary.

'It's getting late,' said the nurse. 'The best thing you can do for your little boy is to go home and get some rest so that you can come back and see him tomorrow.'

'I can't leave him.'

'You must, my dear,' said the older woman, putting her hand on Daisy's arm in a gesture of comfort. 'We'll let you know if there's any change.'

'How? We don't have a telephone.'

'We'll send someone round.'

Daisy couldn't bear to say the word out loud but she knew the woman meant the police and they only came in the case of the very worst news.

'I really think you should go home and come back tomorrow,' insisted the nurse.

'Come on, sis,' said Mary, taking her sister's arm gently. 'Let's go home.'

'I feel as though I'm deserting him,' she said.

'Not at all,' said the nurse. 'You are leaving him with people who know their job and will do their very best for him.'

'I suppose so,' Daisy agreed at last but she cried all the way home.

Mary had got her old job back at the Co-op but she stayed off work the next day to give Daisy some moral support. They checked with the doctor about the rules as regards their own infectiousness and after checking them over, he assured them that quarantine wasn't necessary for them as Sam was in isolation. Daisy spent a lot of the day watching her son through the window and there didn't seem to be any change, except perhaps that he was crying a little bit less.

Daisy had known since giving birth that to be a parent was to feel permanently vulnerable but Sam's illness had made her feel helpless too and that was frightening. She knew without a doubt that she would give her life to save his. This reminded her of her own mother and, despite everything, she wished she had been here with her during this ordeal. Her presence would have given her confidence. It was only a few days since Sam had fallen sick but it felt like a lifetime spent in hell.

Hester finished her shift at the organ on Saturday night and went to look for Daisy just to say hello.

'Where's Daisy tonight?' she asked Doreen. 'I haven't seen her around.'

'You've not heard then.'

Hester's brow furrowed. 'Heard what?' she asked, looking worried.

'Her little boy has scarlet fever and is in the isolation ward at the hospital.'

'Oh, the poor little mite,' cried Hester.

'It's awful for him and Daisy must be going through hell,' said Doreen. 'Her sister called in to tell Mr Pickles she won't be at work for a while. The worst part is that she isn't allowed to be with her boy because he's in quarantine. She can only look at him through the window.'

Hester felt Daisy's pain almost as her own. As a mother herself she could imagine what that must be like. 'Oh poor Daisy,' she said, wondering how she could help.

'Yes, I feel sorry for her too,' said Doreen. 'Not a very good start to peacetime for her, is it?'

'It certainly isn't,' agreed Hester.

'Good afternoon,' said a woman behind the counter in the reception area of the hospital. 'Can I help you?'

'Yes please. Can you tell me how the little boy with scarlet fever is? His name is Sam. I'm afraid I don't know his surname because I don't know his mother's married name.'

'You're not a relative then.'

'No, just a friend of his mother.'

'I'm afraid I can't give you any information,' she said. 'Family only. Hospital rules.'

'It's only information I'm after,' Hester said. 'I'm not asking to see him or anything.'

'It's more than my job is worth.'

Hester was pensive. She'd deliberately stayed away from the Blake house because to visit seemed intrusive and she wasn't sure if they were in quarantine. But she desperately wanted to know how Sam was, and his mother, who must be out of her mind with worry.

'The thing is,' she began, looking persuasively at the woman. 'I am very fond of Sam and his mother. I really do need to know if they are all right.'

The receptionist tapped her chin with her pen thoughtfully. 'Well ... if it's just Sam's mother you want to see and not the boy you'll probably find her down the corridor looking into the ward through the window at her son. She'll give you the information you are looking for.'

'Thanks very much, dear.' Hester headed for the corridor.

Daisy felt a hand on her shoulder and when she turned to see Hester there, a rush of warmth and relief coursed through her. It was as though her own mother had come back to comfort her.

'He'll be all right, love,' said Hester, sounding strong. 'He'll come through this.'

'Will he?'

'I think so.'

Daisy didn't want to know what the other woman's view was based on; she needed optimism, which her father and sister tried to give to her in abundance but it never rang true because they were as frightened as she was and never quite able to hide it. 'Thank you so much for coming, Hester,' she said, putting her arms around her, the tears falling. 'I feel so much better now that you're here. You're such a calming presence.'

'Your dad and sister are too closely involved to give you much comfort, I expect,' the older woman said. 'They'll be as worried and upset as you are.'

'Yes, they are both very anxious,' sobbed Daisy. Even in her disturbed state it occurred to her that Hester was even more involved with Sam than Dad and Mary albeit that she was unaware of it. 'It's only natural.'

'Your boy will probably start to improve in the next few days. But you won't be able to go in there to see him for a while.'

'How do you know?'

'Because my Al had the same thing when he was little. And he grew up to be a fine healthy fella, didn't he?'

The words were pure balm. Daisy so needed to hear something positive. 'He certainly did,' she said.

'So keep your chin up and look forward to having young Sam home soon.'

'I'll try to do that, Hester. And thanks again for coming.'

'A pleasure, love.' Hester was praying she hadn't given Daisy false hope. It was true that Al had come through the same disease but she had no more idea than Daisy if Sam would make it. Yet the poor woman had been in desperate need of hope so that's what she had provided.

Sam's condition began to improve over the next few days to the extent that he looked for his mother at the window. In a way it was even more troubling because she wanted to be with him, but was so thankful that he had been spared she knew she could be patient.

It was a month before he was finally discharged

and no event had been more eagerly awaited. Unfortunately it was a huge disappointment because the dear little boy who had gone away to hospital had been replaced by a monster child who demanded his own way, refused to do as he was told, was cheeky and quick to tears if things didn't go his way.

'He's turned into a spoiled brat,' said Daisy after an incident when he'd refused to go to bed and had been forcibly carried upstairs by his mother. 'But although the nurses were good to him in hospital, I'm sure they didn't spoil him.'

'It's all the upheaval I reckon,' suggested her father. 'He's been through a lot and he's been away for a long time. A few weeks are an eternity to a child and he's been in a different routine with new people.'

'But what can I do, Dad?' she asked. 'I can't let him get away with being cheeky and badly behaved just because he's been ill. I don't want to be going on at him all the time but he's so naughty now I have to be firm.'

'Of course you do, however hard that is, or he'll carry on pushing his luck,' advised Bill. 'We'll all have to keep him in check. But I reckon he'll calm down and get back to normal after a week or so.'

'He starts school in September, doesn't he?' put in Mary. 'Perhaps he's ready for that now.'

'He might be but I'm not,' said Daisy with a wry grin. 'I was looking forward to these last few months of having him at home. The way he's behaving at the moment though...'

'Children do reach a stage where home isn't enough for them,' said Bill.

'Mm, I know, Dad,' sighed Daisy. 'It's just that school is the next stage and I want to keep him close for ever.'

'I expect all mums feel like that when it's time to hand their kids over.'

'In the meantime I have to get him back to something resembling a normal human being,' said Daisy.

'You're not on your own,' Mary reminded her. 'We're right here beside you.'

'I vaguely remember something similar when Al came home from hospital,' said Hester, having witnessed Sam at his worst; he'd thrown himself on the floor, screaming because Daisy wouldn't let him have another biscuit. Daisy was mortified by his behaviour, especially in someone else's house.

'How did you deal with it?' asked a desperate Daisy, having made her snivelling son leave the room.

'It's a long time ago but I think I did what you're doing, living through it and staying firm. As far as I can remember it just passed eventually. He reverted to normal on his own. It's probably because Sam was used to all the attention in hospital; that and the low feeling we all have after we've been ill. We can cope with it; kids don't understand so they react in the only way they know by being downright naughty.'

There was a tap on the door.

Daisy went over and opened it to her red-eyed, disconsolate son. 'You're not coming in until you say sorry, Sam.'

She waited, feeling tense. This was the part where he refused to apologise and went into another tantrum. But he said, 'Sorry Mummy,' in a voice muffled from crying.

Welcome back to the human race, she said silently, hoping that this was the turning point. But out loud she said, 'That's better. Come and give me a kiss.'

He went into her arms and sat on her lap on Hester's sofa, and behaved normally for the rest of the visit.

'It's a start,' she said to Hester, smiling.

'Indeed,' Hester agreed.

As the longed-for peacetime continued it soon became clear to everyone that their hardship wasn't likely to end at any time soon as shortages and rationing became even more severe for some products. In July the Labour party had a landslide victory in the General Election; ordinary people wanted a better Britain with somewhere to live and prospects and didn't trust Mr Churchill to give it to them.

In August Japan surrendered and there were more celebrations but the VJ partying was a pale shadow of VE Day. In spite of that it was a great relief for people with relatives serving out there.

Now, with all the celebrations over and Sam back to his normal self and Daisy back at work, she knew she could wait no longer to try to right a terrible wrong. Her first move was to speak to Mary and her father about it, knowing that she must hurt them in doing so. But she had agonised about it and couldn't see any other way. She was too close to them to keep such a thing secret from them.

'So what's all this about, Daisy?' inquired her father one August evening when she had asked for her father's and sister's attention. 'I was going out for a game of darts tonight.'

'You can go later,' she said. 'But there's something I have to tell you both.'

'Blimey Daisy, you aren't half making a drama of it,' said Mary 'I want to wash my hair. Can't you tell us another night?'

'No. I have left it long enough already and any excuse and I'll put it off again.'

'Something we're not going to like then,' Mary assumed.

'You won't be half as upset as I am but no, you won't like it.'

'Let's hear it then,' said Mary.

'When I went up into the attic to get the flags and bunting for VE Day, I made a discovery,' she began. 'I found out what Mum was trying to say to you just before she died, Dad.'

'Oh.' Bill's brow furrowed. 'You found out who Eve is, did you? How on earth could you do that in the attic?'

'I know what Mum meant but Eve isn't a person.'

'What else could it mean then?' he asked, becoming emotional as he remembered the terrible event.

'Mum was trying to say eaves,' Daisy explained. 'While I was in the attic I noticed that the small door to the eaves wasn't closed properly so I had a look and found out why.'

'And?' said Mary.

'There was a bundle of letters hidden there and they were blocking the door.'

'What letters?' asked her father. 'Your mother and I never wrote to each other because we were never apart.'

'They were letters from me to Al and him to me,' she said.

'What on earth were they doing there?' asked her father.

'Mine were never posted and Al's were never given to me.'

A puzzled silence filled the room.

'It seems that Al didn't turn his back on me, as we thought,' she explained. 'He never even knew I was pregnant. If you remember, Mum used to post all our letters when she went to the shops but it turns out she never posted mine to Al and his were intercepted somehow by her and I never got to see them. She must have looked out for the post and taken mine before I even knew they were there. So I thought he had rejected me and he thought the same about me. There are several letters from him begging me to tell him why I had stopped writing. He must have been as devastated as I was, and him away fighting for his country too.'

'There must be some mistake,' said Bill, pale with shock. 'Your mother wouldn't do a terrible thing like that.'

'That's what I thought at first. But I've con-sidered every possible alternative explanation and drawn a blank. It appears that she would and she

291

did. I know it's upsetting for you, Dad, but I had to tell you. All those lives upset. Mine, Al's, John's and even Sam's even though he's too young to know any different.'

'I can't believe it,' said Mary. 'I mean Mum was very dominant and interfering but she wasn't evil. That is the act of a wicked person.'

'Yes it is, but I don't think she saw it as evil,' said Daisy. 'I believe she thought she was doing the best thing for me and if she had to break the rules of common decency to do it so be it. She didn't like Al from the start and when he went away she was probably glad, hoping that I'd meet a nice respectable boy and forget all about Al. But he was the love of my life, which is why my marriage to John was a disaster. I think Al might have got some of my very first letters but all the others are here in this house, now rescued from the attic and in one of my drawers. You can have a look at them if you don't believe me.'

'Of course we believe you,' said Mary. 'But it's very hard to accept such an awful thing of your own mother. I wouldn't dream of looking at something so private. Would you, Dad?' She looked at him as he appeared to be lost in thought. 'Dad, are you listening?'

'Yes, I'm listening, and of course we don't need to see the letters,' he said.

'Why didn't she just destroy them I wonder,' said Mary.

'I don't know,' said Daisy.

'I think your mother realised how precious the letters were so couldn't bring herself to destroy them,' suggested Bill hopefully. 'Perhaps in some corner of her heart she wanted them to be found and the truth to come out at some point in the future. She was very misguided but not inherently bad. That is what she was trying to tell me. She just couldn't manage the last part but she wanted you to know before she died, Daisy, I have no doubt about that.'

The sisters exchanged glances. Their father's loyalty to his wife knew no bounds. It wasn't easy for them to think ill of their mother either. But was there something in what he said about Bertha's last words?

'Yeah, that must have been it, Dad,' said Daisy.

'Hang on a minute,' began Mary. 'You found the letters before VE Day so why wait so long to tell us?'

'You can imagine how devastated I was when I realised how Al and I had been duped in the worst possible way. I wanted nothing more than to share this with you and have you comfort me. But the end of the war was such a huge event in all our lives, I couldn't bring myself to spoil things for you two. No sooner were the celebrations over than Sam got sick and that dominated my thoughts. But this awful thing has hung over me since that day in the attic. I can still hardly believe that Mum would do such a thing to me. We all know how domineering she was but this was downright manipulative. What makes a person do such a thing?'

Bill had been silent for a few minutes. He was struggling with a dilemma. Did he tell his daughters, what he believed had made their mother so dominant over them to the point of wicked interference, and in doing so hurt one of them deeply?

Or did he let them believe there was no excuse for her behaviour to spare the feelings of one daughter? He knew he must do the right thing for Bertha.

'There's something you don't know about your mother,' he began. 'And I am going to tell you about it because I believe it made her the way she was; always wanting to organise both your lives. It's no excuse but it might help you to understand why she did what she did.'

They waited, looking puzzled.

'When she was a young girl she got pregnant and the boy didn't stand by her,' he said quickly as though forcing himself to utter the words. 'Things were even harder for unmarried mothers in those days than they are now.'

'Blimey, they must have been bad then,' said Daisy.

'They were,' confirmed her father gravely. 'And her parents were very strict, almost to the point of cruelty at times. Anyway, she and I had been friends since we were little and used to tell each other everything; we lived in the same street.' He paused because this was the really difficult bit. 'To cut a long story short, I married her to save her good name. Unlike Daisy's marriage of convenience ours worked really well and we grew to love each other in our own way.'

'Which was why she thought it would be the same for John and me,' said Daisy.

'Exactly,' he said.

There was a silence while the girls digested this breathtaking information.

'So what happened to the baby?' asked Mary.

He looked at her sheepishly. 'I've always loved you as my own, Mary,' he told her.

'Me! Oh my God,' she said, flushing up then turning pale. 'So you're not my dad and Daisy isn't my sister.'

'She's your half-sister and I have always loved you as my own daughter,' he repeated.

Mary was very pale. 'Was she courting my father ... I mean, er, it wasn't rape was it?'

'Oh no, nothing like that,' he assured her.

'Thank goodness. I should hate to think I was the result of something like that.'

'Your mother and this boy were seeing each other on a regular basis, though they were very young and he was a bit of a Jack the lad,' he went on. 'He moved away soon after she told him she was pregnant and she never heard from him again. That was why she was always so terrified the same thing would happen to you two girls. I think Al reminded her of the boy who let her down; he was good-looking and sociable. She didn't think Al was right for Daisy because of her own experience. Anyway, Al wasn't around later on when Daisy got pregnant so he couldn't save her good name.'

'But you stepped in to save Mum's,' said Mary.

'Yes. We told her parents that the baby was mine and by God did they make me suffer. They never let up. But it was worth it for me because I'd always loved Bertha and I was proud to call you mine, Mary.'

Both his daughters were wet-eyed.

'Nothing has changed, sis,' said Daisy, hugging her. 'I'm still your half-sister. We still share the same blood. You're not gonna get rid of me. I can promise you that.'

'And there was me thinking I could shake you off,' said Mary, pretending to make light of it; but she was actually devastated.

'Anyway, back to Sam and Al, Daisy,' began Bill. 'What are you going to do about it?'

'Al must be told what happened,' said Daisy. 'I want nothing from him; the time has passed for us. But he needs to know that I didn't discard him. And of course I want him to know about Sam. If he has no place for him in his life, I'll accept that. But he must be told of his existence.'

'I agree,' said Mary 'But it means he'll have to know what Mum did.'

Daisy nodded. 'Yes I have thought about that and I can't see a way around it without making up a pack of lies and there has been too much deceit already.'

'How do you feel about that, Dad?' asked Mary. 'Will that be too painful for you, having your wife exposed?'

'It's painful for me whether other people know about it or not,' he said. 'But your mother is beyond being hurt.'

'That's what I thought,' said Daisy.

'When will Al be coming home?' asked Mary.

'I don't know,' replied Daisy. 'Hester and I carefully avoid any mention of him. I don't think she knows when either of her boys will be back. No one seems to know when their people will be back from the war. I get the idea they are told to expect them when they see them.'

'Hester needs to be told about Sam right away

though,' Bill stated categorically. 'Enough time has passed as far as that's concerned.'

Daisy stared at him in astonishment. 'You think I should tell her before him then.'

'Under the circumstances, most definitely. I've been telling you she should know the truth for a while,' he reminded her. 'Now that we know that Al didn't let you down so you won't cause any trouble, there is no reason why not.'

'Surely he should be the first to know.'

'In normal times yes, of course, but he isn't around and you are on friendly terms with his mother,' said Bill. 'More importantly, Sam is in her life so she deserves to know that she is related to him. If Al doesn't want to be involved with Sam all the better that the boy has Hester to love him. She can come here to see him if Al doesn't want Sam around. At least he'll have a grandma, even if he doesn't have a dad.'

'Mm. There is that,' said Daisy. 'I don't want Al to hear about it from his mother though. That wouldn't be right.'

'Make sure she knows that,' he said. 'I don't think she would mention it without your permission anyway.'

'Actually Dad, it will be a relief for her to know,' she confessed. 'I've sometimes found it a burden keeping it from her when I see her being so obviously fond of Sam.'

'There's no need to hold back now, is there?' he said.

'No there isn't.' She turned to her sister. 'What do you think, Mary?'

She was lost in her own thoughts, still recovering

from the personal blow her father had just given her.

'Mary...'

'Everything isn't about you, Daisy,' she snapped. 'There are other people in this family besides you. I might just be a dirty little secret but I have feelings too. I'm going out for a walk.' As Daisy went towards her she added, 'I want to be on my own so don't you dare come after me.'

Daisy stayed where she was as Mary left the house, shocked and angry with herself for being so wrapped up in her own affairs as not to realise how utterly devastating Dad's shock revelations must have been for her sister.

Mary's eyes were hot with tears as she headed for the river in the summer evening. She felt like a different woman to the one who had got out of bed that morning. She had always been closer to her father than her mother and to find out that she wasn't even related to him biologically had left her reeling.

She had never fully recovered from the feeling of rejection she had experienced when her affair with Ray had ended so horribly. Now it was many times worse. Her beloved dad wasn't her father. He was just a bloke who had helped her mother out when she was in trouble. Wasn't that a smack in the face?

There were a lot of people about on the riverside, many of them couples walking hand in hand, engrossed in each other. This added to her sense of desolation. She didn't even have a boyfriend and her dad wasn't her dad. What a mess!

It was a humid evening, the sun almost done for the day, the muddy-coloured river tinted with olive green in places, the air heavily scented with the earthiness of incipient autumn. The familiarity of it all made her want to cry. This area was all she'd ever known; she'd grown up here and had always felt she belonged. Now she felt like an interloper. She hadn't been conceived from the love of her parents as she had always believed. She was just a mistake that had forced them to be together.

'Whoops,' said a male voice and she realised she had almost walked into someone. Looking up, she saw it was John.

'Sorry,' she said thickly. 'I was miles away.'

'Somewhere not very nice by the look on your face.'

With that she burst into tears.

'Feeling better now?' John asked after she had blurted out the whole story in the garden of a riverside pub.

'A little,' she said. 'I think it might be the gin and orange you were kind enough to buy me though.'

'I think the occasion demanded something a little stronger than lemonade.'

'Nothing will have changed when it wears off though, will it?'

'Your attitude towards it might have, though, when you've had time to think it through properly,' he suggested.

She shrugged. 'My dad, my lovely dad, isn't my father,' she said. 'I was just a nasty little mistake.'

'Don't say that,' he urged her. 'All right, so you

don't have your dad's blood but you have his love. From what I know of your family he thinks the world of both you and Daisy. You are still who you are, Mary; the same person you were this morning. All right, maybe we all want to know where we came from but it isn't going to change your life because the man you know as your father didn't actually create you. Surely the fact that he's brought you up and loved you is the really important thing.'

'Yeah, I suppose so,' she said and suddenly she really did feel a little better. 'Yes it is, John, of course. It's just a bit of a weird feeling that's all. I need time to get used to it.'

'It might be a good idea not to brood on it though,' he said. 'Especially as you can't change what happened before you were even born.'

She looked at him. 'How come you are such a calming influence?' she asked.

'I'd much rather be an unsettling influence on women but they nearly always see me as a friend,' he said with a half-smile. 'So that seems to be my role in life, sadly.'

Managing a watery smile she asked, 'What are you doing around here anyway?'

'Being stood up by one of your lot,' he said.

'Oh?' she said, interested.

'I had a date with a woman from work. We'd arranged to meet outside the Adelphi. But she didn't show up so I was walking off my disappointment.'

'So I'm not the only one feeling low.'

'No, you're not.'

'I'm sorry to hear that.'

'Don't feel sorry for me, please,' he requested. 'That would kill off my confidence completely.'

'For what it's worth I think the woman who didn't show up is the loser.'

'Really?'

'Yes, I always found you rather a dish.'

'Now I know you're trying to make me feel better.'

'No I'm not, honestly, John,' she said. 'You've just given me a lecture about liking myself despite my dodgy ancestry. Now I'm giving you one about having confidence despite your bad luck with women, and that's all it is, bad luck. And luck can change.'

'I didn't realise you could be so sparky,' he said.

'You lived in the same house for quite a while. I should think that might have given you a clue.'

'Yeah, there is that,' he said with a wry grin.

'Anyway, I suppose I'd better get back,' she said.

'I was hoping you'd stay for another drink.'

'I would like to but I left the house in such a miserable state, Daisy and Dad will be worried.'

'Maybe we could meet up another time then,' he suggested.

'I'd like that, John,' she said. 'But what about you being my brother-in-law?'

'The marriage to Daisy is over in every way except on paper,' he reminded her.

'Yes, there is that,' she said. 'So, yes I would really like to meet up again.'

'I have a night off on Wednesday,' he said. 'We could have a drink and a chat or whatever you fancy doing. If you're not doing anything.'

'I'd really like that.'

'Shall I call for you at the house?' he asked.

'Better not, John. I think I'd feel a bit funny about it.'

'I'll meet you outside Hammersmith Station then,' he said. 'Shall we say eight o'clock?'

'I'll be there.' She turned to go. ''Bye for now.'

'Cheerio.'

'Oh, there you are,' said Daisy when Mary arrived home. 'You went out in such a state Dad and I have been worried.'

'Sorry about that,' said Mary.

'You seem to have cheered up.'

'Yes, I've managed to get things into perspective, thanks to your ex, Daisy.'

'John?'

'I ran into him down by the river and I poured my heart out to him over a gin and orange in the garden of the Dog and Pony.'

'Nice,' said Daisy.

Mary shot her a look. 'Are you being funny?'

'Not at all,' she said. 'I'm glad he helped you through it. John is very good like that.'

'I'm meeting him again as it happens,' Mary blurted out.

'What, for a date?'

'I suppose it is. You don't mind, do you?'

'Of course not,' Daisy said. 'He's a free man as far as I'm concerned.'

'I'm pleased about that,' said Mary. 'I wouldn't want to upset you. But I like John. I always have.'

Their father came into the room. 'Oh, you're back then, Mary, that's good,' he said. 'Sorry to have dumped that news on to you out of the blue. But I had to make you see what made your mum what she was when all this other stuff came out.'

'It's all right, Dad,' she said. 'I think I can cope with it now.'

'She's been talking to John and he's cheered her up.'

'What? Your John?'

'He isn't my John now, Dad,' said Daisy. 'Mary is going out with him on a date.'

'But he's a married man,' said Bill.

'Only on paper, Dad.'

'I am going out with him, not intending to marry him,' Mary made clear.

'Yes, of course. I'm sure it will be fine.'

Chapter Fifteen

One morning in early September Daisy gave her adored son a valedictory hug then handed him over to a complete stranger and left, fighting back the tears as she walked away.

'It's a big day for them,' said one of the other mums as a group of them headed out of the school gates.

'And for us,' said Daisy. 'I feel as though I've just abandoned my boy.'

The other woman laughed shakily. 'I'm wondering how I'll get through the day too.'

'We're soft, aren't we?' said Daisy. 'I mean, they are more than ready for school and it's the next stage in their development. But I loved having him around, even if he did sometimes drive me mad.'

'They'll never be quite the same once they've rubbed shoulders with the outside world without us there to protect them,' said the other mum.

Daisy was feeling so emotional she found herself laughing on the verge of tears. 'I suppose that's why we're upset; because we know they'll change,' she said, her voice cracking.

'Still, life goes on,' said her companion. 'At least we can have a cup of tea in peace.' She paused. 'Do you fancy joining me for a cuppa before we start the chores?'

Daisy would like nothing more than a chat with a mother of about her own age on this memorable morning. But there was something more import-ant she must do that could be put off no longer. There was no excuse now that she had free time without Sam.

'Any other day I'd love to but I have to go some-where straight from here,' she told her.

'That's fine,' said the woman pleasantly. 'See you later on when school is out then.'

'Can't wait,' said Daisy and hurried on her way.

Hester listened to what Daisy had to say in a state of shocked silence.

'How dreadfully sad,' she said when the young woman had finally finished speaking. 'How devastated you and Al must have been.'

'I was broken-hearted,' said Daisy. 'I imagine Al would have been upset too.'

Hester was only human. She wanted to expel a

tirade of abuse towards Daisy's mother along the lines of her being an evil witch to do such a dreadful thing. But that would only hurt Daisy so the words must remain unspoken.

'But today you have given me the most precious gift I could ever have: a grandchild who I already adore,' she said, casting aside her anger towards Bertha. 'I am so proud to be Sam's granny and I will be the best I can whatever Al decides to do about him. I promise you that, Daisy.'

'I'm so glad you're pleased, Hester,' said Daisy.

The older woman hugged Daisy as though she would never let her go.

'So how did it go with Al's mother this morning?' asked Mary that night.

'She was really sweet about it and didn't say a word out of place about Mum, though she must have felt like it,' said Daisy. 'She's thrilled to be Sam's gran as I knew she would be. She promised not to say anything to Al when he comes home; not until I've explained the whole thing to him.'

'That's good,' said Mary. 'It would be awful for him to hear about it second-hand, a bombshell like that.'

'Exactly,' said Daisy. 'I'm not looking forward to telling him but it has to be done. He has a right to know.'

'Still, it might be a while yet before you have to worry about that,' suggested Mary. 'It's taking for ever to get all the troops home from abroad.'

'That's true. And when he does turn up I don't know if he'll be as polite about our mum as his mother was and I probably won't be able to help myself making excuses for her.'

'It's only natural that you would. We always defend our own no matter what they've done. We can criticise them but God help anyone else who does.'

'Mm, it's funny the way that works,' said Daisy.

It had been quite a day, what with Hester becoming aware that she was a granny and Sam becoming a schoolboy. Both had turned out well as it happened though Sam hadn't quite grasped the fact yet that school wasn't something you only went to when you felt like it.

A few evenings later Hester walked up the garden path and knocked on the Blakes' front door.

'Hello dear,' she said when Mary opened it. 'My name is Hester Dawson. Your sister may have mentioned me.'

'She certainly has.' Mary smiled at her. 'Though nothing bad I promise you.'

'Is your dad at home by any chance?'

'Yes sure, please come in.'

Hester followed her into the Blakes' homely but somewhat drab living room where Bill was sitting in the armchair reading the newspaper; he rose politely when he saw that they had a visitor.

'I'm sorry to call on you out of the blue,' said Hester, having greeted him. 'But I recently found out that we share a grandson and I just wanted to say that if there's anything I can do to help at any time, I'd be happy to do it. I know you both look after Sam while Daisy is out at work. If you ever wanted to go out, for instance, please feel free to call on me. I do teach piano some evenings but am always free at the weekends and I know that Daisy works then. I was playing the organ at the Adelphi on a Saturday night for a while but that's finished now that people are coming back from the war.'

'It's very good of you to offer,' said Bill stiffly. 'But I don't go out of an evening.'

'You do sometimes like to go out for a game of darts with your mates, Dad,' Mary reminded him.

'Only very occasionally,' he said, looking at his daughter in an admonitory way. 'But you are here then anyway, Mary, to look after the boy.'

'Yes, but I might like to go out at night at the weekend sometimes,' she said, with John in mind. He had recently gone into the repair side of projectors so no longer had to work evenings. 'So it's good to know that we have some back-up. Thank you very much, Hester.'

'No trouble,' she said. 'I wanted to come and see you in person rather than sending a message through Daisy. I thought it only right as we have young Sam in common. I knew Daisy would be at work but it doesn't matter because it was you I wanted to speak to. I don't know if my son will want to take a part in Sam's life when he comes home and is told the truth but I have told Daisy that I want to be Sam's grandma whatever Al decides to do.'

'And we are very pleased about that, aren't we, Dad?' said Mary, shooting her father a look.

'Of course,' he said dutifully.

'Young Sam would be fine with me, in case you have doubts,' she said. 'I've brought up two boys of my own. Sam knows me quite well anyway.'

'We don't doubt your capabilities, not for a second, do we, Dad?' said Mary.

'Of course not,' he said. 'It's very good of you to offer, especially after what's happened.'

'That was none of your doing, was it?' she said. 'Anyway, I'd rather look forward than back.'

Bill nodded. 'Quite so,' he agreed.

'Would you like a cup of tea?' offered Mary. 'I was just about to put the kettle on.'

'Thank you but I must be going,' she said. 'But don't forget, if ever you need me, Daisy will tell you how to find me.'

'We'll definitely bear it in mind,' said Mary, and showed her to the door.

'What a lovely woman,' she said to her father when she went back into the room.

'She does seem all right,' he said. 'We won't need her though, will we?'

'We very well might, Dad,' she said in a firm tone. 'I don't want to spend every single Saturday night stuck indoors and it would do you good to get out now and again. She wants to help so why not let her?'

'I'm quite happy here at home of an evening with the wireless and the newspaper and I'm not being forced out because Al's mum wants to be involved with her grandchild.'

'You shouldn't be indoors, every single night of the week,' she said. 'You'll be old before your time.'

'I'm old already according to you.'

'Compared to me, of course you are. But you're not quite past it yet. Anyway, I'm very glad Hester came to see us. It will be nice for Sam if his grand-parents know each other.'

'I don't suppose we'll see much of her.'

'If you have your way we won't see anything of her,' she said. 'I don't know why you've taken against her.'

'I haven't,' he denied. 'She isn't the sort of woman I am used to, that's all, so I feel awkward.

'As far as I can make out the only woman you've ever known is Mum.'

'For all you know I might have had a lurid love life before I met your mother.'

'As you weren't much more than a boy, I very much doubt it. Not all women want to be like Mum was, you know. Just because Mrs Dawson is a bit out of the ordinary that doesn't mean she isn't nice.'

'I haven't suggested she isn't,' he said. 'I'm not comfortable with that sort of woman, that's all.'

'She a musician, Dad, and artistic people aren't usually run of the mill.'

'Exactly. I don't know what to say to her. I feel uncomfortable.'

'I suppose you'd be like that with any woman as you never mix with any,' she suggested. 'I think she's quite good-looking for her age.'

'I can't say I've noticed.'

'Did you lose your eyesight when you married Mum then?' she asked.

'There's no need to be rude.'

'Well, honestly,' she said. 'We get Sam's grand-mother round here begging to be involved with him and you give her the cold shoulder.'

'I didn't, did I?'

'Well you didn't exactly roll out the red carpet.'

'That isn't my way,' he said. 'Anyway, her son got my daughter into trouble.'

'Oh Dad, don't throw that one in. Daisy was nuts about the bloke so I doubt if he seduced her.'

'That isn't nice, dear.'

'Nor is you being offhand with Sam's grandma,' she said. 'And while we're having words, I don't want to hurt you but you need to know that I intend to carry on seeing John even though he is still legally married to Daisy. I really like him, Dad.'

Oh dear, he didn't seem to be making much of a job of being a dad to his daughters. They lived in a different world to him: Daisy getting knocked up; Mary going out with a married man. Then he remembered the circumstances of his own marriage and realised that nothing had really changed, except that he was the older generation now.

'Maybe they'll get a divorce eventually,' he suggested hopefully.

'I should think they would at some point but I don't know for sure, Dad,' she said. 'For the moment I'm just enjoying his company and not looking beyond that.'

'That's up to you, Mary,' he said. 'I'm long past the stage where I have an influence over your life.'

'I'll always be influenced by you, Dad,' she said. 'But I am old enough to make my own decisions.'

'Quite so.' He looked ponderous for a few moments then said, 'I will bear Mrs Dawson's offer in mind. You never know when we might both want to go out. So if she calls again I will try to be nicer to her.'

'Thank goodness for that,' she said, smiling at him.

The new year of 1946 brought no lessening of the austerity that gripped Britain, an odd reward for having won the war, many people thought. Rationing was still severe and the bomb damage remained untouched except by weeds and stinging nettles which flourished on the bombsites. People grumbled but hoped for better things to come.

Now that Bill and Mary no longer worked long wartime hours Daisy was able to take on a few more evening shifts at the Adelphi, with her sister's and father's full co-operation and Hester's offer on hand if needed.

'Nice to have you around more often, Daisy,' said Doreen one night when they were on duty. 'We make a great team, you and me.'

'We certainly do,' she agreed. 'The cinema still seems to be people's favourite pastime, doesn't it? I thought the numbers might drop after the war now that people don't need to escape but it's still packed out every night.'

'There's no danger to escape from but life is still pretty dismal out there,' said Doreen. 'A night at the flicks is still one of the best pick-me-ups.'

'Quite a few new faces among the staff lately,' Daisy remarked.

'All the grannies have gone back to being housewives now that the war workers are back. But I reckon that you and I have been here longer than any of them.'

'Mr Pickles' old favourites,' said Daisy.

'Not so much of the old.'

'Longstanding then.'

'That's better.'

'Have you heard from Dickie Dawson lately?' Daisy inquired casually.

'Not for a while but in his last letter he said he was hoping we could meet up when he finally gets back.'

'How do you feel about that?'

'Pleased. It will be good to meet him and see what happens,' Doreen said. 'I only know him through letters and the night he had his crisis so we might not hit it off under normal circumstances. But he does seem nice. I've been a widow for quite a while now so I'm completely out of the habit of male company. I suppose it's time I made an effort to put that right.'

'I've got an ordeal to face when Al finally makes it back,' said Daisy, having already confided in her best friend about the letters in the eaves. 'The truth must be told.'

'Yes, I suppose so.'

'I'm really nervous about it and feeling guilty about what I have to tell him.'

'You've done nothing wrong,' Doreen reminded her. 'You don't need to feel bad.'

'You know what they say about shooting the messenger,' she said. 'Anyway, it was my mother who did the deed so it will rub off on me, naturally.'

'He won't blame you,' said Doreen. 'He's too much of a nice bloke to do that.'

'Yes, I always found him to be rather lovely. But that was a very long time ago.'

'Indeed,' Doreen agreed. 'We've all changed since those pre-war days.'

It was spring before Al finally got back and he arrived one evening and made his homecoming as ordinary as possible. He simply pulled the key through the letterbox with the string, opened the door and called out, 'I'm home, Mum. Are you in?' as though he had only been to the corner shop to buy a newspaper.

There was no such holding back from his outgoing mother though.

'Al,' she cried, hugging him and letting the tears flow. 'Oh my boy. Home at last.' She drew back. 'Let me look at you. Oh my word, you're just as handsome as ever.'

'And you're as biased in my favour as you've always been.' He grinned.

'Of course I am,' she said. 'But you're still my boy. Sit down, let me get you something to eat and drink.'

'Don't fuss, Mum,' he said gently. 'Let's just sit down and you can give me all the news.'

'You're the one with all the news,' she said. 'I haven't been anywhere. You've been to foreign parts. You must have lots of interesting things to tell me.'

'I've been away at the war, Mum, and that's the same wherever you are in the world, I should think,' he said. 'I wasn't on a sightseeing tour in France and Africa. The best thing about it was my mates and I had some great ones.' He decided not to add that some of them had perished in the line of duty. 'I'd rather hear about you and what's been going on here. Is Dickie back?'

'No, not yet.'

'I don't suppose he'll be long; they are doing their best to get everyone home as soon as they can.'

He was still her lovely Al; warm-hearted and caring. But the gleam in his eye had gone, which wasn't surprising considering what he must have been through. What that had been exactly, she would probably never know. He certainly wasn't going to tell her at the moment, anyway. But it was so good to have him home.

When Al went up to bed that night, he thought how unreal it felt to be home for good. For nearly six years he had lived in a male environment with all its roughness and jovial vulgarity. His mates had been everything to him; all in the same boat and longing to be home but rarely short of a joke or two. Now it was just himself and Mum and he felt confined even though he loved her dearly. Fitting into a household routine was bound to feel strange at first, too, after the hurly-burly of army life which had been strictly structured but full of company.

His brother would be home soon and tomorrow he would go and see if any of his mates were back yet and also find out what the chances of employment were. He had to wait until he was formally demobbed before he could make any serious moves but there was no harm in making a few inquiries.

As he got into bed with crisp, clean sheets it felt like luxury. It was so good to be back. He would

314

enjoy his demob leave.

The next morning Hester waited for the right moment to broach a certain subject. She and Al had sat talking until late last night but she thought she would let him have a night's sleep before she mentioned it.

'Lovely porridge, Mum,' he said.

'Is it really?' She was surprised because as a rule porridge was far too commonplace to inspire compliments.

'Oh not half. After six years of army porridge it tastes like heaven. No one makes lumpy porridge like the British Army. Me and the lads used to say they had the lumps made specially and put in after it was cooked to stop us being fussy.'

She laughed. 'You haven't lost your sense of humour then.'

'Without that you wouldn't survive in the army during a war,' he said. 'I'm lucky. I inherited mine from you. You always enjoy a joke don't you, Mum?'

'I have my moments,' she said.

'You haven't had it easy here on your own with all the bombing,' he said more seriously. 'I was worried about you. I expect Dickie was too.'

'A sense of humour came in handy then too. But it's all over now, thank God.'

'Yeah. We must look to the future now. Are you still teaching, Mum?'

'You bet,' she said. 'I lost some of my pupils to evacuation but I'm back to full strength now.'

'Did some of them lose interest while they were away and not come back to lessons?'

'A few didn't return but there are always new people wanting lessons.'

'Must have been hard for you with Dickie and me both away.' Unwittingly, he had given her the opening she had been waiting for.

'It was but I managed and people were very good, the neighbours and so on.' She paused. 'Actually, Al, I have become quite friendly with your ex-girlfriend Daisy and she's been a good friend to me.'

'Daisy,' he said, his face working as he said her name.

'Yes. That's right.'

He put his spoon down and looked at her. 'That's a bit odd isn't it, Mum? You two being friends. I mean the mother and the ex-girlfriend.'

'People look out for each other in wartime,' she said. 'And she looked out for me because she knew I was on my own. We ran into each other one day at the shops and it went from there. I'm very fond of her as it happens so I will be continuing with the friendship, which is why I wanted you to know. But don't worry, she won't be coming here.'

'Good,' he said and resumed eating.

'The thing is, Al, she wants to see you when you have some time to spare.'

He looked up sharply. 'What would she want from me after all these years?'

'She doesn't want anything from you,' Hester told him. 'I can promise you that. And it will be a one-off.'

'But why on earth does she want to see me?'

'She'll tell you that herself. I told her I would

pass on the message, that's all.'

He knew his mother inside out and he could tell from her tone of voice that she would say no more on the matter. Mum and Daisy friends, well that was a turn-up for the books. 'Where is she living, now that she's married?'

'The family home,' she replied. 'She never moved away from there anyway but her marriage didn't work out so they split up a while ago.'

'Oh.'

'Maybe you could call round there sometime when it's convenient for you. She only works in the evenings so she's around during the day, apart from shopping. Her little boy is at school and she hasn't found a suitable day job yet so she's on her own.'

'What about that bossy mother of hers?' he said. 'She'll not be pleased to see me.'

'Daisy's mother died, Al,' she told him, frowning. 'She was killed in an air raid.'

His features stiffened and his neck coloured up. 'Oh dear, I'm sorry. I didn't realise.'

'Of course you didn't, how would you?'

'Exactly. Anyway if I happen to be in that area with time on my hands, I'll call in to see Daisy,' he said casually. 'But I won't put myself out.'

'That's up to you,' she said. 'I've done my part by passing on the message.'

'What this cinema needs is a really good organist,' said Bert Pickles, chatting to Daisy and Doreen in the foyer on their way to their places for the evening performance that same night. 'We haven't had a decent one since before the war.'

317

'I wouldn't say that, Mr Pickles,' said Daisy. 'There have been a few good ones. Hester Dawson was excellent.'

'She was about the best since before the war,' he agreed. 'But she left to make way for people returning from the war and we haven't had a decent one since.'

'Oh I don't know, Mr Pickles,' said Doreen. 'They've all been proficient.'

'Proficient, yes, but lacking that something special which boils down to personality and that shows in the way they play as well as their rapport with the audience,' he said. 'The best one we've ever had was Al Dawson. Is he back?'

'Not as far as I know,' said Daisy. 'But I think he's expected at any time.'

'If you hear he's home, could you let me know,' he requested. 'I'd love to get him back.'

'I'll let you know if I hear anything,' she said.

'Thank you, now off you go to your places,' he said. 'You're in the stalls tonight.'

As Daisy walked away, her stomach was churning at the mention of Al's name. She was particularly sensitive because she had things to tell him when he finally turned up and, as a letter wouldn't be appropriate in this instance, she would have to see him for a proper conversation.

After spending the day looking for mates only to find that they were either still away or out somewhere, Al went to the local pub that night. It was odd to think that before he went away to war he hadn't been old enough legally to drink alcohol. Now he could down a pint like a veteran. Nights spent in the NAAFI, when they'd had time off from duty, had taught him that.

So what was next for him after his official demob? Britain was in a state of austerity and jobs wouldn't be plentiful until the country got going again and manufacturing was fully underway. The war had apparently left Britain broke and in debt to America so it might take a while.

But there was always his music. His plans to make a full living from it had been scuppered by the war; maybe this was his chance to make it work. He'd lost six years of his life to the army so he ought to give it a serious try. Now that his father's debt was paid off and the war over there was no excuse – he would go to the newsagent tomorrow and order *The Stage*. They usually had jobs in his line of work advertised in there.

It was an odd thing to realise that, after longing to come home with all his heart, it now seemed a bit of an anticlimax. He felt lost here at home and lonely without his army mates around him. When he'd left school at fourteen and got a job in a factory with music as a second string to his bow, he'd thought he had it all planned out. Now he had to start again in his mid-twenties.

He ordered another drink and was beginning to feel better. Having to go away to war had taught him that there were not many things in life you could rely on. But one of the few certainties was that a pint or two always cheered you up. It never failed. When you'd been in combat there was a need for that.

He turned his mind to Daisy Blake and wondered again what she could possibly want with him after giving him the elbow all those years ago. He didn't want to be in too much of a hurry to go round there after the way she had treated him but he suspected that curiosity wouldn't allow him to leave it too long.

Two days later he stood at the front door that held so many memories for him. It was dark red and the paint had seen better days, like all the others in the street. But it seemed like yesterday since he had last been here. More nervous than he cared to admit, he lifted the knocker.

Daisy opened the door and stood there staring at him because she was so pleased to see him. She'd seen him briefly at the cinema the night he had played there but she'd been too startled to study his looks. Now she could see how much he'd changed. She remembered him as fresh-faced and boyish. In the intervening years his features had firmed and matured. He was still very good-looking but not in the same way. The youthful bloom was absent, as was the beaming smile, understandably given the circumstances but it was more than that. There was something missing: the light in his eyes.

'I heard you wanted to see me,' he said at last.

'Yes, I'm sorry to keep you standing there,' she said, opening the door wider. 'Thanks for coming.'

'Mum seemed keen for me to do so,' he said as they went into the living room, which was exactly as he remembered with its traditional and rather dull furnishings.

'Yes, I asked her to mention it to you.'

'Sorry to hear about your mother,' he said politely.

You probably won't be when I've told you what I have to, she thought, but said, 'Thank you. It was a terrible shock. It shouldn't have been since bombs were raining down on us but when you've been getting away with it for a few years you start to think your luck will last for ever.'

'Yeah, I'm sure.'

'Would you like a cuppa?' she asked.

'No thanks,' he said. 'I'd rather just know what it is you want to see me about.'

'Please sit down.'

He did as she asked, carefully avoiding the sofa which he had shared with her on so many occasions, hardly able to keep their hands off each other back then. Now he tried to avoid looking at her but was unable to stop himself. Her physical appearance had altered. When they had been together she had been a very pretty girl. Now she was a sublimely beautiful woman.

As a girl she had been part of that bright, pre-war world when anything had seemed possible. He'd grown up since those gloriously heady days. Seeing her again brought back the pain and desolation he'd felt at the time she'd disappeared from his life when he had been away from home and afraid, even though he had put up a front for his mates. He never wanted to be that vulnerable again.

'I'd better get on with it then, hadn't I?' she said.

'Yeah, I think that would be a good idea.'

Hester was waiting in the queue at the green-grocer's. News had got around that they would be having some onions in at ten o'clock and women had answered the call in abundance. There were a lot in front of Hester but she was determined to wait because now that Al was back she made more of an effort than she would just for herself to make decent meals.

'He won't start selling 'em until the dot of ten,' said the woman in front of her, turning around companionably. 'They're buggers for that. He's probably had them there since nine.'

'The traders want to be fair to everyone I suppose,' suggested Hester.

'They like to keep us waiting I reckon because they have all the power, which they won't have when things are plentiful again,' said the woman.

'There might be something in that,' agreed Hester.

'By the time it gets to our turn they'll probably be sold out,' said her companion.

'I've had that happen to me a good few times too,' said Hester. 'You wait for ages and come away empty-handed.'

'I didn't think we'd still be queuing and short of food a year after the end of the war, did you?'

'No I did not. I think we all thought that everything would go back to normal right away. I suppose we should have guessed it would take time.'

'Not this long though. I don't think anyone expected this.'

Hester nodded in agreement. The woman turned around and Hester drifted into her own thoughts and the thing that was most on her mind.

Would Al go to see Daisy today? She'd not mentioned it again since telling him his ex-girlfriend wanted to see him. She didn't think it was her place.

She was very fond of Daisy and adored Al. The two of them had seemed so right for each other all those years ago. In a perfect world or a Hollywood film they would run into each other's arms when the truth was out. But she knew that was unlikely to happen because real life wasn't like that.

If Daisy's mother hadn't interfered they would have been celebrating his homecoming together. The woman must have been deranged to do such a terrible thing. But she supposed when you had daughters you'd do anything to save their reputation. Mothers of sons were just as protective. Hester's biggest fear had been one of her boys getting a girl they didn't love into trouble and being forced to marry them. Many lives were ruined that way.

'We're on our way at last,' said the woman in front as the queue began to move.

Oh well, thought Hester, Al and Daisy would do what they wanted no matter how much she worried, so she must leave them to it.

Chapter Sixteen

Al listened without interruption as Daisy told him the whole story, his expression becoming grimmer with every word.

'Well, it isn't like me to be lost for words but I really don't know what to say, Daisy,' he said, which wasn't strictly true because he had plenty to say about the meddling of Bertha Blake but he knew Daisy's filial instinct would be to defend her and, even after all this time, he didn't want to hurt her.

'I was very shocked when I found the letters and realised what had happened,' she said. 'I can still hardly believe that Mum would do such a thing.'

'It does seem very extreme,' he said in a controlled manner. 'I was always aware that your mother never took to me but I didn't know her feelings went that deep.'

'She'd already died by the time I found out so I never had the chance to talk to her about it,' she explained. 'This might sound a bit naive but I was wondering if the fact that she tried to tell us about the letters and didn't destroy them means that she regretted what she'd done and wanted the truth to come out at some point.'

'Maybe,' he said tactfully but he wasn't in a frame of mind to think well of Mrs Blake.

'It wasn't only our lives she messed with; it was

John's too,' Daisy went on to say. 'He only stepped in so that I could keep the baby. She would have forced me to give him up otherwise.'

He winced at the heartlessness of it. 'It must have been very hard for you.'

'It was awful and I was very grateful to John. He was always a good friend but that didn't last long after we got married. It was a complete disaster because friendship wasn't enough for marriage for us, especially with a baby to care for with all its noise and disruption. I know it works for some people but it didn't for us. It was a mutual decision for him to leave. We'd have grown to hate each other if he'd stayed any longer.'

'So you were on your own again.'

'Single, yes, but never on my own because I had the family behind me. Apart from the moral support they also made it possible for me to work which I need to do with a child to bring up.'

He was still too shocked to be able to think straight but said quickly, 'Obviously I will help with that once I'm working again.'

'That isn't why I asked you to come here,' she made clear in a confident manner. 'I thought you deserved to know the truth; that I didn't desert you and I was as hurt as you must have been when I thought you had turned your back on me. I also thought you had a right to know that you have a son. But I want nothing from you, Al, honestly. I think I'm doing a pretty good job of bringing Sam up but you can be involved in his life if you wish. Of course, because of the way things are, it would have to be on my terms. I am very protective of him and I won't have him hurt or let down. So if you do decide to take part in his life you need to be serious about the commitment. Don't come and see him a couple of times then disappear. He's a lovely kid but all children are naughty and difficult from time to time. I won't think ill of you if you'd rather not.'

'Anyone would think you are trying to put me off.'

'No. Not at all,' she said. 'I just don't want my boy to be hurt, that's all.'

'I don't know much about kids but I've never seen myself as a child beater,' he said sharply.

Daisy turned pink. 'I suppose I asked for that.'

'You are coming on a bit strong.'

'My maternal instincts are going a bit haywire I suppose after being a single mum for such a long time. But it must be a huge shock for you to suddenly find out that you have a five-year-old child. So if you need time to think about it before you decide what you want to do, that's fine with me.'

'I'll be thinking about nothing else,' he said. 'But I will let you know.'

He went over to the sideboard and picked up a framed photograph. 'Is this him?' he asked.

She nodded.

'A fine boy; looks very much like you.'

'Yeah, everybody says that,' she said. 'He really is the most darling child.'

'Not surprising, considering who his parents are,' he said with a wry grin.

She managed a smile but the atmosphere was far too tense for humour.

'So when will you get officially demobbed?' she

inquired, glad to change the subject.

'Not long now and I'll be collecting my demob suit,' he said. 'I can't wait to get out of this uniform. I was proud to wear it but enough is enough.'

'Do you have any definite plans?'

'I'm hoping to get my music career off the ground. If I don't try now I never will. I can only fail and there is no shame in that. Trying is the important part. Meanwhile I shall need to earn a living so I'll get a day job of some sort.'

'I wish you well with that but I hope we haven't seen the last of you at the Adelphi.'

'I'm sure you haven't,' he said. 'In fact I might go along and see if they might want me back after I'm officially demobbed. I'll need steady earnings while I try to build some sort of career with the piano. In fact, I might offer to do a one-off there while I'm on demob leave. Is Bert Pickles still the manager?'

'He certainly is and I'm sure he'll welcome you with open arms. Funnily enough, he mentioned you the other day; said you were the best organist we'd ever had and asked me to let him know if I heard you were back.'

'Oh what a nice thing to say, though I'm sure it isn't true.'

'No need to be modest, Al,' she said. 'It doesn't suit you.'

He shrugged, grinning.

'Anyway, if you'd like to take the letters to read on your own, you are very welcome. But I'll have them back when you've finished with them if you don't mind.'

'Of course.'

She gave a nervous laugh and blurted out, 'It seems odd, us being here like this, awkward with each other. When you think how close we were all those years ago.'

He doubted if he would ever forget. If this revelation had happened sooner they might have been able to carry on where they had left off. But too much time had passed and they didn't know each other now. The vulnerable girl he had been in love with was now a confident woman who knew her own mind and wasn't afraid to call the shots. A different person altogether and he didn't feel at ease with her in the way he used to. 'It was a long time ago and life moves on. So much has happened. What with my being away at the war and you becoming a mum, we're not the same people now.'

'No. We are serious grown-ups,' she said and added swiftly, because the atmosphere between them was so uncomfortable it was embarrassing, 'Anyway, that was all I wanted to see you for, just for you to know the truth. If you'd like to see the letters, I'll get them for you.'

'Yeah, I might as well take a look,' he said, not really knowing if he wanted to see them or not. As the late Mrs Blake had successfully demolished their relationship there didn't seem to be much point. But Daisy seemed to want it and there was no harm in having a glance at them.

He left with the letters in a brown paper bag. He should have been glad to know that Daisy hadn't deserted him but all he felt was cheated of something precious.

Daisy felt deflated after he left without really knowing why. She was a sensible woman and hadn't been expecting any suggestion of reconciliation after all this time; she didn't know if she would want it if the subject had come up. But she had felt about as close to him as a stranger in a queue, which was a disappointing way to feel when they had once been so very close and she had loved him so much. That was what came from working in a cinema, she thought wryly; you got to believe in all those happy endings.

Al sat on the edge of his bed reading the letters. He was going through them in date order and the early ones were love letters. He smiled at the romantic language. It was hard to believe he had ever been that soppy. As he worked his way through the missives they became sadder and more desperate as both he and Daisy thought they had been abandoned.

He remembered exactly how he'd felt at that time and he could feel her pain as she wrote a letter telling him she was pregnant and begging him to get in touch. It was too much and he put his head in his hands and wept.

At the risk of getting her head bitten off, Hester decided to dispense with tact that evening over their meal.

'Did you go to see Daisy, Al?' she asked as he had said he might go that morning.

'Yeah.'

'How did it go?'

329

'All right I think, but we both felt awkward.'

'Inevitable I suppose, after not seeing each other for such a long time and the drama of what happened with Daisy's mum.'

'Yeah, I'm still trying to come to terms with the antics of Mrs Blake,' he said.

'It was a terrible thing to do. She was obviously a very possessive mother.'

'She must have had a cruel streak as well,' he said. 'She never liked me. She made that obvious to me, though she kept her dislike hidden in front of Daisy when it became clear that the rest of the family liked me. But she was always warning me with those mean eyes of hers.'

'Well, she isn't here to defend herself so I think we should change the subject and concentrate on happier things. How do you feel about being a dad?'

'Terrified.'

She laughed. 'It must have been a shock. But it isn't that frightening surely, though I suppose it could seem a bit overwhelming coming out of the blue like that.'

'Five years old and I knew nothing about him,' he said. 'Some men would run a mile.'

'You won't though...'

'Of course not, Mum. I won't shirk my responsibility. I shall pay maintenance to Daisy as soon as I'm working again. I've told her that.'

'You're only going to be involved financially then,' she said.

'I'm not sure yet. If things had been normal and I'd known him since he was a baby it would be the natural thing. But suddenly having to become a dad to a five-year-old boy; that is seriously scary, especially as I don't know anything about kids.'

'So you've fought in a war and faced danger on a regular basis and you're scared of getting involved with your own little boy?'

'It's a bit more complicated than that, Mum,' he pointed out. 'It's a serious commitment. Daisy has made it very clear that she's in charge and I risk letting him down at my peril. She's changed a lot since I knew her. She's very sure of herself now.'

'Most mothers are when it comes to their kids; they are protective of their offspring. It's only natural. But you're not the sort of man to let him down.'

'No, but I might not always get it right,' he said. 'That's what I'm afraid of.'

'Nobody gets things right all the time,' she reminded him.

'I suppose not,' he said. 'But I don't have to be involved with him at all if I'd rather not. Daisy made that very clear. It's entirely up to me.'

'Hmm. But I know that you'll regret it if you don't become a dad to him, albeit just a part-time one.'

'I don't know Mum,' he said. 'I mean, what do I know about little kids?'

'You'll soon get the hang of it,' she said. 'I fell in love with him when I first saw him and when Daisy told me I was his grandma I was overjoyed. Apparently her father told her to go ahead and tell me and not wait until you got back because he thought no more time should be wasted. He thought I should have been told right away after

Sam was born, apparently, but Daisy was worried it would cause trouble between you and me because she thought you had turned your back on her and she knew I wouldn't approve of that. Anyway, such a move would have upset her mother.'

'Mr Blake was always much nicer to me than his wife,' he said. 'That's the sort of thing he would do because he seems like a decent bloke.'

'Anyway, it seems young Sam missed his other gran after she died,' she said. 'For all her faults Mrs Blake was a very loving grandma.'

'I bet you are too.'

'I adore him. And I think you would too if you got to know him.'

'We'll see. I need time to think about it. It's a very serious commitment. I have to be really sure that I can make a decent job of it.'

'Don't leave it too long,' she advised. 'Every day missed of a child's life is a tragedy.'

'Don't go all poetic on me, Mum,' he said. 'I've got a lot on my mind. How I am going to earn a living for start.'

'You're not even officially demobbed yet.'

'I soon will be so I need to think ahead and make a few inquiries.'

'I suppose so.' She knew her son wouldn't waste any time before looking for a job. He'd proved what a hard worker he was in the past. She wondered if he would pursue his music career or look for something safer. But now wasn't the time to ask. She'd pushed her luck far enough for the moment. He might be her son but, as a grown man, he was entitled to his privacy.

'Dare I ask if you heard any more from Al?' asked Doreen as she and Daisy walked home from work together one night. 'Or is it too personal?'

'No to both questions,' she said. 'No I haven't heard from him and of course it isn't too personal. I miss seeing his mum but I don't feel able go round and see her as I normally would because he'll be there.'

'Does that matter?'

'It does to me. I'd feel awkward, as if I'm pursuing him. If he wants to be involved in Sam's life it has to come from him without any influence from me. I think I was a bit hard on him actually. You know, warning him not to get involved if he isn't serious about it.'

'He wouldn't think you are pursuing him if you go round there. He knows that you and his mum are friends.'

'I suppose so.'

'He hasn't seen Sam yet, has he?'

'No.'

'Mm, that's strange.'

'Not at all,' said Daisy sharply, instinctively defensive of Al. 'It was a shock for him suddenly hearing that he's got a child. Of course he needs time to think about it, especially as he knows that if he does come into Sam's life he'll have to be serious about it or he'll have me on his back.'

'All right, Daisy, no need to snap my head off.'

'Sorry.'

'Anyone would think you still cared for him.'

'I expect I'll always feel something for him as the father of my child and because I loved him so much all those years ago but it's been too long for what you are suggesting. I want to be fair to the man, that's all. He'll be in touch about Sam when he's ready.'

'Yeah, course he will,' said Doreen diplomatically. 'Anyway, here's my turning so I'll say goodnight. See you tomorrow.'

''Night Doreen,' Daisy said and went on her way.

Al knew he should have returned the letters to Daisy but he didn't want to part with them and wasn't quite sure why. Maybe because they were evidence of something very special, long gone. He had once heard that nostalgia didn't start until you were forty, in which case it had visited him early, if that was what was causing all this sentimentality. But he really must get them back to her. If he went round there during the day the boy would be safely out of the way at school. He wasn't ready for that particular challenge yet and he was deeply ashamed about it.

Sitting on his bed he realised that he had come home from the war thinking all his troubles were behind him. Instead he had walked into a whole load more. In a way it was easier being on the battlefields than wrestling with these emotional problems. There it was kill or be killed: there were no choices. Now he was constantly thinking about personal matters when he should be worrying about the future and how he was going to earn his living.

He put the letters back into the bag and picked up his copy of *The Stage* and lay on his bed reading it to see what jobs were available.

'Hello Mrs Dawson,' said Bill Blake on opening the front door to Hester the following evening. 'Daisy is out at work.'

'Yes I know, and that's why I'm here,' she said. 'It's you I've come to see. I wonder if I might have a word with you about something that concerns us both.'

'Of course,' he said, opening the door wider. 'Come on in, please.'

'Thank you, and the name is Hester.'

'I'm Bill,' he told her as they went inside.

The next morning after breakfast, when Sam was playing outside because it was Saturday, Daisy's father had something to say to her.

'I'm very sorry, love, but something has come up and I have to go out tonight so I won't be able to look after Sam.'

'And I've already arranged to go out with John,' added Mary, looking concerned.

'Oh blimey, that's a blow,' said Daisy.

'I'm ever so sorry love,' said her dad. 'But they want me in the darts team because someone has fallen ill and dropped out and I can't let them down because they are good mates. I didn't realise that Mary would be going out when I told them I would do it.'

'Sorry, sis,' said Mary.

'That's all right, both of you.' Daisy appreciated what they did for her and knew they were entitled to their own lives. 'You do more than enough for me. I'll pop round to the Adelphi as soon as they open and tell Mr Pickles that I won't be in today.

He won't be best pleased, this being Saturday and our busiest night, but it can't be helped.'

'Why not ask Sam's grandma if she can stand in for us?' suggested Bill. 'She has offered to have him any time and I think she would love it.'

'Mm, that's a thought,' said Daisy. 'It would mean I wouldn't have to let Mr Pickles down as well as save a night's wages. It's very short notice though.'

'The sooner you get round there to ask her the better then,' said Bill.

'I'd rather not go round there,' she said.

'You'll have to, won't you? Since we're not on the telephone and neither is she. Anyway it's only right for you to ask her yourself rather than one of us going round there for you. She'll be ever so pleased to see you. You said you haven't been round there lately.'

'Mm, I suppose so,' she agreed thoughtfully. 'Would you look after Sam for me while I pop round there then to save dragging him away from his play? I'll be as quick as I can.'

'Course we will,' said Mary, seeming more than happy to oblige.

'Daisy,' said Hester with a beaming smile as she opened the door. 'How lovely to see you. Come on in.'

'I'm after a favour actually,' explained Daisy as they went into the living room, relieved that there was no sign of Al.

'What is it you want then, love?' asked Hester.

'I'm stuck for a babysitter when I go to work later,' she said. 'And I wondered if you might be able to help me out.'

Hester appeared to think about it for a moment. 'I'll willingly do it but I'll have to have him here initially because I have a pupil coming round later on. Not for a lesson; just to go over a few points for an exam she has coming up. I'm doing it as a special favour. She won't be here long but I have to wait in for her.'

Daisy was doubtful, wondering if Sam would be happy out of his own environment without her, and also mindful of the fact that Hester had other things to do. 'I don't want to interfere with your arrangements,' she said.

'You won't be. The pupil won't be here for more than ten minutes or so. I'll give Sam his tea here then take him home and put him to bed and stay with him until you get home from work. I'll enjoy it.'

That sounded better so Daisy said, 'If you're sure.'

'Absolutely.'

'Thanks Hester. You're a real pal.'

'A pleasure.'

'Al's not around then,' Daisy blurted out, much against her better judgement.

'Still in bed,' said the older woman. 'He's making up for six years of early mornings in the army.'

'I don't blame him,' said Daisy. 'I haven't had a lie-in since Sam arrived.'

Hester smiled. 'So you'll bring young Sam over later then.'

Daisy nodded.

'I'll look forward to it,' she said.

Daisy was far too grateful to her for solving her

babysitting problem to notice the satisfied gleam in Hester's eye.

It was late that same afternoon and Al was on his way home from the West End where he had had a meeting with a man about a job with the famous dance band, the Ted Scott Orchestra. Having previously shown what he could do on the piano at an audition, this discussion had taken place in the bar of a hotel near Piccadilly. Musicians didn't always work office hours or hold interviews in traditional venues.

It was a very exciting opportunity for Al. His interviewer was acting on behalf of the bandleader and the job was regular pianist with the band. It was a dream job for Al and the man had given out positive signals but said he would let him know for definite later on. Unfortunately there was a major snag but Al would decide what to do about that if he was actually offered the job. Until then he would keep it to himself.

It had felt good to be looking for work again and had given him a feeling of normality after years of uncertainty and a way of life that had been forced upon him. He had enjoyed the break from the emotional trauma that had plagued him since certain events had come to light too. As he approached the house he was looking forward to a nice quiet cup of tea with his mum.

He turned the key in the lock, opened the door and called out, 'I'm home, Mum. Are you in?'

'Hello,' said a bright young voice and, looking down, he saw a blond-haired boy emerge from the living room. 'I'm Sam. I'm having tea here today.'

'Are you?' said Al thickly, having known immediately who he was and almost too emotional to speak.

'Yeah. Granddad and Auntie Mary can't look after me today while Mum is at work so Hester is doing it.'

'I see,' said Al.

The boy thrust forward a small fabric bag that made a chinking sound when he moved it. 'Do you want to see my marbles after tea?' he asked. 'My mum got them for me in the market.'

'I'd like that, Sam.'

'She queued up for ages for them,' he said proudly.

'You must have a very nice mum.'

'My mum can do anything. She says I'm the best boy in all the world.'

Al's mother swept on to the scene. 'You two have met then,' she said.

'Sort of,' said Al.

'Tea will be ready in a few minutes. So if you could take Sam to wash his hands please, Al, we can get started. I'm taking him home after we've eaten and I don't want him to be too late to bed.'

'Come on then, little 'un,' said Al, leading the boy towards the kitchen sink. 'Let's get some Lifebuoy soap on to those hands of yours.'

Hester was smiling as she lit the gas under the kettle. So far so good; father and son were together for the first time. What happened next was out of her hands but the first step had been taken. Sometimes people needed a prod to send them in the right direction. It was amazing what you could do with a little co-operation. Bill Blake was a decent sort of a bloke to go along with her plan and suddenly be unavailable for babysitting today. They had agreed that a few porky pies had been forgivable under the circumstances.

That Saturday teatime proved to be one of the most joyful experiences of Al's life. Sam had to be told several times by his grandmother to stop talking and eat his food. But Al was so taken with him he just watched and listened as this little miracle, who had come from Al and was a part of him, went about the business of being a little boy. He chatted about his family, his friends, his toys and his great wish to have a pet, preferably a cat.

'All my friends have got an animal living with them,' he said. 'Some have a dog but I like cats best. The people next door have got a lovely black one. He sits on our coalshed in the sun and lets me stroke him.'

'Do your mum and your granddad not want one in the house then?' asked Al, finding himself riveted by the boy's every word.

'My grandma wouldn't have an animal in the house; she said they were too smelly and made a mess,' he informed them. 'So that's why we don't have one.'

'I see.' Al thought it best not to remind him that his grandma wasn't around now. The family must have their reasons for not having a pet.

Al hadn't expected to feel such a strong rush of love for the boy, unlike anything he had ever experienced before. He knew beyond a doubt that he wanted to be with him, to protect him, to do things for him and be a part of his life. He would go to see Daisy tomorrow to get something organised.

'Next Saturday,' exclaimed Al the next morning in the privacy of the Blakes' front room. 'Surely I can see him before then.'

'He's at school during the week,' said Daisy.

'What about this afternoon?'

'Mary and John are taking him to the zoo,' she replied. 'The arrangements have already been made and he's looking forward to going out with them.'

'But I'm his dad and I want to get to know him,' he said, irritable because he felt so let down. 'How can I do that if you're not going to let me see him?'

'Stop being so dramatic, Al,' she admonished. 'Of course I am going to let you see him but I can't change everything to suit you on the spur of the moment. He'll be disappointed if he can't go out with his auntie. He's very close to her.'

'He'd get close to me if he was given the chance to get to know me.'

'Oh for goodness' sake,' she said, exasperated. 'I want you to be a dad to Sam, of course I do, but he's a child, not a toy; children are creatures of routine. They need stability in their lives.'

'Anyone would think I was going to drag him off abroad or something,' he said. 'All I want is some time with him.'

'And you can have it. But in such a way as not to upset him.'

'That is the last thing I would want to do.'

'I know you wouldn't mean to,' she said in a

341

softer tone. 'But I have to be confident that you'll be around for the long term and won't disappear when the novelty wears off. Don't forget, Al, when you start work again you won't have so much time on your hands as you have now and he doesn't need to get used to seeing a lot of you only to have it cut down because you are busy working.'

'All fathers have to work,' he pointed out. 'Anyway, when did being a dad become all about rules and regulations?'

'When the child's parents aren't together and the father is a stranger to the child, I suppose,' she came back at him.

'You never used to be this stroppy, Daisy,' he said.

'And I didn't used to be a parent with responsibilities when I knew you before,' she said. 'As we have both already agreed, we are different people now and life is more serious. Sam means everything to me and I have to look out for him.'

'I want to do that too.'

'In time I'm sure you can. But for the moment, slowly does it. Why don't you have him on Saturday afternoon as I suggested? Perhaps you could take him out somewhere, to the park and the sweetshop maybe. He usually goes with his granddad but I'm sure Dad won't mind stepping back. Then he could have tea with you and your mum again and you could bring him home in time for bed.'

'I suppose that will be all right,' he said.

'Right, we'll settle on that then, shall we?'

'Yeah,' he agreed. 'Sorry I've been a bit awkward. I didn't expect to feel so strongly towards him.'

'That's all right.'

'Oh and Daisy,' he began. 'I want him to know that I'm his dad. I want things to be right.'

'Yes, we do need to do something about that,' she agreed. 'He needs to be told your mum is his grandma too. I'll find the right moment and tell him. It probably won't mean much to him yet because he's so young.'

'Has he said anything about not having a dad?' he asked.

'Not yet but he will start to ask questions soon if he isn't told, I expect. Some of his friends at school lost their dads in the war so he won't have felt different to everyone else for the moment.'

'Good.'

'Oh and while we are on the subject, I named you as his father on the birth certificate even though I was married to John,' she said. 'I couldn't lie about an important thing like that.'

'Thank you,' he said. 'I appreciate that.'

'Some men wouldn't.'

He shrugged. 'I can only speak for myself and I'm really pleased.'

This warmed Daisy's heart. Her boy was wanted by his father and that meant a lot to her. She would do what she could to help the two of them to form a bond.

A few evenings later Al went round to John's house and invited him to the pub for a drink.

'I just wanted to thank you for stepping in to help Daisy when she was in a mess because of me,' he said.

'That's all right, mate,' said John, putting his drink on the bar counter where the two men were standing. 'You weren't in a position to do anything about it and Mary has told me you didn't know anything about it either.'

'That's right. But cheers anyway.'

'It wasn't one of my best ideas as it turned out but at least Daisy got to keep Sam.'

'She said it didn't work out for the two of you.'

'It was hell, mate, for both of us,' John admitted. 'Daisy and I were very good friends before we got married. That soon changed afterwards. You need that special something to live with someone, especially when there's a baby around. I didn't become close to young Sam. I don't know why.'

'I'm hoping to do exactly that,' Al said.

'I expect it's different when it's your own. He isn't a baby now so it should be easier. At least you can talk to him and do things with him. When I was around all he seemed to do was yell and I couldn't cope.'

'He's my son and I really want to get to know him. Be a proper dad.'

'Good luck with that.'

'So I gather you're going out with Mary Blake now,' mentioned Al casually.

John nodded. 'Yeah. Mary and I get on really well. I've got high hopes in that direction.'

'Is it a bit awkward with you being married to her sister?' queried Al.

'Not for me, not at the moment anyway though I think it bothers her dad,' John said. 'Obviously something will have to be done if we stay together.

But at the moment we're just enjoying each other's company.'

'You weren't carrying on with her when you and Daisy were still together, were you?' said Al in the blatant way men have about these things.

'With Bertha Blake in the house, don't make me laugh.' John grinned as he spoke. 'But no. I wouldn't have done a thing like that. Mary and I always got on well though when I lived there. We used to have long chats sometimes when just the two of us were around. But nothing untoward, God no. I ran into her one day in town long after Daisy and I had split up and we got chatting; went for a cup of tea in Lyons and realised that we got on. It just went from there.'

'Good for you, mate,' said Al.

'You were always the apple of Daisy's eye,' said John. 'No one else could even come close.'

'Back in the day, maybe, but not now. She's changed completely since I knew her. The adoring young girl she once was seems to have disappeared altogether. She's a confident woman now who isn't afraid to speak her mind.'

'She's had a lot to cope with one way and another. And I suppose you have to stand up for yourself when you have a child.'

'She does that all right.'

'So what are your plans for after demob?' asked John by way of conversation.

'Music I hope,' Al told him. 'I've been looking to see what's around and I have one possibility in the pipeline. A very exciting opportunity as it happens.'

'No more Adelphi for you then.'

'I wouldn't rule it out. I always rather enjoyed working there though I do need to make progress as a pianist now. Anyway, I haven't got the job yet and am not sure I'll take it if I do get it.'

'Really?'

'The problem is, John,' he began and went on to explain the difficulty.

Chapter Seventeen

The Saturday afternoon outing with Sam began well enough. The boy held his dad's hand as they walked to the sweetshop and Al loved the feeling. It brought his protective instincts to the fore and made him feel like a proper dad, looking after his boy and keeping him safe.

Things began to go downhill in the sweetshop because Sam wouldn't make up his mind and the female assistant became irritable.

'It's only natural for him to take his time choosing,' Al said to her, powerfully defensive of his son. 'The sweet ration isn't exactly huge so kids like to make sure they get what they want. There weren't these restrictions when you and I were little so we should count ourselves lucky and be patient.'

'There are other people waiting,' the assistant pointed out briskly.

Al turned round to see a long queue. 'Come on, Sam,' he said. 'Choose what you want sharpish.'

'I don't want any sweets,' the boy said.

'Don't be daft, of course you do,' said Al.

'No I don't.'

'Can you move out of the way and let other people who do want to buy something get to the counter please,' said the assistant, who clearly wanted to see the back of these time wasters.

Al led Sam towards the shop door. 'Now we'll have to queue up again when you finally make up your mind.'

He looked up at Al, his blue eyes shining with tears, his cheeks bright pink. 'I want to go home,' he said.

'Home,' said Al, devastated. 'But we're going to the river to see the boats and feed the ducks.'

'I don't want to go. I want my mum.'

'We could find another sweetshop,' Al suggested hopefully.

'I want to go home.'

'How about the park?'

The boy shook his head and Al knew he must admit defeat; he physically ached with disappointment.

'Back so soon,' said Daisy, frowning as she opened the door to them and Sam rushed to her and flung his arms around her.

'He wanted to come home,' Al explained miserably.

'Come in, Al,' she said, ushering him inside. 'Sam, why don't you go and see Granddad, he's gardening out the back.'

The boy did as she suggested and Al went into the hall and followed her into the living room, which was empty.

347

'It's all my fault, Al,' she said as they sat down in the armchairs.

'Of course it isn't,' he said. 'How could it be when you weren't even there?'

'Exactly. I shouldn't have left you alone with him the first time. I mean, you're a stranger to him. I told him you are his dad but he doesn't know you at all so he probably didn't feel comfortable.'

'How will I get to know him if he doesn't want to be with me?' he asked.

'I need to be there with you until you and he get better acquainted,' she suggested. 'I could kick myself for letting it happen. I'm usually so careful when it comes to Sam.'

'That was probably because of the pressure I was putting on you to let me spend time with him. I know I was getting a bit stroppy about it. I want to be his dad so much it's colouring my judgement. I should have known it wouldn't be easy. What was I thinking? I've probably put the poor kid off me for good and all for barging in with my size nines.'

'Give yourself a chance, Al, it's only one time.'

'There is that, I suppose,' he sighed. 'But supposing he doesn't want to go with me again?'

'Why don't the three of us go tomorrow afternoon? It's my Sunday off so I can do it. Give him a chance to get used to you while I'm there.'

'I'd really like that,' he said.

'That's settled then. We'll take him to see the boats on the river and then maybe the park. We'll see how it goes.'

Mary came into the room. 'Hello stranger,' she said warmly to Al. 'I heard you were here. It's been a long time. You're still a handsome devil, I see. The war hasn't ground you down.'

'I'm a tough bugger.' He got up to shake her hand. 'It's good to see you again.'

'Are you staying for a cuppa?' she asked in a friendly manner.

'No, I'd better get off.' He said this because he thought Daisy would rather he left and he knew she had to go to work.

'All right,' she said breezily, heading out of the room. 'See you again soon I hope.'

As she left Bill came in. 'Al,' he said, offering his hand. 'Glad you made it back from the war in one piece.'

'Me too,' said Al, shaking his hand.

'How did it go with the nipper?'

'Badly.'

'Oh. Well, it was bound to take a bit of time,' Bill said cheerfully. 'Better luck next time.'

Al nodded. It felt good being back in this house again. He'd always got on well with the Blake family, except for Bertha. Even though he and Daisy were no longer together, they still felt like friends.

'Oi oi, anyone at home,' said a voice from the Dawsons' front door that evening and in walked a soldier.

'Dickie,' cried Hester, rushing over and throwing her arms around him. 'You're a sight for sore eyes.'

'Al's home too, I see,' he said, looking at his brother who was waiting to greet him.

'Good to see you, mate,' said Al, shaking his hand.

'Likewise,' said Dickie. 'There have been times

when I thought I would never see you two again. But here we are all together again just like old times.'

'I'm a lucky woman,' said Hester tearfully. 'I have both my boys back safe and sound. Not every mother is so lucky.'

'No need to cry about it, Mum,' said Dickie.

'She enjoys a good old weep, don't you, Mum?' said Al affectionately.

'Only under certain circumstances and this is one of those special occasions.'

'It certainly is,' said Al. 'So you go ahead and do whatever comes naturally.'

They all began talking at once; there was so much to say.

'Well, you look all right anyway,' observed Hester after she had made tea and sandwiches for Dickie. 'You're not hiding any war wounds under that uniform, are you?'

'No, Mum, nothing like that.'

'How did you get on with being in the thick of it?' inquired Hester.

'It wasn't so bad, Mum,' he said. 'It would take more than a few Germans to get me down.'

Only two people knew how deeply his war service had affected him and he trusted them not to say anything. In actual fact he had found combat terrifying and barbaric and had hated every single second of his service. He hoped he never had to do anything like that ever again.

Sam held on to his mother's hand tightly as the three of them headed for the river the next day. The day was bright with a light breeze moving through the trees. Hammersmith Bridge, in all its green and golden glory, shone decoratively over the water. The war had taken its toll on the town but the riverside still had its special feeling of space and light. There were a few people working on their moored boats but the tide was out so there was no passing river traffic, just the muddy river bed.

Because Al so wanted to do things right with his son, he was feeling anxious as they headed in the direction of Chiswick but tried hard to get some sort of a rapport going.

'Look at the swans, Sam,' he said as they stopped near Chiswick Eyot, which was a haven for wildlife and nesting place for swans.

'What are the swans doing?' asked Sam.

'Just waddling around being swans,' replied his mother.

'Can I go over and see them closer?' he asked.

'Through all that mud, not likely,' she said, though it was possible to walk to the island at low tide.

'I could take my shoes and socks off and walk there.'

'You are not doing that, Sam,' she said firmly. 'The swans wouldn't want you getting too close anyway.'

'Why?'

She turned to Al and said quietly, 'Questions, questions it drives me nuts sometimes.'

'I think it's sweet.'

'You don't have to come up with all the answers.'

'I hope I can help out with that from now on.'

'I'd like that, Al,' she said.

'Why don't the swans want me near them,' Sam persisted.

'Because the island is their home, not yours,' she said. 'You might scare them.'

'Why?'

'Because you are not a swan.'

Al chuckled at this but it seemed to satisfy Sam for the moment and they walked on until the boy began to lag behind.

'Are you tired, Sam?' asked Al.

'No.'

'Oh. Well if you were I could give you a ride on my shoulders.'

'I think we ought to turn back now anyway,' suggested Daisy. 'His legs are only little.'

'I'm not tired but I'd like a ride,' said Sam.

'Come on then, up you come.'

As they headed back along the towpath, with Sam safely perched on Al's shoulders, he and Daisy chatted and it felt so right, so natural.

A long queue at a small café attracted their interest and when it transpired that it was for ice cream they joined it excitedly. Having ceased manufacture throughout the war this luxury had become available again recently but was still in very short supply.

They sat on a bench in the sun to eat their treat and when they continued the walk home with Sam chattering away, Al felt a strong sense of belonging. He still had a way to go to win his son's affections completely but he'd made a start.

'Maybe we could go to the park next time, Sam,' he said as they made their way back, Sam walking now. 'We could take a ball perhaps.

Would you like that?'

'Yeah, but I want Mummy to come too.'

'I think you two will be all right on your own now that you've got to know each other,' said Daisy.

'I still want you to come with us, Mum.'

Daisy looked at Al and their eyes met properly for the first time since she'd seen him again. They both knew that this was a seminal moment. He was a little older and sadder, she more mature and responsible, but they were still the same people, their own special magic still there.

'I want you to come too,' said Al, looking at Daisy, the lost years melting away.

'Yes, I would like that as well,' she said.

Al put his mouth close to her ear and said, 'I love you, Daisy, and want us three to be together for always, not just for an afternoon out. You and me and our beautiful boy.' He put his arms around her and pulled Sam towards him too. 'That's what I want for the rest of my life.'

They moved to the side to let people past. A couple in love and their boy, arms entwined. 'Me too, Al,' she said, from the heart, the complications put to one side.

'Please may I have another ice cream?' asked Sam, bringing a touch of normality into the romance of the moment.

'Afraid not, son,' said Al. 'Strictly one per person and we've had ours.'

One day in the not too distant future, if the government were to be believed, treats wouldn't be so few and far between. Al wanted to embrace that bright new world with Daisy and Sam beside him. And if the good times didn't come, they would face that too, *together.*

Hester decided it was time for a party. A belated celebration for the return of both her sons and also to mark the engagement of Daisy and Al. So one Saturday in the summer of 1946 the Dawson residence was crowded with people. The event began in the afternoon so that Sam could enjoy it but Hester thought that some of her guests would probably still be here well into the evening when the booze was flowing.

But for now it was teatime with just a glass of something stronger for a toast and time for Hester to say a few words.

'Thank you all for coming for this double celebration. They took their time to get here, more than a year after the end of the war, but they got here in the end. Welcome home, boys.' Glasses were raised to the Dawson brothers amidst cheers. 'We are also here to celebrate the engagement of Daisy and Al and I'm sure we all wish them well for the future with their lovely son Sam.'

Up went the glasses again and Daisy was overwhelmed with emotion because she was here with the man she loved and her son and she had thought that day would never come. They weren't yet able to get married but the legal wheels had been set in motion for a divorce, which John also wanted now that he and Mary were serious about each other. It would be a lengthy process but they were prepared for that.

Doreen was there that day as Dickie's guest, the two having been seeing each other regularly since

354

he got back. Daisy was glad that her dad was here too with Mary and John. As the Dawsons and the Blakes were going to be related by marriage it made sense for them to be included. Dad and Hester got along well together now that they were better acquainted and often kept each other company while babysitting Sam.

Al was back at the organ at the Adelphi, much to Mr Pickles' joy, though Daisy knew that Al was hoping to further his career as a pianist as soon as he could. So all things considered Daisy could ask for nothing more from life.

Al was thinking much the same thing. Everyone he cared for was here in this room. When he'd been away at the war he'd never dreamed he would be sharing his life with Daisy again. To have Sam too made it extra special. He looked across at Daisy and smiled. He would never tell her what he had given up to be with her. A position as resident pianist with the highly regarded Ted Scott dance orchestra, his favourite dance band and the job of his dreams.

But it would have meant being away from home as the band was going to work in America. Al had been keen on the job and thrilled to be offered it, but he'd wanted to be here with Daisy and his son more. So for the moment he was supplementing his income from the Adelphi by working at the music shop.

Maybe there would be other musical job opportunities at some point in the future and he might sometimes have to be away for his work as a musician. But now there was only one place to be, here at home with the love of his life, Daisy, and their beautiful son.

As soon as they were married and in their own place he would see about getting a much-wanted pet for Sam; a kitten would be nice.

The publishers hope that this book has given you enjoyable reading. Large Print Books are especially designed to be as easy to see and hold as possible. If you wish a catalogue please ask at your local library or write directly to:

Magna Large Print Books
Cawood House,
Asquith Industrial Estate,
Gargrave,
Nr Skipton, North Yorkshire.
BD23 3SE

This Large Print Book for the partially sighted, who cannot read normal print, is published under the auspices of

THE ULVERSCROFT FOUNDATION

THE ULVERSCROFT FOUNDATION

... we hope that you have enjoyed this Large Print Book. Please think for a moment about those people who have worse eyesight problems than you ... and are unable to even read or enjoy Large Print, without great difficulty.

You can help them by sending a donation, large or small to:

**The Ulverscroft Foundation,
1, The Green, Bradgate Road,
Anstey, Leicestershire, LE7 7FU,
England.**
or request a copy of our brochure for more details.

The Foundation will use all your help to assist those people who are handicapped by various sight problems and need special attention.

Thank you very much for your help.